ALLIGATOR HERETICS

written by **Joshua Sobel**

developmental edit by **Erin Bledsoe**

copy edit by **Sydney Rain**

cover illustration by **Emily Gerich**

What Readers Are Saying

"Bravely pushes the boundaries of the coming-of-age genre by giving us a unique, yet extremely relatable perspective on growing up with autism and enduring religious trauma."
—*Tiffany Keyes, Former Mental Health Clinician*

"The story is engaging, the autism representation is spot-on, and the characters are fully human with three entire-ass dimensions."
—*Alexis Record, Author of Bedtime with Bitsy*

"A fascinating and realistic depiction of fundamentalist Christian culture. I couldn't put it down, literally; I read it in one day."
—*Emily Anderson, Freelance Editor*

"A brilliant and creative portrayal of growing up in fundamentalist culture from a perspective that desperately needs to be heard."
—*Name Redacted, Former Missionary*

"Josh creates characters that you can't help but invest in, telling a story that leaves you satisfied, and wanting more."
—*Marla, Former Fundamentalist Christian*

"I couldn't put it down! Believable characters and a great build to the climax. I gasped so many times. Loved it!"
—*Anna, Beta Reader*

"Alligator Heretics is a gripping mystery novel with compelling characters. Anyone who grew up in religion and has questioned things, especially if they're neurodivergent, is sure to relate."
—*Chris Freihofer, Neurodivergent Former Christian*

Special Thanks To...

Alexis Record, **Emily Anderson**, and **Ellie Bain**, for selflessly proofreading my early drafts and providing invaluable feedback.

My **friends** and **beta readers**, for being endless soundboards as I struggled to find the best way to tell this story.

My **parents**, for raising me in a way that allowed me to escape purity culture without significant trauma.

My **therapists**, for helping me work through my baggage and come to terms with my autism.

My **high school teachers**, who I might disagree with on many things, but who nonetheless treated me with kindness and respect to the best of their abilities.

The real *Alligator Heretics*, my **high school classmates**, for keeping me grounded during my adolescent journey.

Author's Preface

I grew up surrounded by Christian fundamentalism, both at church and school. This story is loosely inspired by events from those years, experienced by myself, my friends, and my classmates.

Although *Alligator Heretics* is a work of fiction, I put great effort into ensuring I accurately represented the emotional turmoil teens in these types of institutions commonly struggle with.

As such, take this as a content warning. This book contains potentially triggering subject matter, such as homophobia, physical abuse, and mental abuse. Please read at your own discretion.

Please also be aware that experts rolled Asperger syndrome into autism spectrum disorder in 2013. This was due, in part, to its namesake—a member of the Nazi party. For era accuracy, characters in the book refer to it as Asperger syndrome.

Table of Contents

Prologue: Humid Memories

Despite sharing my hometown with dozens of alligators, they rarely concerned me. Gators don't feel empathy, at least not how many other creatures do. They travel alone, lacking all care for the lives they destroy, animal or otherwise. They don't know any better, and I never judged them for it. People, however, should know better.

The adults surrounding me throughout my adolescent years in South Florida instilled in me a visceral desire to avoid "worldly" experiences. As a result, I never snuck booze from the top cabinet for a night of curious inebriation. I never skipped school for a spontaneous road trip. I never spent seven minutes in heaven with a crush during a game of spin the bottle. Instead of living my teenage years to their fullest, I pushed away potentially meaningful friendships by policing those around me to behave more like Jesus Christ.

To my teachers and pastors, I followed the righteous path. But the harmful ideas placed in the heads of my classmates and me stretched far beyond basic overprotection; the discipleship practices on display at my school and church hindered our ability to function ethically. Even when my classmate disappeared because of the faculty's negligence, they failed to seek growth.

As easy as it is to dwell on the dark underbelly of my high school experience, there's a silver lining. When empathetic creatures suffer together, unbreakable bonds form. Nobody should've been thrown into those waters, but we were. Through those challenging times, we found each other.

1. Altar Calls and Queso

Sometimes I wonder if my inability to absorb information through lectures was responsible for my eventual sprint away from the church. On the last Saturday night before my senior year of high school, if you asked me, "Hey Arthur, what was the youth ministry sermon you just sat through about?" I couldn't have told you.

I spent roughly half my time in services at Righteous Christ Church shifting my husky body in the trendy chairs, dragging my fingers across my bushy eyebrows, and obsessively tracing the shapes of the large room's acoustic paneling with my beady blue eyes. Occasionally, I'd push my poofy brown hair away from my forehead, or wipe the oil off the bridge of my pale nose with the collar of my t-shirt. I also adjusted my cargo shorts more than was socially acceptable. Few boys in their late teens were as fidgety and distractible as I was, so focusing on public speakers was a nearly insurmountable challenge.

Aside from Pastor Robbie's impromptu parody of OutKast's "Hey Ya," containing the lyrics "My Jesus don't mess around, because He saved me so, I'll never perish, fo' sho'," the message, to my perception, might as well have been about chips and queso. And no, that's not as random as it sounds—dinner with friends at Chili's after service was the main reason I looked forward to church back then. That's right, dinner; the hip churches in the mid-2000s hosted service Saturday and Wednesday evenings, as well as more-traditional Sunday mornings.

It wasn't like I didn't want to listen. At the time, I saw God as the sole source of all the good things in my life. I wanted to know the capitalized Him, deeply and righteously. His presence was the key to bypassing my sinful desires in favor of spreading love and kindness to my friends and neighbors. If only I could focus, I could continue down a path of holiness.

As an eighteen-year-old diagnosed with what was then referred to as Asperger syndrome (now known as autism spectrum disorder), my mind would often ignore my surroundings in favor of daydreams; sometimes about my next meal, a video game, or collecting Yu-Gi-Oh! cards—a supposedly demonic pastime I kept well hidden from my pastors. I may have strived to mirror God's image, but I wasn't beyond *all* adolescent rebellion.

I glanced at the clock at the back of the room, wondering how much longer I'd have to pretend to listen. The clock was almost invisible next to the enormous sign featuring the youth ministry's recently rebranded name, *Spóros*, the Greek word for seed. The church had spared no expense on the modern graphic design of the logo. The striking branding may have helped the church "spread the good word" by standing out from the traditional crowd, but it did little to ensure the ninety-minute sermons held my attention.

Fifteen minutes, I thought. *I can do this. A good Christian would* want *to hear from the pastors in their life. Time to focus.*

Pastor Robbie, the head of youth ministry, stepped away from the pulpit to sip some water as the worship team took to the stage.

Crap. I tuned out the whole sermon again. Maybe I'll absorb some of the sermon next week.

I rolled my eyes at the new worship leader: Samuel—my classmate, and Pastor Robbie's son. Seeing my bully of three years celebrated on stage made my face scrunch. He probably wasn't as awful as my biased memories convey, but he exuded at least a small amount of performative pompousness through his trendy flannel shirt, unnecessary infinity scarf, and shaggy blonde hair. His words "let us worship" carried a confidence that only comes from practicing line delivery in the mirror dozens of times. In my experience, he was far from the example of Christ he deliberately emulated on stage.

The lights dimmed, and the musicians filled the room with a slow acoustic ambiance no different from the instrumental score of an indie flick's funeral scene.

The modern decor of the youth ministry's faux sanctuary enhanced the emotional vibe. Those new churches knew how to entice America's youth with flashy lights, colorful chairs, and gigantic projector screens featuring mesmerizing stock footage screensavers.

After a few minutes of tone setting, a spotlight welcomed Pastor Robbie back to the pulpit. Like most pastors in those sorts of churches, he was a charismatic, conventionally attractive White man. He was tall and had jaw-length, wavy brown hair, not unlike the mainstream depictions of Jesus. A chiseled goatee adorned his chin and upper lip. His desire to appear approachable was evident in his outfit—an untucked button-down shirt with rolled-up sleeves, and blue jeans.

He slowly raised his head and looked back and forth over the roughly three hundred teens in the audience. The tension was palpable.

"My brothers and sisters in Christ… do you feel that? It's not every day I can say without a shadow of a doubt that the Holy Spirit is in the room with us right now. I know many of you came here tonight thinking you'd leave just as broken—just as sad—as you were before. But I have great news. What if I told you there's someone who loves you no matter how often you mess up? What if I told you He could take your pain away like it was never there to begin with? What if I told you He wants to welcome you into the kingdom of Heaven to rejoice for all eternity? And that all you have to do to receive this gift is one thing: Believe. It's that simple."

Robbie and his team knew how to work an audience. As much as I'd love to say I was above it all, I ate it right up, along with the rest of the audience. In the same way no empathetic human can watch the opening ten-minutes of Pixar's Up without welling up at least a little, emotional music and poetic language targeting the audience's most human vulnerabilities is a universally effective strategy. Despite my propensity to daydream, the altar calls captivated me.

"If you feel moved right now; if you feel a welling in your chest that makes you feel like you're about to lift out of your seat… that, my friend, is Jesus knocking. All you have to do is answer."

I couldn't ignore the inspiration in his voice. It was calculated and provided struggling individuals with the hope they so desperately needed.

"If it sounds, my friend, like I'm talking to you… I invite you to join me at the stage to declare Jesus as your Lord and Savior. To admit that you're a sinner—that you are broken and can only be fixed through Him. And if you do this, I promise you… He will take your pain away."

After a few moments, one young woman stood up, crying, with her hand over her face, and approached the stage. She kneeled in front of Pastor Robbie. He placed his hands on her back, and rubbed it back and forth, and back and forth. Soon after, a young man joined her, followed by two more young women. After another few minutes of somber music and an occasional "Yes, Lord" from Robbie, there were about ten individuals on their knees at the stage, ready to heal.

I couldn't help but feel slightly jealous of those currently receiving so much validation from the youth group leaders. I was a bit of a clout seeker sometimes. It crossed my mind that it had been quite some time since I went up during an altar call, and that maybe it made sense to "renew my vows" but I wisely figured that wouldn't have great optics.

Pastor Robbie returned to the pulpit. "My friends… please repeat after me. Dear heavenly Father."

"Dear heavenly Father," they chanted in unison.

"Please forgive me, for I am broken, and have sinned."

The group parroted.

"I know I am beyond repair without your grace, and I accept your love into my heart to be my one and only savior."

Through muffled tears, they repeated what they surely believed were the most-important words they'd ever say. They truly felt peace, and I was happy for them.

Pastor Robbie approached the group at the stage, crouched down, and said, "This is the Grace of God, my friends. Your pain has been lifted. Your sins have been forgiven. Welcome to the rest of your life."

The audience clapped, myself included. Samuel struck an uplifting guitar chord, and the worship team performed an above-average rock-fueled song that, if not for the biblical lyrics, could've easily passed for secular radio music. I sang along while occasionally glancing around the room, curious whether my peers noted my pious engagement.

After the song, the fluorescent overhead lights signaled the end of the service. The crowd trickled out of the youth ministry's meeting room, filled with righteous inspiration. I felt it too, but it was time to focus on something more pressing: finding friends to join me in dunking tortilla chips into beefy, cheesy dip.

*   *   *

After service, about half of the young churchgoers mingled in the meeting room and other indoor areas, such as The Link—a service counter selling chicken tenders, cheese-covered French fries shaped like happy faces, and other standard cafeteria fare. If only I had pulled myself away from my Xbox 360 sooner, maybe I could've arrived at church early and sat next to someone I knew, instead of alone. I walked into The Link and looked around for familiar faces.

I was on the shy side, so I mostly kept my head down, with my hands in my pockets. I blended in with the rest of my at least ninety percent White youth group just perfectly. I stroked my chin, feeling the few prickly hairs I managed to grow, but they'd only survive a few more days, as my school had announced a crackdown on facial hair for when we returned from summer break on Monday.

I didn't recognize any friends, so I walked outside, where the rest of the attendees gathered. South Florida's evening weather was far more bearable for after-service socializing than it would've been after the morning service. Either way, Florida summers were brutal. As my older brother would say before he left for college, it was like living in Satan's ass crack.

Finally, I spotted the lucky Christian occupying the number one slot on my MySpace profile's "Top Friends" section. Benny was a skinny performing arts nerd and had, just two years prior, enlightened me on the joys of taking part in musical theater. He wore colorful shirts and skinny jeans, which I could never pull off. He was Black, flamboyant, and his voice contained a hint of femininity—something I'd heard others mock a few times. He stuck out like a sore thumb in a sea of conservative White Christians.

Being on the autistic spectrum meant classical displays of emotion didn't come naturally to me sometimes. The long summer without Benny had been lonely, and I felt genuine excitement for his return. It just sometimes took a deliberate effort to convince him of my friendly appreciation through my words alone. I took a deep breath and summoned a smile.

"Bennyyyyy!" I called.

He turned toward me as a white grin engulfed his face. "Arthur Morton, my boy! It's been WAY too long." He hugged me so tightly that I flinched a bit.

"Okay, okay," I said, avoiding returning the embrace. "People are gonna stare if they see two guys hugging!"

My fundamentalist upbringing ensured that being perceived as gay was a fear of mine—a common mindset in South Florida as a whole.

"I'm just happy to see you!" Benny patted my back and stepped back. "So, how the frick are ya?"

"I'm pretty good. About the same. Nothing huge to report."

Benny was used to my no-nonsense demeanor, and avoided pointing out how boring my summary was.

Those in the neurodivergent community (people with atypical mental behavior) commonly interpret small talk as torturous, but I had learned enough about socializing by then that I had to at least pretend to be interested in hearing every detail about Benny's summer with his dad.

"So, how was New York?" I asked through slightly clenched teeth.

"Oh my God... err, I mean... oh my gosh, it was INCREDIBLE!!! *Beauty and the Beast* was even more amazing than I expected."

The whole theater gang at school desperately wanted to perform the Disney classic for our senior musical, but it wasn't in the cards.

"And New Yorkers are so genuine," he continued. "It's amazing how eye opening it can be to spend time outside this bubble."

"Ugh, I'm so jealous!" It was easy for me to show genuine interest in Benny's stories when they were about a topic I was actually interested in. "Did you see any other shows while you were there? Did you see *Wicked?* Andrew saw it and said the new casting for Elphaba lived up to Idina Menzel, and—"

"Whoa, whoa, Arthur. Slow down. I just saw the one show. Maybe next year."

I'd often monologue about topics presently occupying the front of my mind, commonly known as autistic hyperfixations. Thankfully, Benny knew me well enough not to be put off by these passionate ramblings.

"Ah, sorry," I said. "Sounds like a great trip overall."

"Absolutely. But the traffic, oh my goodness," said Benny with disgust. "By the way, did you end up getting that car from your grandma for your birthday?"

"I did. It's right over there!" I gestured to the back of the parking lot. "It's a Toyota Camry. Can't really see it from here."

"We have GOT to take it for a ride sometime."

"Definitely. Maybe to Chili's tonight?"

Benny perked up beyond his already elevated personality and said, "Ya know, New York has some amazing food, but I REALLY miss Chili's."

When we were about to head to my car, a man's voice bellowed, "Hey! Arthur! Benny!"

It was Pastor Marshall, a youth ministry leader who had been an usher during that night's service. Like most youth pastors, he dressed in casual modern attire—a polo shirt tucked into blue jeans.

He approached us enthusiastically, followed by a girl in her late teens with dyed red streaks in her dark hair—a bit adventurous for our conservative church. She wore a baggy t-shirt with a wide neck that hung off one shoulder, and tight black jeans. Silver studs lined her belt. To a goody two-shoes like myself, she gave off strong "wrong side of the tracks" vibes.

"Hey, brothers!" exclaimed Pastor Marshall as he caught up to us. "I'm glad I caught you. This is Ella. She's starting as a senior in your class. I was hoping you two could welcome her in and maybe show her around?"

Although I'd be disappointed to postpone Chili's, my desire to help share the good word with a new friend, and possibly gain some brownie points with the pastors, won out.

"Sure, we—"

"We would LOVE to!" interrupted Benny. "Welcome to Righteous Christ! I'm so excited to meet you. I'm Benny. I love your hair, by the way."

Ella smiled slightly. "Oh… thanks."

I envied Benny's ability to convince anyone to like him through genuine love and enthusiasm. He stepped forward to hug Ella but swapped it for a classic Christian side hug at the last second, presumably remembering he wasn't in the Big Apple anymore. She seemed surprised by his hug and winced a little, but Benny was too excited to notice.

Without making eye contact, I muttered, "I'm Arthur. Nice to meet you."

"Nice to meet you both," she said, nonchalantly. Almost as an afterthought, she smiled for approximately one second.

Thrilled, Pastor Marshall said, "Thank you both SO much. I knew you were the young disciples for the job. Anyway, I gotta get back to work. Welcome to the family, Ella! WOOHOO!"

Ella lifted her eyebrows and grimaced. She clearly wasn't used to those levels of youth ministry bro vibes like the rest of us were. "Sooo…"

I asked, "Isn't it a little weird to transfer to a new school for senior year? Did you just move here or something?"

Benny rolled his eyes at my lack of subtlety.

"Nope," said Ella. "South Florida, born and raised. My parents just stuck me in this place so it can turn me into their perfect little girl, I guess. Might as well be my prison."

"Whoa, whoa!" said Benny. "Starting out with the DEEP backstory, Ella? So, what, I'm assuming you were selling drugs?"

"Yes."

My eyes widened. To my knowledge, the closest Benny and I had come to illegal substances were the *DARE* anti-drug propaganda videos they'd shown us in school.

Ella punctured our silence. "Kidding."

We laughed.

"Or am I…"

*   *   *

I checked the time on my foldable hot pink Motorola Razr phone. A few weeks prior, a youth minister had dumped a giant bucket of water on me at a pool party, breaking my blue one. The phone screen read 7:25 p.m. It had been ten minutes since we began our job as Ella's tour guides. I was happy to take part in a discipleship opportunity, but wondered how quickly we could finish. Chips and queso were waiting.

As we strolled away from the *Spóros* youth ministry building, Ella occasionally twirled around to take in the sights. The exterior of Righteous Christ Church contained no steeples, no stained-glass windows, and no bells. Instead, stucco walls covered in painted modern shapes lined the multiple buildings of the enormous campus, all kept in pristine condition. Sporadic gardens and grassy areas broke the concrete pavement up, covered with well-groomed shrubberies and plenty of palm trees.

"Gotta say," said Ella, "this is nothing like the last church my parents took me to."

"Oh, yeah?" asked Benny. "What kind of church was it?"

"I dunno. Catholic?"

Benny's face scrunched as he glanced toward Ella. "Wait, you don't know what kind of church it was?"

"No? I dunno. I haven't been to church in ages."

Church life was all I knew. The concept of not going to church regularly didn't make sense to someone who was a "true" Christian.

Is it possible that Ella isn't a believer like we are? I thought. *If so, it's our job to put her on the right path, so it's a good thing she's here.*

"What kind of church is this?" asked Ella.

I responded enthusiastically. "We're non-denominational Christian!"

"Oh… okay," replied Ella, visibly confused.

Righteous Christ was wholeheartedly an evangelical church, no matter how much they avoided using the term. Evangelicals, also known as "born again Christians," believe that to get into Heaven, you simply have to believe sincerely that Jesus is the savior, and live your life accordingly; usually involving sharing the "good word," or evangelizing to those less fortunate.

The first proper stop on the impromptu tour was The Daily Bread, an impressive bistro that served classy takes on food, such as steak, pasta, and personal pizzas. The smell made me even hungrier. Ella had one word to say about the restaurant: "Damn." Swearing wasn't commonplace at Righteous Christ, but it was entry level at best, so I let it slide.

The next stop was one of the bookstores, full of daily devotionals and memorabilia covered in crosses. The Righteous Christ logo, a silhouette of a cross with a halo resting upon it, adorned much of the swag. The imagery of Jesus was also plentiful throughout the store, and unsurprisingly, they presented him as a handsome White man in every illustration. It didn't phase me in the slightest. It probably bothered Benny, but I hadn't noticed.

Ella picked up a colorful book about Noah's ark and flipped through it. "A bit morbid for a children's book, don't ya think?" she asked.

Benny and I exchanged confused glances.

I responded, "What do you mean?"

"God killed like… almost everyone, right? Kinda weird to tell little kids a story about worldwide genocide through colorful cartoons."

I chimed in, "God gave those people a choice, and they chose to live their lives separate from Him. It's not like they were innocent."

Ella's brow furrowed. "Uhh… a little concerning, but okay. I mean, it's whatever; you do you. But like they say, gay people using the rainbow is fucked… err… messed up. But genocide rainbows are like… way worse? Right?"

The F word made me blue in the face, but Benny just smiled. I noticed she glanced at Benny when mentioning rainbows, but gaydar is all but entirely disabled when you're as religious as I was.

Ella continued, "Eh, forget it. Too much. I'll read the room next time."

"No worries," I said. "I'm kinda just repeating what they told me. I haven't really looked into it."

It was true, but I mostly said it to make sure I didn't push Ella away. I wasn't quite ready for personal revelations like that.

"All good, dude," said Ella.

It's clear Ella needs some discipleship, I thought. *I can't let her end up in Hell.*

As we exited the bookstore, Ella made an observation. "Never expected to see so much capitalism in a church, jeez."

I was immune to her astute critiques.

We walked down an outdoor corridor lined with plants until we rounded a corner.

"And there she is: home sweet home," announced Benny.

Righteous Christ Academy mostly held classes in the colorful, multi-million-dollar building in front of us. A few classes and large assemblies took place in other church areas, including the youth group conference room and the main sanctuary. The relationship between the church and its school was rather synergistic.

The side of the building featured the head of a cartoon alligator, our mascot. "Go Gators!" it read.

"So, I guess I'm a Gator now," said Ella.

Benny bounced up and down on his toes. "Welcome to the RCA family, Ella! We're so happy to have you here. Are you excited about Monday?"

"Eh… not really. I mean, like I said, I'm kinda here against my will. But you guys are nice… I guess."

I added, "We think you're nice, too."

Ella smiled. "Heh. Thanks. Kinda pissed they're gonna make me get rid of the red streaks in my hair, though."

"Oh, bummer," said Benny. "It looks so good!"

"Yeah…" groaned Ella.

We walked back to the parking lot. I checked the time again, and was elated to see Chili's was still open for another two hours.

Benny looked at me and smirked. He glanced toward Ella and said, "Hey Ella, we were gonna head over to Chili's for dinner. Do you wanna come?"

Ella raised her eyebrows. "Ha. Is that a normal thing—Chili's after church?"

"Sure is," I stated definitively.

"Well, maybe next time. They gave me a bunch of transfer student paperwork I need to finish before the first day of school."

Benny frowned. "Aww, bummer. I feel that! Well, we'll definitely see you on Monday! You're gonna love it!"

I added, "Yeah, and it was great to meet you! Let us know if you have any questions about the school or church!"

Ella smiled and said, "Hah, will do. Thanks for the tour, guys. See ya. Oh, and if you wanna add me on MySpace, just search Ella Kent."

"Will do!" said Benny, as Ella left to meet her parents outside the main sanctuary.

"Can we go now?" I asked impatiently.

Benny's eyes zipped toward me. "Oh my gosh, you are INFURIATING! And yes. I'm starving."

As we walked to my ultra-classy, gray 1997 sedan, I glanced back at the church. The bustle of fellowship was lively, even an hour after the service. Leaving while the vibes were still poppin', I almost felt a little left out. Our branch of Righteous Christ Church served as a meaningful source of community for many, including myself. Those who filled its halls, sanctuaries, bistro, and bookstores were generally good people, doing their best to survive the human condition with as little suffering as possible.

However, just like the alligator is oblivious to the suffering its actions cause, the members and leadership at Righteous Christ remained blissfully unaware of the traumas their well-intentioned lifestyle would inflict on the children and teens within their splash zone throughout the coming school year.

2. Godly Gators

BEEP, BEEP, BEEP!

I smashed the wide oval button on my alarm clock and fell back asleep.

Five minutes later, *BEEP, BEEP, BEEP!*

"UGH!" I groaned as I dragged my fingers across the top of the device, eventually finding the tiny button that silenced the powerful speaker.

I rubbed my eyes and dug my face into a pillow on my twin-sized bed to hide from the light. I hadn't woken up to an alarm all summer, and longed for that peace to continue.

Because my autism caused me to have overactive senses, I rarely got a full eight hours of sleep, which resulted in a very irritable mood the next day. A feeling of pins and needles danced across my skin, and my eyes itched.

Just… a little… more… I thought as I drifted away.

Knock, knock, knock.

My eyes jolted open. "Whuh…"

My bedroom door creaked open.

"Honey?" said my mom. "You awake? You're gonna be late!"

"I'm… upwake—I'm up. I'm awake."

She stepped into the room, wearing pale jean shorts and a casual button-down shirt. Her friendly smile and wavy brown hair carried an undeniable warmth.

"Do you need any help?" she asked. "If you're feeling overstimulated, I can—"

I sat up and wiped the oil off my face with the back of my hand. "I'm fine. Please, just let me get ready."

"Okay. Just let me know if you need anything."

I nodded, and she shut the door.

My small bedroom was cleaner than your average high school boy's room, featuring only a few articles of scattered clothing on the floor. In one corner sat a thirteen-inch tube TV with an Xbox 360 connected to it. In another corner was a small computer desk, on which sat a heavy CRT monitor, and just a few meticulously organized sticky notes. I had taped a few cutouts from video game magazines, and some posters for *Star Wars* and *The Lord of the Rings* on the wall.

I walked across the room and slid open the mirrored closet doors that my computer desk all but obscured. At the far end of the closet was a smattering of green and blue shirts on hangers.

I squeezed between the desk and the closet, reached in, and grabbed a royal blue polo shirt featuring the RCA Gators logo. I threw it on my bed, along with a pair of baggy khaki shorts.

After showering and brushing my teeth, I sighed and put on the oddly scratchy uniform. I began to tuck in my shirt when I remembered that RCA axed the "shirts tucked in at all times" rule at the end of the previous year. I smiled at that silver lining as I grabbed my backpack.

As I walked down the stairs of our rental townhouse, I heard my twelve-year-old sister yelling at my mom, though I couldn't tell what they were arguing about.

Same old, same old, I thought.

I poured some Lucky Charms into a cup and emptied them into my mouth—no time for milk or bowls when you're running late on your first day of school.

My mom entered the kitchen with her hands on her hips. "You kids are gonna be the death of me," she said. "Well, not you, sweetie. You've always been such a godly young man."

"Uh huh…" I muttered through a cereal-filled mouth.

"If you're wondering what that was about… your sister was hiding these awful teen magazines under her bed. 'How to score the hottest guys' and such. It was basically pornography!"

I avoided eye contact—I hadn't exactly been the godliest young man when it came to sins of the eyes.

My mom sighed. "I can't believe I only have one more year with you here." She embraced me tight. "Please don't ever change."

"Mom! You're making me spill my breakfast!"

"Yes, your dry, milk-less breakfast. It's the end of the world!"

I slithered free, put my cup in the sink, and walked to the door.

"Honey, you let me know if anyone gives you a hard time at school, okay? Hopefully things will be better this year since I got them to do that Asperger awareness talk last May."

I opened the front door. "I… really don't think that helped much."

"Goodbye, Arthur!" said my dad, peeking his graying head into the stairwell from above.

My father and I didn't share many interests, so we didn't talk much. But I'd take that over a father enforcing masculine stereotypes on his son any day.

"Bye," I said. "Gotta go."

"Bye, sweetie," said my mom. "Make your dad and I proud!"

I smiled and shut the door.

I let loose a sigh of relief. I'd miss the lackadaisical summer vibes, but the freedom of not having to deal with family-related stresses for over half of every weekday made my mind feel ten pounds lighter.

It wasn't that my family were bad people, it's just that my autism always thrived on laxity. Feeling in control of my environment brought me peace, and the pressures of cohabitation and emotional support were akin to drowning. When free of claustrophobic familial expectations, I viewed each day as a smorgasbord of opportunity.

I walked to my car and headed to school, excited to dive into my final high school adventure.

*   *   *

Righteous Christ Academy's back-to-school assemblies were nearly indistinguishable from the standard church services. They took place in the main sanctuary, featured worship performances, and words from a middle-aged man about how to follow in Christ's footsteps. If only my attention span was more effective, the pious young me would've been thrilled.

The enormous sanctuary had a similar vibe to the smaller youth ministry room, but with a bit more elegance. A giant cross was mounted to the wall at the back of the stage. Two massive projector screens hung overhead, next to an assortment of stage lights. There were well over three thousand seats, and they were almost entirely packed. RCA was more than just a high school; they educated elementary and middle school students as well. Despite filling so many seats, each class contained hardly fifty students. Elementary and middle school parents occupied the extra seats that day.

The audience was a sea of green and blue, thanks to the colorful uniform polo shirts, each featuring a small embroidered alligator head on the side of the chest. The other color splotches were from the khaki shorts and slacks on the boys, classic dark plaid skirts on the girls, and a select few mustard-colored "gold" shirts. RCA allowed sweatshirts, but only those without logos. They were scarce, as outerwear wasn't usually necessary in Florida's fall weather.

Principal Randall had been speaking for about ten minutes, and just like at church, I absorbed a fraction of the content. If I drifted off too much, Benny would jab me with his elbow. That had happened twice: once when I became enamored with separating two stuck-together pages of a Bible, and another time when I stared at one of my classmates for a bit too long.

Benny was well aware of my multi-year crush on Jennifer Carrera, possibly the smartest girl in school. She was curvier than most of my classmates and always wore glasses. She was Latina and lived further from the school than most, since her father worked in

Miami. Spending less time on campus than other students was definitely one reason she always had her head on so straight.

Benny made kissing noises.

"Shut up!" I whispered.

The back-to-school assembly reclaimed my attention when they played a highlight reel from the past year. It opened with the national anthem playing over footage of students reciting the pledge of allegiance.

The video continued, showing football games and a theatrical performance, Dr. Seuss's *Seussical*, in which I played a jungle animal. The footage psyched me up for the next musical, which was holding auditions soon.

The video ended with a few interviews with the previous year's seniors, discussing their college plans.

That's right, I thought, *college*. I had barely started researching colleges, though I could worry about that later.

After the video, the RCA cheerleaders took to the stage and performed a dance routine to "Awesome God," a popular worship song. It was cheesy as heck. Despite following the classic "skirts no more than four inches above the knee" rule regarding standard uniforms, the cheer squad showed more thigh than you'd ever expect from such a religious school. Teenage me wasn't complaining.

"Gimme a W! Gimme another W! Gimme a J! Gimme a D! What would Jesus do?! Wooooooo!"

I was all for celebrating my love for Jesus… but that cringy vibe had me burying my face in my hands.

Principal Randall returned to the stage. "Let's have a hand for our RCA cheerleaders! Absolutely beautiful, aren't they?"

The audience clapped.

"I must apologize, parents. I know many of you were looking forward to hearing from our beloved Pastor Tom, but he is unfortunately busy with a church matter."

A few audience members groaned at the news that they wouldn't be entertained by the charismatic head pastor of Righteous Christ Church. Parents around RCC treated Pastor Tom like a celebrity. One of the few times I'd seen him in the wild, he was signing autographs for women in the hallway after giving a sermon. I felt most of his presence in my life through whispers of adoration, sometimes from myself. "I go to Pastor Tom's church," I'd state proudly when the opportunity presented itself. He was a bona fide local celebrity.

Principal Randall cleared his throat. "I will now close us out with a prayer. Dear Father God, I thank you for the opportunity to disciple this next generation of souls to go forth and spread your good news through their works. I am grateful for the chance to touch each of their lives. As the pup suckles on its mother's teat for sustenance, I ask that you guide these children as they learn from our wonderful faculty. As we begin our first day, I pray every student looks to you and your word, your Bible, for guidance on how to best navigate their education. Amen."

*   *   *

Before heading to lunch, the faculty instructed us to proceed to the hallway outside the sanctuary to sign up for homeroom, the fifteen-minute class we'd report to at the beginning of each school day for the entire year.

Benny took the decision seriously. "I do NOT wanna end up with Ms. Branten again; she was an absolute snore last year."

"Yeah," I said. "I didn't love her. Who were you thinking?"

I didn't even hear what Benny said next. Jennifer had gotten into the line at the far end of the hallway. The sign above her read Mr. Crumbull.

I knew my next move. "I think we should sign up for Mr. Crumbull this year. Let's go, before he's taken!"

"Umm… have you lost your marbles? Everyone says he's SO strict."

Frustration quickly replaced Benny's confusion when he saw who was signing the sheet at the table we were heading to.

"Are you serious right now? You're gonna stick us with one of the worst teachers for our entire senior year so you can sit in the same room as your crush and probably not even talk to her?"

I didn't even answer Benny's question; that would require admitting I was being an awful friend, or lying.

Jennifer finished signing up and walked away. Once she was gone, it was safe to approach. I signed the sheet, and Benny reluctantly followed suit.

"The things I do for you…" he said.

As I turned around and walked to the exit, I smashed headfirst into a student, and both our backpacks fell to the ground.

Benny let out a quick laugh. "Oh, HELLO, Jennifer," he said. "Fancy meeting you here…"

"I'm so sorry, Arthur!" said Jennifer, gathering her backpack and adjusting her glasses. "All my fault, all my fault."

A warmth filled my cheeks as I composed myself. "Uh… hey, no worries. I wasn't paying attention."

"I was just having second thoughts about Mr. Crumbull for homeroom," said Jennifer.

Out of the corner of my eye, I noticed a familiar face approaching to observe my total lack of game firsthand—our new pal and discipleship project, Ella. I focused on wrapping up the conversation at hand before she'd arrive.

"Oh, okay," I said. "We just signed up. Would be fun to see you in there, Jenn."

"That would be fun! Well, okay, as long as I know I'll have some friends in there. He can't be as bad as everyone says, right? I know some friends think he's worth it cause he's really smart. He has a doctorate."

"That does sound fun…" said Benny through clenched teeth.

He wasn't much of an academic.

"Well anyway," said Jennifer. "I guess I'll see you guys in homeroom tomorrow! I gotta go meet my mom outside to pick up my lunch. Bye!"

"Bye!" I blurted out a few seconds too late.

"Smooth moves, Artie," mocked Ella. "You blush easily."

Unsurprisingly, she added an off-kilter vibe to how she wore her uniform. She sported a long-sleeve black shirt ripped at the elbows under her green polo, both of which exposed an inch or two of her stomach. Her skirt was definitely over four inches above the knee. She also wore a pair of tall striped socks. Despite having rid her dark hair of the red streaks it featured on Saturday, I was curious if the faculty would give her a hard time about her general style.

Benny threw his hands in the air. "GIRL, welcome to your new home! Stoked to see you again. The hair looks nice, by the way."

"Thanks," said Ella. "So what is all this, anyway? I had my headphones in."

Benny rolled his eyes. "We just signed up for the WORST homeroom. Care to join us?"

"Hard pass." Ella stepped to the closest table and signed it without looking.

"Ouch," I retorted.

"So, are we eating lunch at that fancy restaurant or what?" asked Ella.

"No, that's faculty only during the day," I said. "Follow us, and we can eat a bunch of cheap fried food at the normie cafe next door."

She looked directly at me. "It's okay. I'll just spice it up with some marijuana ketchup." She fished into her backpack.

I didn't fully buy it, but I also wouldn't have been surprised. I'd never even seen pot.

"I'm kidding."

"I know…" I said.

Ella smirked and nodded. "Riiiight…"

*   *   *

After an unhealthy amount of smiley-faced cheese fries and chicken tenders, Benny, Ella, and I stood in a surprisingly long line to receive our locker assignments.

"Here you go! Have a blessed day," chirped the librarian as she handed me the number *48* on a flash card.

Benny and Ella received *49* and *50*, respectively. It turned out they assigned the numbers in order, so the three of us would have neighboring lockers.

This will make it easier to show Ella my example of living biblically, I thought.

The lockers belonging to Ella and me were on top, and Benny's was underneath Ella's. I had lucked out over the years and never had to deal with a bottom locker, which, because of my slightly above-average height, I was incredibly thankful for.

"Thank you, Jesus," I muttered under my breath.

If they assigned me a bottom locker, I would have complained, but Benny was too much of an optimist to care about his misfortune.

Ella started unloading her backpack into her locker, and smirked as she glanced down at Benny, who kneeled to access his.

She smirked and said, "So, does it make you uncomfortable to see a woman be shown more respect than a man?"

Benny laughed. "You've got the wrong guy, Ella. If it were my choice, I'd transfer to a church that allowed women to be pastors."

"Right on."

They fist-bumped.

I was surprised to hear that. It was clear that the Bible instructed women to take on submissive roles toward the men in their lives, allowing the men to lead without question. I wasn't sure how Benny could ignore that. Like most vague ideas touched on in the Bible, my autistic mind interpreted them as hard rules. Subtlety wasn't my strong suit, causing me to view morality and justice in black and white.

Maybe, I thought, *the worldly people Benny surrounded himself with in New York over the summer influenced him to stray from the holy path.*

I kept those concerns to myself for the time being, knowing Ella wasn't ready for such a confrontation. Besides, the purity conference next week was sure to convey that information to all the RCA girls thoroughly.

Benny took a few Broadway playbills from his backpack and stuck them to the inside of his locker door with sticky tack. He stood up and turned around just as Samuel approached. His dark blonde hair looked just as shampoo commercial-worthy as it was when he led worship on Saturday night. His signature flannel shirt and guitar were missing, so he was at least lacking some of his weekend allure. He did, however, make his otherwise-hideous mustard polo look good.

"Sup, Benny?" Samuel's voice would command respect, if not for its belittling cadence. "I heard you made a new boyfriend in New York this summer."

My gullibility prevented me from even considering the rumor could be true. *Benny is a good Christian boy. He'd never sink so low as to partake in such horrific sins. Samuel's just doing what he does best—finding something ridiculous to accuse someone of and convincing everyone else that it's true.*

Ella seemed surprisingly chill, witnessing her new friend get insulted and just standing there. Perhaps she had already learned there's nothing wrong with gayness, and calling someone gay wasn't an insult. Maybe she simply wasn't attuned to the subtle tone of Samuel's bullying yet.

Before Benny could answer, Ms. Flannigan, the drama teacher, entered the hallway. Her frizzy red hair, eclectic glasses, and creative fashion choices stood out in any room.

Samuel immediately straightened up, put his arm around Benny's shoulder, waved, and said, "So nice to see you, Ms. Flannigan."

Her forward momentum was consistent as she walked by, but she put in the effort for a quick on-the-move greeting. "Hello, Samuel! And hello, the rest of you! I'll see you all at auditions for the musical tomorrow after school, right?"

I was ecstatic about the musical. "Absolutely!"

"Definitely will!" echoed Benny.

Samuel shrugged.

"Whoopie!" Ms. Flannigan continued around the corner, winking as she left.

Despite being collectively known as the cool theater teacher, even Ms. Flannigan wasn't beyond Samuel's social manipulations. To the faculty, he was God's chosen young man. As the son of the head youth pastor, Robbie, he was untouchable, but not in a way where he'd get away with obviously horrific behavior. He was an evil genius. He'd treat his classmates like ants beneath his feet, but turn on the charm as soon as an adult walked by. As far as the faculty could tell, he was the embodiment of Christ's image.

With Ms. Flannigan no longer in earshot, Samuel's personality returned to his animalistic default. He turned to face Benny again.

Benny's confidence was all but gone. He stared at the ground, holding his arms across his stomach. "I'm not gay, Samuel. Why would you think that?"

Samuel mimicked Benny with an increased emphasis on his feminine inflection. "Ahmm, I'm not gayyyy, Samuel! Why would you think thahht?!" He returned to the aggressive inflection he featured when adults weren't around. "Even when you say you're not gay, you sound like a frickin' faggot."

Back then, the "F slur" was an entirely normalized casual insult, especially in an environment where homosexuality was so heavily frowned upon. As long as he used "frick" instead of "fuck," Samuel was living the life God supported. Even Benny wasn't very phased, at least not on the outside.

Ella's nostrils flared as she clenched her fists. She broke her silence, shoving Samuel away from Benny.

"What the fuck's wrong with you?!"

Samuel smiled and looked Ella up and down. "You're feisty. I like that."

He stepped toward her and put one hand against the locker over her shoulder, pinning her against the green metal. Her eyes narrowed.

He asked, "What's your name?"

"Not my first time being threatened by a monumental bitch like yourself. You sure you wanna do this, Garnier Fructis?"

Before Ella could enact what would've likely been a legendary smack down, Samuel spun around and morphed his personality toward innocence yet again, though it wasn't a performance for an adult. His on-again, off-again girlfriend was approaching.

Rachel Bristol still wore her cheerleading outfit from the assembly, though she covered it with a green sweatshirt featuring the RCA Gators logo. She had pulled her blonde hair back into a classic cheerleader ponytail. Rachel was one of the prettiest girls in school, though her timid personality didn't flaunt it.

Samuel tilted his head, reached his hands forward, and approached her. "Babe. Hey. I was just looking for you. You look beautiful, by the way." He placed his hands on her waist and kissed her.

I chirped, "Hey, no PDA on campus!"

"Public displays of affection" were against school rules. My self-righteous, autistic drive to police my classmates when they strayed from "God's path" was less severe than it was during previous years, but it was still one of my least-attractive qualities.

"Hey," said Samuel. "Why don't you mind your own business, retard? Go back to organizing your pencils or whatever."

I lowered my head and took a step back.

"Samuel, that's not okay," said Rachel. "Apologize, now."

Samuel glanced vaguely in my direction. "Sorry, dude." He turned back to Rachel. "Good?"

Rachel nodded.

"Alright," said Samuel. "Let's get outta here."

He grabbed Rachel's hand, but she pulled it away.

Rachel glanced toward Ella, then looked at Samuel. "Hey… before I came over here… were you flirting with that girl?"

Ella, Benny, and I turned toward our lockers and pretended not to eavesdrop.

"Babe. You know you're the only girl for me. But I dunno. Sometimes I just can't help myself, ya know?"

"Right, right." Rachel's brows furrowed. "Was it my fault? Am I not… meeting your needs?"

"I mean, it *is* your job to look hot for me. But also, like… look at her. She's dressed like a frickin' slut."

Rachel looked Ella up and down. "I think she looks cute, though. You wouldn't like it if I dressed like that?"

Ella cracked a smile into her locker.

"Of course I would. Just… don't do it around everyone. You can't go flaunting that body around here like this new chick. You're gonna cause the other guys to stumble."

"Okay. You're right. I'm sorry."

"That's my girl." Samuel smacked Rachel on the bottom.

She closed her eyes and flinched. Samuel grabbed his books from his locker and looked over at Benny.

"See you later, fairy."

Finally, Samuel was gone.

Ella rolled her eyes as she buried her head into her locker. She turned around, ready to burst. Rachel had walked to her locker, three over from our little cluster. Her aggressive body language made it clear she was experiencing some emotional discomfort.

Ella approached Rachel. "Hey… I'm Ella."

Benny and I snooped from behind our locker doors.

Rachel wiped a tear from her eye. "Oh… hi. Ya know, you really shouldn't dress like that. It could cause the guys here to lust after you. Besides, the first teacher who sees you will tell you to order longer skirts and shirts without holes."

"Funny. I could've sworn I heard you say my outfit was cute."

Rachel seemed taken aback. "Oh. Umm. I mean… it is cute."

"Thanks. Yours's pretty cute too. My old school wasn't fancy enough for a cheerleading squad. You looked great onstage."

Rachel blushed. "Oh… thank you so much. That's very sweet."

Ella smiled. "Ya know, we *can* make decisions without consulting what a man thinks about it."

Like an automated phone robot with predetermined responses, Rachel attempted to parrot what she'd heard all her life. "But the Bible says—"

"Fuck the Bible," said Ella.

Rachel blurted out a guffaw and covered her mouth. "Ha! Oh my goodness, you swear like a sailor. I've never heard anyone around here say something like that."

Ella folded her arms and cocked her head. "More where that came from. And, by the way, the Bible says that if a man's eye causes him to sin, he should pluck it out. Just sayin'."

"Oh… Well, the Old Testament covenant doesn't really matter any—"

"Matthew 5:29. Jesus said it."

Rachel's eyes widened. "Oh. I see you do know the Bible."

"Just the parts that come in handy."

"That's fair. I'll have to study that verse again and see what it says." Rachel composed herself and cleared her throat. "Anyway. I just think it's our responsibility to make sure we stay in our lane when men are trying to be good leaders. Our bodies are just gonna distract them from making wise decisions."

Ella shrugged. "Maybe if they can only be good leaders when they're not turned on by a fully clothed woman in a hallway, they shouldn't be the de facto leaders."

"That's… I mean. Sure. But… that's just how things are, and I know you don't like it, but that's what God wants us to do."

"Well… guess I can't argue against God." Ella placed her hand on Rachel's arm. "Just do me a favor. If a guy's treating you like shit, run away! I mean y'all say God is love, right? I don't think a loving God would want him to treat you like that. And based on my ten minutes of knowing your boy… you deserve better. Like, way better."

Rachel's eyes almost welled up. "Thank you. I appreciate that. I'm sorry for what I said. You're very sweet."

"Anytime. You're sweet too."

Ella reached into her backpack and grabbed a pen. She wrote her AOL Instant Messenger screen name on Rachel's arm—*hardxcore247*.

"Here's my name on AIM if you ever wanna chat. I'm usually on after school."

"I'll definitely add you. But in case I forget…"

Rachel took the pen and wrote her screen name on Ella's arm, *cheer4jesus23*.

"Yikes," said Ella.

Rachel blushed. "I know, I know. It's like four years old. I really need to change it."

Benny and I decided amongst ourselves that the tension had died down enough to approach.

"Hey, Rachel," I said. "I see you met our new friend."

Rachel and I were friendly, but not very close.

"Hey, Arthur. Hey, Benny. And yeah, we're gonna be AIM friends, so you know it's real."

I dryly voiced my approval with the hippest lingo. "Woot woot."

Benny's morale was still low from the encounter with Samuel. I could tell he struggled to think fondly of Rachel while she was associated with Samuel, but he wouldn't actually hold it against her.

"How was your summer, Rachel?" he asked.

"It was pretty good! Spent lots of time with Samuel and his dad. Oh, and sorry if Samuel was giving you a hard time earlier."

Benny paused. "No worries…"

Rachel was quick to change the subject. "I ended up doing the theater summer camp, actually."

"Oh, no way!" I was surprised—Rachel wasn't much of a theater nerd. "I almost went to that."

"Yeah, it was so fun! I hadn't sung since I was a kid. It was great getting back into it. I sang *Blackbird* by The Beatles for the showcase."

"Sick."

I refrained from mentioning the embarrassment that was my complete lack of experience with music outside of film and game soundtracks, musicals, a few punk rock bands, and that one album by Evanescence.

"Oh," Rachel continued, "I wanted to ask you guys a question. I was thinking of trying out for the musical since it's our last year and all. Do you know when auditions are?"

Benny came to life. "Oh my gosh, that would be so fun! They're tomorrow after school in the theater. You can pretty much sing anything, and they will give out the scripts for character readings there."

"Oh, thanks so much! I'll definitely do that! Ella, are you gonna audition too?"

Ella winced a little. "Oh, uh… I'm not much of a singer."

"That's fine," Benny chirped. "There are usually plenty of background roles. It's just so fun to be part of the ensemble."

Rachel rubbed Ella's arm. "Come on, it would be so fun!"

"Uhh… sure?"

Benny squealed. "OH MY GOODNESS. Ella, I am so excited. Your first musical! And Rachel's, too!" He stepped between the girls and draped one arm over each of their shoulders. "My heart is so full. This is gonna be the best senior year ever."

It was a very nice thought—the four of us hanging out in rehearsals over the coming months. Sadly, it was too good to be true.

3. Garden of Submission

Mr. Crumbull's seating chart ensured that Jennifer and I sat at opposite corners in homeroom. Just my luck. But of course, being me, I felt partially elated that I had an excuse to avoid talking to her. That didn't stop Benny from darting his eyes back and forth between her and me, smiling wide with his head resting in his hands.

There were still four minutes left until 8 a.m., so if I was gonna talk to her, I had to act fast. After a few moments, I took a deep breath, stood up, and walked straight toward her without giving myself a moment to think. "Hi, Jennifer. How are—"

"Good morning, class. Mr. Morton, please return to your desk."

Teachers at RCA often had a thorough knowledge of every student in the small school—even those they'd never met.

Mr. Crumbull had a beer gut, a thick mustache covering his upper lip, and was balding underneath his very European hat. He wore his glasses for practical use only—no style whatsoever. He wore a standard button-down shirt covered by a buttoned vest.

"Everyone, please rise for the national anthem."

Mr. Crumbull's strict dictation gave me a new excuse to bail. Before I could even assess Jennifer's reaction to my partial question, I was back by my seat, standing extremely straight, looking ahead, deep in thought.

I bet she was confused. She probably thought I was creepy. What was I even thinking? I should just leave her alone. She's better off with someone less awkward.

Another thought occurred to me: *I could pray.*

Under my breath, I muttered, "Dear God, please, if it's in your plan, please make Jennifer like me. It would make me so happy. Amen."

"… one nation, under God, indivisible, with liberty, and justice for all." I hoped nobody noticed my verbal tardiness.

"And now, the Christian flag." Mr. Crumbull's dull inflection indicated he very much missed summer vacation.

I followed in step with the class. "I pledge allegiance to the Christian flag, and to the savior for whose kingdom it stands; one savior, crucified, risen, and coming again with life everlasting to all who believe."

"Today the—Mr. Connell, please remove your sweatshirt until you can get one without a brand on it. Thank you. Ahem… today, the administration has asked for us to read from *Devotions for Young Minds*. Please turn to page 147."

His lack of enthusiasm wasn't the most-effective way to get his students energized about the coming school day.

Devotions were bite-sized reminders of how to live your best Christian life; kind of like reading a daily horoscope if everyone was the same sign, and the instruction was always about gleaning information from the same source—the Bible. No fortune telling angle, though. Well, aside from the impending rapture and apocalypse, of course.

"Lessons From the Sermon on the Mount." He cleared his throat. "Jesus once said, 'blessed are the poor in spirit, for theirs is the kingdom of Heaven. Blessed are those who mourn, for they will be comforted. Blessed are the meek, for they will inherit the Earth.' Matthew 5:3-5."

Mr. Crumbull continued to read about the biblical benefits of humility. Young me was oblivious to the hypocrisy of reading that passage on a multi-million-dollar campus with two restaurants and bookstores.

A few minutes later, our first homeroom session ended. The bell rang, or rather, the bulky tube TV by the ceiling corner chimed. The permanent burn-in the digital clock had imprinted on the TV always bothered me.

On my way out, Benny approached to lambaste me about my lack of game, right on schedule. "That was brutal, man. Did you even get one word out?"

"Barely. It's fine. All in God's plan… right?"

I entered the combination to my locker.

"Sure," said Benny. "But if everything is God's plan, that doesn't mean you sit there and do nothing. Do you really think his plan is for everyone to do nothing?"

"Obviously not."

Benny shook his head slowly. *"Tch, tch, tch.* Gotta make some moves, my man."

"I will, I will…"

*   *   *

To my surprise, Jennifer was in my first class. I should've expected it—she was always in the advanced placement classes. It was my first AP course; I was a solid B- student, but over the summer, my fascination (or neurodivergent obsession) with computers allowed me to show enough drive to get into AP Science.

Right off the bat, Mrs. Till surprised us with a verbal pop quiz, just for extra credit.

"Question 1: What is the primary element used in the construction of central processing units for modern computers?" She sounded almost giddy.

Jennifer's hand immediately raised.

"Yes, Jennifer?"

She adjusted her glasses, adorably. "What is silicon?"

"That's correct!"

Oof. Was it getting warm? It wasn't news to me that intelligence turned me on, but hoo boy. I knew she was smart, but knowledge of computer construction was a new level of hot.

The quiz contained a few more questions, though none were about computers, much to my dismay. Jennifer answered three in total. I answered one about electricity. Jennifer smiled at me when I got it right. I think my heart skipped a beat!

After class, hyped up on adrenaline from my one question streak of scientific genius, I finally summoned the courage to talk to Jennifer. I approached her at her locker and tapped her on the shoulder. "Hi." That's it. Just "Hi."

"Hey there, Art. I didn't know you were gonna be in my class. Welcome!"

"Thanks! Yeah, I built a computer over the summer and they saw that as enough initiative, I guess."

"Oh, sick! What kind?"

Careful when asking a neurodivergent teenager for details about their nerdy hobbies. "It was a PC, obviously. Nvidia 7600 GT, Intel CPU… made of silicon…"

"Eyy…"

"A 512 gigabyte hard drive. I don't actually remember how much RAM, sorry."

"Oh, don't worry about it, you kinda… lost me, actually." Jennifer giggled. "I haven't kept up on computer builds too much lately, but I have dabbled. So cool that you built one, though!"

As was common during conversations about my hyperfixations, my mind waited anxiously for my next turn to speak, which manifested in impatient nodding. "Yeah, yeah. It's working really well. I've been playing *FEAR* at ultra settings. It almost hits sixty frames per second at 1024 by 768 resolution." I rarely remembered that the other ninety-nine percent of the world didn't give one crap about video game tech specs.

"Wow, that's so smooth! My rig can't crack forty."

I gulped. Jennifer was in my tier of nerd. I laughed for some reason.

Jennifer tilted her head. "What's so funny?"

"Oh, nothing. Sorry." I glanced at the floor. "I just do that."

"You're good, dude. But hey, class is starting, so I gotta run. Umm… here…"

She grabbed a pen and flashcard from her sweater pocket and wrote something down: *PikachuButtcheeks2.*

"You're on AIM, right?" she asked. "That's my name. Message me if you see me on?"

Butterflies fluttered in my stomach as I took the card. "Wow, great name. And definitely I will."

"Oh, I almost forgot. I hope you don't think I'm a bad Christian for saying this, but some of the stuff in this science book… it's just not true. Since you're new to AP, I'm not sure how caught up you are."

"What do ya mean?"

"Well, for starters, the earth is billions of years old. We would never have evolved into humans if we only had a few thousand years."

"Wait, you aren't one of those people who think the universe exploded out of nothing and that we used to be monkeys, are you? Oh… sorry. No offense if you are."

"This is science, Artie, not conjecture. Mrs. Till agrees, by the way. She's not super public about it 'cause the other teachers would rat her out to the board. But she gives it to us straight."

"Wait. I don't understand. I thought Christians couldn't believe this stuff?"

"There are lots of Christians who believe in evolution. Not everything in the Bible needs to be taken literally, ya know? For one, the Earth wasn't created in six days and seven nights. Many Christians think God intended it to be poetry. If we discover facts about the universe, our subjective readings of the Bible need updating, not the science. It doesn't mean God isn't real. Just means it's… not as simple as some of the other teachers would tell you."

I was dumbfounded. I was too deep in my feelings to see this as a deal breaker, but there was no denying it was a red flag.

Jennifer could tell she made me uncomfortable. Conveniently, her next class was starting. "Just food for thought. I really gotta run, though. Let's talk later! See ya!"

"Yeah, see ya."

I'd never heard anyone talk so critically about the Bible before. *Could there be other ways to interpret it? How could that be if it was the infallible word of God?* In any case, I'd process that later. And besides, it was Jennifer. She was amazing. *I'll hear her out next time*, I thought as I headed to my next class.

*   *   *

Three o'clock in the afternoon was a time of celebration for many students at Righteous Christ Academy because it signaled freedom. For me, three o'clock could be the start of a few fun activities. I could head home to play video games with cutting edge Xbox 360 graphics. I could eat a burrito at the hot new restaurant, Chipotle Grill. I could check the mail to see if the DVD rental service, Netflix, had shipped three new episodes of *Lost* for what once qualified as binge watching. In reality, though, three o'clock signaled the beginning of the best part of my day: theatrical extracurriculars. That Tuesday was the first afternoon of the year that we theater nerds gathered for the sake of fun, art, and friendship. The theater was an outlet for our most eccentric selves.

We didn't have a show to rehearse yet, but the excitement surrounding the impending musical auditions permeated the air more than sweat in the boys' changing room.

They weren't the kind of auditions we were used to. Ms. Flannigan emailed our parents over the summer to let us know what to expect. We were to prepare a song to audition with—any song—and simply show up. She provided no further details—not even the name of the show.

Benny, Ella, and I gravitated to seats in the corner of the newly built theater on the ground floor of the main school building. The room itself was a bit hideous. The shockingly vibrant rainbow color scheme covered the chairs, carpets, and walls of the auditorium. The on-stage curtain was a bombastic purple. Color choices aside, it was a proper theater, and we were ecstatic to finally perform in it.

"This is beyond sick," said Benny with wide eyes. "I heard they almost postponed it for another year, but Ms. Flannigan stepped in to make sure it got done for us."

"Heh. Sucks to be last year's seniors." I reeled in my candor slightly. "I mean… glad we get to use it!"

It was lovely to see my theater friends again, scattered among the first few rows of the massive auditorium. I exchanged waves with Andrew, a tall boy of low energy who was frequently cast in roles that accurately mirrored his religious fervor and kind heart. Unlike Samuel, Andrew actually represented the character of Jesus, with as much authenticity as humanly possible.

Rachel entered the theater, her blonde hair bouncing on her shoulders rather than tied into her usual cheerleader's ponytail. We waved her over to join us and exchanged pleasantries. Although we all fed off the excitement in the room, Rachel seemed lower energy than usual. Her social status generally revolved around being a hot cheerleader, and dating Samuel, the son of the head youth pastor, Robbie. She was a fish out of water among theater nerds.

I wasn't sure how she was gonna focus on the musical effectively, so I asked plainly, "Hey, how are you gonna balance this with your cheerleading?"

"Oh, I'm actually skipping cheering this year."

Benny turned toward her and raised a brow. "Wow. But isn't that like… your main jam?"

"Yeah… I just… it's time to focus on more important things, like college."

Ella, sitting next to Rachel, sat up and removed her iPod headphones from her ears. She leaned in close to Rachel. "You know this isn't study hall, right?"

Rachel swung her head to mirror Ella's and struck a silly expression. "It's not?!"

Ms. Flannigan arrived a fashionable seven minutes late. Her red hair was almost hidden among the vibrant theater palette. Her bandana featured The Magic School Bus, a deliberate parallel to her fictional doppelgänger, Ms. Frizzle.

"Hello, my babies!" she said. "I missed you so much!"

Three small yells of "woop!" leaped from the audience. One was from Benny.

"Now, I know you're all wondering how this audition process is going to work. I thought I'd make it more fun this time. Instead of signing up in the hall and sitting around doing nothing, I figured it would be a better time if we turned this into a show itself!"

"Oh my goodness…" Rachel squirmed in her seat and glanced at the exit.

"After all, you're all here to be performers, right? Let's get that stage fright out of the way! Now, should we get started or am I forgetting something…"

"WHAT'S THE SHOW?!" I couldn't tell who asked first, but nearly everyone echoed them soon after.

"Oh, right! The show… WELL. We're doing something a little different this year. Over the summer, I attended a playwriting workshop and met the most amazing songwriter there. We may or may not be dating now. Anyway, we teamed up and wrote an original musical that nobody has ever seen before, and we want YOU to be the first actors and actresses to perform it. How does that sound?"

The audience reaction probably wasn't as enthusiastic as Ms. Flannigan was expecting, but it was still pretty energetic. There was certainly disappointment that our final performance wasn't going to be a musical we had petitioned the faculty to approve, such as *Les Misérables*, or the much turned down (for some reason) *Beauty and the Beast*. That being said, depending on what our eclectic director and her mysterious lover had cooked up, it could possibly be very cool.

"The musical is called… drum roll, please."

A few students smacked their hands against the backs of seats. I lazily slapped my thigh a few times.

"*Eden*. We wrote a musical about the Genesis story. Adam, Eve, and the snake. Oh my gosh, you are going to LOVE IT!"

A look of disappointment struck most of the students sitting in the green and purple seats. A few of the most devout students made an audible "ooh" or "ah," but who knows if they were sincere. Well, other than Andrew, who was predictably thrilled by the biblical subject matter.

Ella was the first in our friend clump to voice our collective letdown. She leaned toward Benny and me and whispered, "Are you kidding me right now? I'm supposed to get on a stage and act out a Bible story for hundreds of people?"

"One thousand people. And maybe it will be good?" I tried to stay positive.

What kind of Christian would I be if hearing that our musical was Bible-themed made me sad? I thought to myself. *And this would, of course, be beneficial for Ella's growth in the spirit. Win-win. Right?*

"And don't worry," Ms. Flannigan continued, "nobody is gonna be naked onstage. I have some ideas for outfits covered in leaves. Oh, and there will be a kiss. A stage kiss, of course. I cleared the approval through Principal Randall already. Turns out, when you say you're gonna put on a show based on a Bible story, the approval process just flies by."

The students in the audience gossiped amongst themselves. None of us had performed an onstage kiss before.

That's some serious PDA, I thought.

After some technical troubleshooting, Ms. Flannigan played a select few tracks from the demo CD for *Eden* over the theater speakers.

Halfway through the first song, I wasn't impressed, but wasn't horrified either. There are plenty of musicals out there with questionable opening numbers. The emphasis on the Earth being created in "six days and seven nights" stuck out for obvious reasons, and caused me to distract myself with daydreams of Jennifer for a brief moment.

The Act 1 *I want* song that many musicals feature, sung by Eve and performed by Ms. Flannigan, was surprisingly emotional.

"Will I ever stand alone, when I'm made from Adam's spare rib bone? Maybe I should just return to dust."

I had never heard the Genesis story pitched in such a cynical way, but I was too swept up in the emotional melody to feel bothered. Andrew, however, wore a conflicted expression.

Oddly enough, the musical portrayed the snake, AKA Satan, as somewhat of a misunderstood hero. We were meant to feel sympathy for him. He felt passionate about pursuing knowledge. He saw the pain Adam and Eve felt, trapped in a garden with little autonomy. He wanted to free them. It was tragic, because he was broken by default. He was incapable of understanding God's love.

Adam was portrayed as rather misogynistic. One of his lines was, "How can I trust her word? She's just a woman; her mind is not assured."

The most powerful song in the musical, by a mile, was Eve's third act empowerment anthem, *More Than a Rib*. "If I had a garden of my own, no man, no snake, no Father would hold me down. But here I sit, Adonai. I accept this holy role, larger than I." Teenage me did not see the full breadth of the story's progressive profundity.

By the end of the demo, most of us were sold. It was a bold, possibly risky musical to perform at a Christian school. As edgy theater nerds, we were all about it. I had my hesitations, but the message in the end supported what I had been taught, so I figured it was acceptable. As it would turn out, the controversial nature of much of the show would not go unnoticed by the more devout faculty for very long. For the time being, though, it was incredibly exciting.

Benny cheered. "WOOOOOO!"

The other students clapped with enthusiasm.

Andrew seemed conflicted, as did Ella. Their claps were on the softer side. I definitely noticed Ella smirk during a few of Eve's more validating moments, so maybe she'd stay onboard.

Rachel, on the other hand, sniffled during more than a few songs. She seemed to relate strongly to Eve's struggle.

Ms. Flannigan welled up, brought her hands to her face, and bowed a few times. "Thank you… Thank you so much."

The show was a representation of a would-be independent woman's struggle to accept her role in life. Ms. Flannigan might have been hurting just as much as the coming school year would hurt us, but we were too naïve to notice.

After a five-minute break, auditions began. The first few performances garnered a modicum of enthusiasm from the students. Not terrible, but not amazing, either.

Benny was predictably good in his performance of the duet *I'll Cover You* from *Rent*. He played both parts. The performance set a record for the amount of applause for the day, though it wasn't exactly a standing ovation. Benny was a real talent. If anyone from our little theater troupe would make it on Broadway, it would be him. Along with a few other guys, Ms. Flannigan asked him to read for the role of God in addition to Adam.

"You still down, Ella?" asked Benny after he returned to his seat.

"Ugh. I'm supposed to follow that?"

"Aww, you're making me blush. Now get up there!"

Ella grunted and trudged up to the stage.

"Please don't be awful, Ella…" Benny whispered to me.

"Hi, my name is Ella Kent. I'll be singing 'Tire Swing' by Kimya Dawson."

Ella had mentioned in passing that she loved the movie *Juno*, which that song had featured in.

Her singing voice sounded pleasantly indie. Nobody performed with accompaniment that day, so some a cappella awkwardness was unavoidable, but she made the most of the moment. The almost-talky song didn't provide much evidence that she'd get cast in a leading role, but she impressed us, nonetheless.

Benny stood up and clapped loudly when she finished singing. A few other students echoed his joy, including myself and Rachel. Ella then read for Eve, like most of the girls.

Andrew's audition was predictably pleasant. He sang a classic church hymn with an operatic vibe. He read for Adam and God.

I was up next. I didn't show it, but I was terrified. My song choice was "Any Dream Will Do" from *Joseph and the Amazing Technicolor Dreamcoat*, another biblical musical. I had workshopped the song at summer theater camp two years prior.

My singing wasn't top-tier. It was well known that I struggled with pitch, but I had definitely improved over the years. Could senior year be the first (and last) time I'd get to sing a solo onstage in a musical?

My song garnered a few claps, and, predictably, a "woop!" from Benny.

Ms. Flannigan seemed lost in thought. "I'm actually gonna ask you to read for a different character. Can you please read for the snake?"

"Sure thing." I grabbed the page from Ms. Flannigan's hand at the front of the stage.

I was admittedly a little sick of being typecast as creepy animals in almost every play, but the snake had one solo, so it would definitely be a win if I got the role.

I struck the creepiest inflection I was capable of. "Dear Eve. I can offer you happiness… All you have to do is… eat the apple. Heh, heh, heh…"

Ms. Flannigan offered some notes. "That was super creepy, but remember, we're not portraying the snake as evil. Black and white characters aren't interesting. Try it again, but with more sympathy."

"Totally." I cleared my throat.

I repeated the line but without the evil laugh. Ms. Flannigan nodded. I continued through the remainder of the paragraph.

"Yes, very good, Arthur! Thank you for that."

I took my seat, beaming with pride.

"What a creep," Ella teased.

"Thanks?"

Before anyone else was called to the stage, Pastor Robbie entered the theater via a side door, followed closely by his son, Samuel. Robbie waved. "Hello! Don't mind me. I'll just be a second."

Rachel pulled her hoodie over her head.

"Trouble in paradise?" asked Ella.

"Something like that. I guess the stuff you said yesterday kinda stuck with me."

Ella smirked. "Oh, yeah?"

Rachel squirmed in her seat. "We had a big argument last night. I'm just… so over the pressure, ya know? Between him, his dad, and my parents… they just want me to be so perfect, and to exist basically just to make Samuel look good." She looked at Ella. "I just want to focus on finding myself."

Ella smiled. "Yikes, over share much?"

"I… uh…"

"Relax, I'm kidding! I think that's great."

Rachel smiled.

Pastor Robbie approached Ms. Flannigan. He placed his hand on her shoulder. I couldn't hear what they were discussing.

After a few moments, he patted Samuel on the back, said something to him, and left the theater. Samuel took a seat, spreading his arms across the tops of the empty seats on either side of him.

"Well, it sounds like we have a last-minute addition to the roster. Pastor Robbie's son, Samuel, needs an extracurricular credit, so he's going to participate in the musical with us. Welcome, Samuel!"

Ella groaned as I rolled my eyes. Rachel sank into her seat, and Benny scoffed.

"Welcome," muttered a few students.

"Would you like to be next?" asked Ms. Flannigan.

"Oh, uhh… sure." Samuel stepped onto the stage. It wasn't a surprise that the worship song he sang sounded great. He was the youth group worship leader, after all.

"Woo!" Ms. Flannigan was impressed.

Samuel read for Adam. Ms. Flannigan had him read a second scene, which had only happened with two other auditions so far.

Finally, Samuel's audition was over.

Up next was a pretty girl with long black hair: Jade Parnacle. Her face was coated in expensive-looking makeup, and her clothes displayed no wrinkles. Peeking from under her shirt was the uniform of the RCA cheerleaders, of which she was the captain. She belted out "Defying Gravity" from the musical *Wicked*. I was impressed.

"Amazing, Jade!" said Ms. Flannigan.

"You're welcome," said Jade, curtsying.

Rachel rolled her eyes. "Ugh. That girl always hated me. I still can't tell if she was thrilled or pissed when I quit the cheer squad."

Ms. Flannigan checked her sheet. "Last, but probably not least. Rachel? Are you here?"

Rachel lowered the hoodie from her head. "I'm here. Hi."

She tripped a little on her way up to the stage.

Samuel whistled a cat call. "Yeah, Babe!"

Rachel didn't acknowledge it.

Ms. Flannigan pushed her glasses toward her eyes. "Well, Rachel. What will you be singing for us?"

"I'll be singing 'Blackbird' by The Beatles."

"One of my favorites." Ms. Flannigan smiled. "Let's hear it."

"Okay." Rachel took a deep breath, clasped her hands in front of her, and closed her eyes.

By the end of the first line of song, the room fell silent. Rachel had a lovely voice. She started with some hesitancy in her inflection, but she came into her own by the end. There was no disagreement in the audience—she was a star. For someone like me who had no familiarity with The Beatles, her song was a great introduction. After the powerful performance, Rachel finally opened her eyes.

"Wow. That was beautiful, Rachel." Ms. Flannigan's post-audition praise had not been of that intensity until then.

"Thank you so much."

Rachel then read two scenes for Eve. They were powerful. Rachel's delivery and body language emotionally conveyed Eve's pain.

When she sat back down, we absolutely lavished her with praise.

"That was SO good!" I said.

I wasn't a great liar, so it was rare that I was that enthusiastic.

Benny upped the energy level even further. "OH. MY. GOODNESS. Rachel, you are a star."

"Uh, thanks… That's so nice."

Ella leaned in. "Yeah, Rach. That was powerful. You've got skills."

"Thank you… I was so nervous. I hate feeling like everyone is looking at me and judging me."

For the final twenty minutes of auditions, Ms. Flannigan called a few audience members to the stage in pairs for chemistry readings. A few read for Adam, including Benny and Samuel, opposite Rachel and a few others for Eve. I was called to read for the snake in the background of a few Adam and Eve pairings, along with one other student.

Rachel showed hesitation when asked to read opposite Samuel, but she played along.

"I think I've seen enough," said Ms. Flannigan. "This has been so fun. I'm very excited. The cast list will go up Monday. You should all be very proud of yourselves."

It was a grueling two hours, but I was happy to have theater back in my life. That being said, it was time for a very slow five days of uncertainty. Waiting for the cast list to go up was always excruciating.

*   *   *

Benny had promised that the following night would be more than a standard Wednesday night youth service. He pitched it as a game night, though with little detail. It wasn't hard for Benny's charms to persuade Ella and Rachel to join us, though Ella did at least show a tiny bit of resistance.

Pastor Robbie gave a fairly standard sermon about the power of Satan's demons. Predictably, I tuned out most of it. I did absorb one part about how the *Harry Potter Series* was proof of Satan sending literal demons to pull us away from God. I thought that was ridiculous, as I had read a few of the books myself and enjoyed them. I winced a little as I questioned whether a good Christian would doubt their pastors like that.

"These books also encourage acts of violent rebellion. The 'hero' inflates his aunt into a balloon using demonic incantations, and she floats into space to die, simply because she asked him to do something he didn't feel like doing. God asks us to obey our parents and authority figures unconditionally, because it prepares us to obey Him unconditionally. My brothers and sisters in Christ... do not be swayed by Satan's latest seductions."

After the sermon, Pastor Marshall, the minister who introduced Benny and me to Ella, took the stage. "Hello, disciples! I'm so excited for you to get to play Underground Church with us tonight! The rules are simple. It's basically Mafia, if you've played that. We'll divide you into two teams: Christians and police. The lights will be off and it's the job of the Christians to find good hiding places. Two of the police will try to find Christians and escort them to prison!" He made a spooky gesture with his hands. "One of the police is an undercover Christian. He or she will try to find and bring Christians to a room that he or she designates as a church. If all the Christians gather at church, they win. If the police bring all the Christians to jail, the police win. It's gonna be so fun! Oh, and if you can somehow manage to sneak past us, jailbreaks are allowed."

We gathered in the lobby and received slips of paper with our assignments. After they handed out the last one, all the lights in the building went dark with a loud thud.

"Woooo!" shouted a few teens.

Benny pulled Ella, Rachel, and me in for a rousing huddle-style side hug. I squirmed a little in response to being hugged by a boy in public.

"Alright, everyone!" yelled Pastor Marshall over the youthful hullabaloo. "Police, please report to the station upstairs to receive your flashlights! Christians, scatter and avoid persecution at all costs!"

"Prepare to be arrested, criminals!" taunted Benny as he headed upstairs.

Ella rolled her eyes.

Rachel, Ella, and I booked it to the gym and onto the stage at the far end. When Ella groaned and fell behind, Rachel pulled her along by the hand.

"Ooh, under there!" said Rachel as she pointed to a long table covered with a black floor-length cloth.

We crawled underneath.

"Aren't you having FUN?!" said Rachel, jabbing Ella in the side.

"I mean… it's not *not* fun."

After a few minutes, we heard the creaking of metal steps. Ella and Rachel giggled conspicuously.

"Shh!" I whispered.

Ella pressed her hand over Rachel's mouth, and Ella did the same to her. I could still hear two muffled giggles as a flashlight drifted by.

The footsteps and light faded after a few moments.

"Well," I said, "I'm not getting caught thanks to y'all's giggling!"

Just as I lifted the cloth, Benny spun around with his policeman's flashlight, illuminating all three of us fugitives. "Ahhhh!" screamed Ella and Rachel as they booked it through the stage door behind us.

I hopped the stage rail and sprinted through the gym toward the lobby, but Benny was faster, tagging me from behind.

"Gotcha, Christian filth. Off to jail with you."

"Run!" I yelled to Rachel and Ella as Benny hauled me off to prison. "Run and survive!"

He escorted me up some stairs and into a smaller ministry room commonly used for middle school services.

"Got a live one, boys," he announced to the youth ministers posing as prison guards before heading down the stairs to hunt more Christians.

Pastor Robbie stepped toward me. "Welcome to Hell. Arthur, right?"

"That's me. So, what am I in for?"

"Well, we wanted to use this as a teaching experience. Christians have always been persecuted and always will be. You need to be prepared for what it will be like when you share God's word throughout the world."

I gulped and looked around the room. Two others had already been taken to jail and given their punishments. One of them was blindfolded, and she was squatting. I leaned to the side for a better look and noticed she held a wooden plank between her thighs and calves, which I assumed the ministers instructed her to not let fall. The visible part of her face was tensed. The other captive Christian was doing push ups while another youth minister counted in a harsh tone.

Pastor Robbie picked up two buckets of ice water from the side of the room and placed them in front of me. "Your hands. Ten minutes."

I stood in silence. The hypersensitivity of my autism made the proposed punishment sound extremely uncomfortable.

"Now, Arthur!" Robbie crouched in front of me. "You think you're gonna have a choice when you're a missionary overseas? They'll chop your hands off. You've got it easy."

I closed my eyes and slowly pushed my hands into the freezing buckets. I handled the first few seconds with little drama, but then the stinging started. I yanked my hands out and shook my head back and forth with the force of a hairy dog after a shower.

"I can't do this! I won't!"

Without even registering Pastor Robbie's insults that surely followed, I bolted down the stairs and into the furthest room I could find. I hid in a sound booth under a desk in the fetal position and waited for the game to end.

My mind sat somewhere between shock and fear. I was mentally frozen; uncomfortable, and unable to confront what I was actually feeling.

After at least twenty minutes, the lights boomed on.

I made my way to the lobby and reunited with my friends. Rachel and Ella were giggling. Benny seemed to be in goofy spirits, too.

"I think I got lost," I said. "Who won?"

"The police," said a smirking Benny. "Duh."

I turned to Ella and Rachel. "How did jail go for you?"

"Well, because we've got such epic skills," said Rachel, "we were the last two to get caught. Didn't even have to go to jail. How was jail for you?"

"Oh… it was fine. No big deal."

Internally, I struggled to reconcile my guilt over failing to live up to my pastor's expectations. I also felt concern for the ethics they showed, which added even more guilt, since judging my pastors was heavily frowned upon.

We stepped outside, and Benny headed off to meet his mom for a ride home. Ella and Rachel decided to get dinner at Chipotle. Even if it had been Chili's, I just wasn't hungry.

That night, self-deprecating thoughts kept my mind too stimulated for sleep.

If I want to walk a holy path, I need to toughen my skin.

I had no idea that my simulated prison experience was just the beginning of the year from Hell.

4. Sexy Trees

Thanks to the impending cast list, the first week of school felt like it lasted a month. The teachers didn't share much information of substance in my classes, as was expected for the first week in a school year. Instead, I sat through countless introductions, explanations of lesson plans, and prayers for the coming year. The next morning would herald the beginning of the year proper, starting with the cast list.

Before a restless night of anxiety-ridden sleep, I had some time to kill. I sat at my desk and turned on my bulky desktop PC. The monitor flickered on, revealing the classic rolling hills every Windows XP user was so familiar with. I clicked the icon of a little yellow person in mid sprint: AOL Instant Messenger.

In the mid-2000s, texting wasn't very practical, since most phones didn't have full keyboard access, digital or physical. We accessed the alphabet by pressing large number buttons multiple times to cycle through a collection of letters. Full sentences took commitment. If you wanted to chat with someone properly, you needed to clear some free time, sit yourself down at a computer, and log on to AIM. That night I was determined to start an instant message rapport with Jennifer, who I hadn't spoken to since I insulted her for believing in evolution.

Krr, krr, krr. The door-opening sound signaling a friend signing on would be forever etched into my brain. Sadly, it wasn't Jennifer. It was Andrew.

JesusLyfe321:

hey arthur! are you xcited 4 the cast list to go up tmrw?

FFXpert89:

umm duh. wat role are you hoping to get?

My screen name represented my obsession with the video game Final Fantasy X. I didn't notice it then, but the story of that game was easily the most anti-religious story I'd ever consumed. It just may have influenced me.

JesusLyfe321:

there arent that many named roles… embarrassing but i would luv to play adam…

FFXpert89:

yeah that would be cool. i have a feeling that if i get a named character it will be the snake. im always typecast as evil animals.

JesusLyfe321:

well thats cause ur so good at playing them! ur wolf in narnia was inspiring to me!

FFXpert89:

haha thx.

JesusLyfe321:

rats, my moms calling me. g2g. ill pray 4 us to get the roles god wants 4 us 2nite. bye!

FFXpert89:

me 2. ttyl.

Ka-chunk. The sound of a door slamming signaled goodbye for Andrew.

To kill time while waiting for Jennifer to appear under *Buddies,* I updated my away message. All the cool kids used song lyrics as the message that automatically appeared when someone messaged you while set to the *away* status. I decided on "Bring Me to Life" by Evanescence, a song I knew Jennifer was a fan of.

Krr, krr krr. My heart skipped a beat. At last, Jennifer was online. But I couldn't be so lame as to message her the second she appeared online. I had to wait a bit first.

After what felt like five minutes but was likely closer to thirty seconds, I double-clicked her name. I took a moment to formulate the ultimate opening message.

FFXpert89:

sup

PikachuButtcheeks2:

Hey!! How r u?

Jennifer's online lingo seemed slightly more proper than I was used to. And by more proper, I mean used capital letters. So, I adapted.

FFXpert89:

Im pretty good. Just nervous about the cast list going up tmrw.

PikachuButtcheeks2:

Oh right! You auditioned for the musical!

FFXpert89:

Yeah! Im really excited. Also im sorry about the other day. U obviously know way more about science than me.

I still thought she was probably a little misguided, but I wanted to get back on her good side.

PikachuButtcheeks2:

Oh ur good! Don't even worry about it. :) And I'm sorry too. I shouldn't have pushed all that on you.

FFXpert89:

Haha ok kool. No worries.

There was silence for a minute, so I changed the topic.

FFXpert89:

Did u hear about the purity conference happening this week?

PikachuButtcheeks2:

Yeah. I actually think im gonna skip it. My parents rnt big fans of that kinda thing.

FFXpert89:

Oh ok.

Her words confused me, but I had learned my lesson already. I'd let Jennifer do her thing. She seemed like a godly person, for the most part.

PikachuButtcheeks2:

I hope it's a good time 4 u tho! Maybe you can give one of those purity rings to a lucky girl. ;)

FFXpert89:

Ooh ya. Maybe.

PikachuButtcheeks2:

Got someone in mind??

FFXpert89:

Haha no. Unless u want one?

PikachuButtcheeks2:

Hehe im ok. I appreciate the gesture though. :)

I didn't know what to say next, and I wanted to get a good night's sleep, so I led the conversation to a close.

FFXpert89:

Ok well I'm gonna hit the hay. See you at skool!

I quickly activated my rad away message so Jennifer would see it when she said goodbye.

PikachuButtcheeks2:

See ya!!

Your away message has been sent to PikachuButtcheeks2.

Success.

*   *   *

Monday at 8 a.m. there was already a gathering of students outside the theater, waiting for the cast list to go up.

"I CANNOT contain myself!" squealed Andrew. "Jesus, take the wheel."

Benny approached. "My boys. We got this. Here's to an AMAZING last-ever high school musical."

Rachel and Ella casually joined the group, chatting amongst themselves as they walked. They clearly weren't as stoked or anxious as the rest of us.

It wasn't long before Ms. Flannigan appeared at the lobby entryway, sheet of paper in hand. It felt like she had to walk a mile to reach us.

"Guess what I have here…" she taunted.

She held so much power at that moment.

Before long, she pinned the sheet to the wall and danced away while mumbling goofy sounds. The students gathered in a messy huddle around the cast list. I couldn't make it out from my position on the outskirts. Excited cheers and words of congratulations surrounded me.

After the students by the cast sheet took pixelated photos on their flip phones, they petered out from the human cluster. Finally, we could see the results.

I scanned the list and then I saw it: *Arthur Morton—The Snake.* Not a big surprise, but I was elated. It would be my first and only solo song onstage in a musical.

I heard Benny's voice from next to me. "Bow to me, plebeians."

I glanced back at the list. *Benjamin Bertrand—God.* Casting a Black boy as God the Father was a pleasantly progressive choice for such a conservative school.

The sheet listed Ella Kent as *Garden Animal #6,* to which she expressed a reaction entirely neutral.

Jade Parnacle checked the list and then spun around, scowling. She walked past us, bumping into Rachel with her shoulder.

"Whoops," said Jade. "Sorry, skank."

Rachel scoffed. As she approached the cast list, Andrew patted her on the shoulder and said, "Congratulations, Rachel. You're gonna crush this!"

Rachel stepped up to the list and saw her achievement. *Rachel Bristol—Eve.* The look on her face resembled something between elation, sadness, excitement, and dread. She brought her hand to her mouth.

Ella grabbed the limp Rachel and hugged her. "Girl. Holy sh—cow. You did it!"

"Yeah… thanks, Ella." After a moment, she smiled and hugged back.

I understood Rachel's conflicted feelings when I read the cast list in more detail. Despite not swinging by to receive news of his achievement, Samuel had been cast as Adam.

*   *   *

One perk of attending a small private school was the wiggle room in the curriculum. As a standout in art classes over the years, pitching the faculty on a year-long independent study in which I'd teach myself 3-D animation software using internet tutorials was easy peasy.

I had known I wanted to major in animation for a while, as it was the logical midpoint of my biggest interests: performing arts, computers, and art. Behind-the-scenes videos on DVDs like *The Lord of the Rings* and *Finding Nemo,* which pitched the animation industry as a professional playground where everyone wore shorts and rode scooters around the office, definitely helped too. As for what college I'd attend, that was a problem for Future Arthur to solve.

I sat in the back corner of the assigned computer lab. My smile gave away my giddiness to get started. As students from the main class in the lab funneled in, I plugged my headphones into my iPod

Shuffle, turned on some John Williams film scores, and explored the animation software for the first time.

A YouTube tutorial walked me through modeling a hammer. My assumption of how 3-D modeling would work in the digital realm was far from accurate, but I got the hang of it quickly.

When I finished, I beamed with pride. I glanced around, but, since I was sitting in the back row, nobody was around to give me validation.

I looked around the room to see what the class was up to. On the students' monitors were various typing games. One featured a penguin jumping across small ice platforms on water, and in another, a chameleon used its tongue to slurp up ants carrying letters.

Rachel was in the class and noticed me people-watching. She smiled and waved, and I returned the friendly gesture.

Having vaguely learned the concepts of basic 3-D modeling, I decided to sculpt something more interesting from scratch. I looked up drawings of gundams—large piloted mechs from the animated Japanese TV show, *Gundam Wing*. Modeling the highly detailed design was much harder than I anticipated, but the result wasn't completely unrecognizable.

"So, whatcha makin' there?" asked a voice from behind me.

I took off my headphones and spun my chair around to see Mr. Snirdley, the art teacher appointed to oversee my independent study. He had a finely groomed mustache, a stocky build, and always tucked his dress shirt into his pants.

"Oh, hey there," I said. "I'm just getting started teaching myself the software, like we discussed in our emails over the summer."

"Great, great. What's that you're making, though?"

"Oh, it's a gundam from *Gundam Wing*." I pointed at the drawings in the second window. "This one is piloted by Heero Yuy, and—"

"I don't know if this kind of stuff is such a good idea to be making art of," said Mr. Snirdley. "I've heard these Japanimations contain so much demon worship." He pointed at the metallic crown on the head. "And look at the Satan horns on that thing!"

I cleared my throat. "Well, I made this hammer, too." I opened the hammer model.

"Ah, yes. Fine work there. Keep making stuff like that, okay?"

"Mm-hmm…" I said.

After making sure he left the lab, I switched back to the gundam model. Five minutes later, I felt guilty and started modeling an apple.

*   *   *

The first rehearsal for any show exudes extremely high energy, and *Eden* was no different. The cast and crew bustled with excitement, flipping through the scripts we had just received.

Ms. Flannigan stepped to the center of the stage. "Welcome, thespians! I cannot express how grateful I am to have you all here to craft the first ever performance of *Eden*."

A few students clapped, including Benny.

"Today, we will read through the script in its entirety, in character! We'll play the studio recordings of the songs as we reach them; no need to sing today."

The cast read-through was very fun and painted the story of *Eden* in a more thorough light. Even though very little forethought had gone into that afternoon's performances, the cast and I brought our A-game.

Rachel brought to Eve the struggle of a woman yearning for independence. It was obvious that her authenticity would lead to a tear-jerker of a performance.

Her other theatrical half, Samuel, failed to match her emotional portrayal. Clearly, Ms. Flannigan cast him for his musical presence, but hopefully his acting chops would improve by showtime.

In everyday conversation, Benny hid his booming radio voice, and his casting as God allowed it to shine. He commanded the room with its power.

For my snake, Ms. Flannigan had to remind me again to bring more sympathy to the role when I launched into my creepy voice. I'd get there, eventually.

The garden animals, including Ella, didn't have much to do. They were mostly in the show for the sake of background vocals and to add a sense of life to the garden. They had very few lines, which Ms. Flannigan read, since she had not assigned them yet. Ella seemed quite bored, checking her electronic Tamagotchi game more than twice.

Before we knew it, we had read and experienced the entirety of *Eden*. We headed home, hungry to interpret it on the stage.

Our first proper rehearsal took place that Tuesday. The call sheet listed the snake, God, Adam, and Eve. The rest of the cast was always welcome to watch from the audience, though few showed up when not required.

Ten minutes after the call time, Ms. Flannigan removed her glasses dramatically. "Where on Earth is Adam?"

Taking part in the musical against his will, Samuel hardly prioritized it. He was late on the first day of proper rehearsal.

"It's fine, it's fine… We'll just start with scene five. Rachel, that's your song, *My Garden*."

I could tell by Rachel's jittery body language that she was very nervous. "Good luck, Rachel!" I said.

Rachel smiled, grabbed her sheet music, and headed to the stage. At the piano on the side of the stage, Mrs. Prada, the music teacher, fumbled through her songbook to the correct song.

Ms. Flannigan was in full-on director mode. She paced at the front of the auditorium.

"Okay, Rachel. No pressure, but this is the most important moment in the musical. If we don't nail this, the entire show falls apart. All eyes are on you, okay?"

"Oh. Wow. Okay. Umm… I'll do my best!"

Rachel sang, "I don't remember a life without him. But still, I want to know." She started softly, but belted ferociously as the song continued. "Maybe I should listen to the snake. This garden is mine to take!"

She had clearly been practicing. She sounded amazing.

Jade Parnacle rolled her eyes and began distracting herself with her phone.

Ms. Flannigan interrupted halfway through Rachel's song for notes. "Now Rachel, I want you to really get into Eve's head. In this song, she discovers her inner confidence. She's discovering her sexiness. So be sexy!"

Rachel smiled. "I think I can do that." Rachel really turned it up for the next verse. She sang out instead of in, emoted using far more body language, and seemed to have a lot of fun.

Ms. Flannigan was pleased. "Much better. I can feel her desire now. Let's hear it one more time from the top."

Halfway through the song, Samuel arrived. Rachel's demeanor shifted almost instantly. Her vocal power shrunk, her body language halved, and she sang in instead of out again.

Ms. Flannigan showed mild frustration. "Where did the passion go, Rachel? Let's make sure we bring it back to the level you showed earlier next time. Great stuff, though. Samuel, can you please join Rachel on the stage and flip to scene three? And also, please get here on time tomorrow."

"No prob, Ms. F," Samuel responded. He climbed onto the stage.

Ms. Flannigan rubbed her hands together. "Alright, now let's see what my leading couple has got!"

They read the script while Ms. Flannigan planned out the stage blocking. Every once in a while, Benny or I would be called up to the stage to read our lines in the scene.

It didn't take long for everyone to make one unfortunate observation silently: the chemistry between Samuel and Rachel just wasn't there. In solo scenes, she shone brightly, but when she had to act opposite her will-they-won't-they counterpart, something shut her down.

Ms. Flannigan's frustration was noticeable, especially when she removed her glasses and rubbed her face. "Okay everyone, that was a… decent first day. Let's study up on those lines and step it up next time, okay? Have a great evening!"

Samuel approached Rachel. "Ya know, I think she needs you to be sexier. Everyone in the audience is gonna be expecting it. Maybe wear some makeup next time."

Rachel was not having it. "Eat dirt, you pig."

Oh snap, I thought.

"I see your new BFF is rubbing off on you. But it's okay; I'm kinda into it."

Rachel stared him in the eyes. "I said back off, Samuel. I'm not about this anymore."

Samuel grabbed her hand, on which sat a fake silver band—a purity ring. "You made a commitment to me, and to God. That means you need to listen when I'm giving you advice."

Rachel removed the ring and threw it at him. "Screw you."

"Oh, okay. Real nice. At least the purity conference is tomorrow. Maybe it will knock some sense into that stupid blonde brain of yours!" He stashed the ring in his pocket and stormed out.

Benny looked at me. "Who hurt him?"

I shrugged.

＊　　＊　　＊

The school dedicated two hours at the end of that Wednesday to the purity conference, a yearly gathering for RCA seniors. It may come as no surprise that a Christian institution would lean toward abstinence-only sexual education, but that would be putting it lightly.

We had no sex ed whatsoever. No science or health teachers were involved in the purity conference, let alone proper classes. Nobody put a condom on a banana. There was no mention of how to avoid catching and passing sexually transmitted diseases. Fairly standard educational failures for schooling in those days, but the messaging RCA layered on top of that created a culture of shame

75

and fear that would cripple the mental health of their students for decades past graduation.

Benny, Ella, and I had just dumped our backpacks and books into our lockers and walked over to the youth ministry building where the conference was being held. The building contained more than the youth ministry auditorium; it also housed a smaller second auditorium, and the school's gym.

We entered the gym, which led to the auditoriums on either side. Above the auditorium entrances were signs with painted handwriting reading *Guys* and *Girls*, respectively.

There were five minutes left until the scheduled start time, so plenty of students were mingling in the gym. As soon as we entered, Mr. Crumbull approached us. He looked at Ella.

"Excuse me. Miss Kent, is it?"

"Yes?"

"I'm going to have to ask you to please refrain from wearing clothing with holes in it."

Ella rolled her eyes. "Oh. I don't have anything else with me."

"That's fine. Just please don't let it happen again."

"Yeah, alright."

Mr. Crumbull continued strolling around the gym, presumably prowling for more students to bust for rule breaking.

"Jeez, that's Mr. Crumbull?" asked Ella. "How do you guys deal?"

Benny scowled in my direction. "GOOD QUESTION!"

Ella then spotted Rachel. "Hey, Rach, over here!" She waved vigorously.

Despite my ongoing concern for Ella's sinful tendencies, it was nice to see a new friendship blossom.

Rachel skipped over to us. She was wearing her green RCA Gators sweatshirt, but with some extra flair—custom embroidered patterns now adorned the sleeves.

"Oh hey, nice shirt," complimented Ella.

"Umm, thanks again, girl. You are so freaking talented. I have no idea how you stitched these little flowers!"

Ella smiled. "I try."

"Umm, excuse me, Miss Bristol," said Mr. Crumbull, looping back toward us. "Those patterns on your sleeves… I'm not entirely sure they're up to code."

Rachel pulled out the puppy dog eyes. "Oh, I didn't know! What rule am I breaking exactly?"

"Well… the rule book says that customizations of uniforms should be kept to an absolute minimum."

Rachel smiled. "Oh, well, it's just a little razzle dazzle on the sleeves. My friend worked so hard on it. I'd hate to have to tell her I couldn't wear it."

Mr. Crumbull grunted. "I… I'm not sure where that line is drawn, I suppose. Just for you, and just this once, I'll let it slide. But be careful, Miss Bristol. You're skirting a fine line here."

"Thank you so much, Mr. Crumbull. You're the best."

He nodded and returned to his rounds as the gym clock chimed, signaling the top of the hour.

Ella turned to us. "See you later, boys. Have fun learning about vaginas."

"Ha ha, okay," I said, uncomfortably.

Ella and Rachel headed to the girls' conference, while Benny and I headed to the *Guys* sign.

At the front of the room normally used for youth group sat a panel of men on stools. Pastor Robbie sat on the first stool, and Principal Randall on the second. On the third stool sat Coach Lopez, someone I spent very little time with, thanks to a doctor's note about autism that let me skip most gym-related classes.

The audience was full, containing basically every male student from grades nine through twelve. Benny and I sat together. The scent in the air featured hints of sweat and Axe Body Spray. Unlike with youth group, the lights were at full blast; no room for emotional vibes that day. It was gonna be some *real talk*.

Pastor Robbie raised his microphone to his mouth. "Hello, my brothers. Let's talk about sex."

"Ooooohhhh, here we go," said Benny, equally excitedly and worriedly.

Sex wasn't exactly a common topic at Righteous Christ Church or Academy. We viewed it as a taboo subject, since the Bible heavily frowned upon all carnal acts, at least before marriage.

There was a vibe of excitement in the room. We were about to talk about what some describe as one of life's greatest pleasures, and about how one day we might take part in it.

Robbie continued. "God loves sex. After all, he made it. He wants you to enjoy sex, but only in the ways He designed it to be enjoyed."

"It's true," added Principal Randall. "I love sex. And my wife loves when I suck on her nipples."

The crowd laughed raucously.

"Oh my," I blurted out.

I wasn't used to hearing the faculty, or anyone, for that matter, talk so explicitly about sexuality.

"Hey," continued Principal Randall, "God designed women with highly erogenous nipples! If you laugh at that, you're laughing at God!"

I was all-too familiar with and fond of this act, at least in video form. I had often seen it late at night after my parents were asleep, on my computer, and through the squiggly green lines of cable TV channels we didn't have.

I better say an extra prayer for forgiveness right now, I thought.

"Dear God, please forgive me for looking at porn and masturbating. Amen." The speed at which I whispered to myself was so fast, even my prayer's intended recipient might have misheard me.

"Okay, let's reel it in, Randall," said Coach Lopez. "I, too, love sex. It's one of God's most beautiful inventions."

Pastor Robbie attempted to calm the audience down a bit. "You see, boys. God designed sex to be performed between a man and a woman, and the Bible is very clear that sexual activity in any other way lessens the significance of that godly act."

I straightened my posture and dialed in my focus.

"If you pleasure yourself," continued Robbie, "you are being selfish. You are betraying God's design. I know some of you have fallen into this sinful pattern."

The room fell silent. I gulped.

"The same goes for pornography. It rots your brain and conditions you to view sex as something that doesn't require a partner. This is wrong because it does not follow God's design."

Coach Lopez chimed in. "Let's not beat around the bush here…"

I chuckled at the unintentional pun.

Coach Lopez continued. "The Bible is very clear. Lusting is a sin. If you lust after a woman, you are sinning. If you act on that lust, your acts are an abomination to God. Better to pluck out your own eye. Also, remember. This isn't just a failing of the human mind. These temptations are Satan's demons trying to pull you away from God."

I noticed my fidgeting had become more prominent than usual. I wiped some sweat off my forehead and shuffled in my seat.

"So, remember this," said Coach Lopez. "The next time you undress a woman in your mind… if you continue down that path, hellfire awaits you."

Nobody in the audience made a peep.

Robbie wrapped up the first portion of the conference. "Before we continue, does anyone have any questions about what we just discussed?"

Quite a few hands raised. Robbie called on one toward the front.

"Umm, yeah. So I have a question about masturbation. You say it's a sin, but is it a sin because you're touching yourself, or because you're thinking about someone that isn't your wife?"

"Great question," said Principal Randall. "It's only a sin because you're picturing someone else and reducing the importance of what could've been a godly sexual bond. It would still be a sin if I masturbated while thinking about my wife, because that's removing her from our sexual relationship. However, I guess it wouldn't be a sin to pleasure yourself if you could somehow do it without thinking of another person."

The student continued, "Okay, so like… would it be a sin if I masturbated while thinking about a tree?"

Principal Randall pondered for a moment. "Hmm… no, I don't think so. But good luck getting aroused by a tree."

The audience was loving it. When the laughter died down, Robbie called on a second hand.

"Is it a sin to masturbate while thinking about a guy?"

Laughter once again filled the room.

Robbie smirked, as if waiting for this topic to be brought up. "You know the answer to that. And if you don't, what on Earth have we been teaching you here?"

The audience went silent.

"In Romans 1, God condemns the act of a man lying with a man, and a woman with a woman. God finds this lifestyle choice to be abhorrent. If you have the desire to lie with a man, or even think about him lustfully, I strongly advise you to seek discipleship. Pray, and have others pray over you. You can be rid of this ungodly sickness."

The boy who asked the question sank into his seat without response.

Benny squirmed in his seat. "I need to use the restroom," he said before abruptly leaving.

Pastor Robbie shifted the tone to something less aggressive, yet just as problematic. "Now, the next topic we need to address is how we interact with the women in our lives. God created Eve from Adam's rib to be his companion. He created us men to be natural shepherds, and women, our sheep. It is our responsibility to lead the women in our lives toward a godly life. We must keep them accountable. Men are visual creatures, and if the way a woman dresses causes us to stumble, we must call them out. Once we marry, if they aren't providing enough relief for our sexual urges, we must correct it. If they are not rising to meet God's requirements for an obedient wife, they need discipleship."

Ella would lose her mind if she heard this, I thought.

"Here's an example. You all know Rachel Bristol, right?"

"Yeahhh!" shouted some asshole. Another whistled a catcall.

"She's promised to my son. They exchanged a commitment of purity last year and I couldn't be prouder. She is a woman of God, and let me tell you how."

Uh oh, is what I should've thought. But no. To someone raised in that culture, it was fine.

"When I first met Rachel, she was a young woman of the world. She showed so much cleavage it's a wonder the boys around her weren't sprouting tents as she walked down the street. She had no respect for the men in her life and hung out with many worldly girls of sinful influence. When she started dating Samuel, me and my son talked with her parents, and together, showed her God's mercy. We explained to her, through love, that her actions were wicked, and that all she needed to do to heal was to ask for forgiveness, defer to the men in her life for leadership, and pronounce God as her one and only savior."

I looked over at Samuel, who covered his face with his hands.

"Now, just look at her. She and Samuel are going strong. She now walks in the mercy of God. That's the change we must seek for the women around us who don't follow in the path God has intended for them. Go forth, men, and glorify God through these women. He literally made them for you."

After the conference, I saw Benny leaning against a wall by the bathroom. "Hey, everything okay?"

"Yeah dude, nature just called is all… I'll be alright."

The girls' conference was just letting out. After a moment, Ella and Rachel emerged. Ella looked deeply angry—even more than usual. Rachel looked very sad.

A boy from our conference walked by. "Hey Rachel, I heard you used to show a lot of boobie. Heh, heh, heh."

"What?" Rachel was dumbfounded.

Another boy walked by. "Hey Rach, I got a boner just thinking about your sweet cleavage in there. Guess I'm going to Hell."

Rachel's face turned pale. She crossed her arms over her chest and stepped back into the corner.

"Watch out, Rachel. I kinda wanna put a baby in you," said another boy, who made kissing sounds with his lips as he walked by.

Rachel put her hand over her mouth.

Jade Parnacle, after chatting with a boy nearby, shot a stink eye at Rachel while strutting by. "I always knew you were just a filthy sinner. Have fun burning in Hell, slut."

Ella turned to Benny and I. "What the ACTUAL fuck happened in there?"

Benny shrugged. "I was in the bathroom for a while. I don't know…"

I explained. "Pastor Robbie was talking about the roles men and women play in godly relationships. He used Rachel and Samuel as an example."

"And he… talked about her tits?"

"Ella, seriously? Language!"

Ella stepped toward me, viscerally angry. "Rachel is traumatized in the corner, and you're worried about my language? Grow up, Arthur."

Ella might have assaulted me if it weren't for Pastor Robbie emerging from the gym with a cocky smile on his face.

She stormed up to him. "What is wrong with you?! Rachel is NOT yours to verbally throw around in your locker room of a church!"

"Excuse me, young lady. You better take a second to—"

Rachel started to cry.

"Whoa, hey…" said Robbie. "Rachel, I didn't mean to hurt ya. I was just using your amazing progress as an example!"

Rachel wiped her tears and speed-walked to the exit.

Robbie followed. "Rachel, it was a compliment. You dress like such a godly woman, and the way you defer to Samuel on important matters is very admirable. A lot of people look up to you!"

"Stay away from me!"

Rachel ran through the doors and out of sight, followed by Robbie. Ella pursued them, but not without stopping to give me the finger.

To my left, Samuel stood in the gym doorway. He shrugged and exited the building.

As I drove home, the events of the previous hour played on a loop in my mind.

We're not supposed to doubt our pastors, but Robbie clearly hurt Rachel… What do you do when your leaders get stuff wrong?

I spent the evening with a pit in my stomach. Despite thinking that Ella was probably in the wrong, I'd begun to really appreciate her as a friend, and felt a deep sadness that I had let her down. I wondered if there was anything I could've done differently.

My pain was real, but so small compared to what was on the horizon. Come Monday, I would receive news that one of my friends had vanished without a trace.

5. Bombshell

The halls of RCA were surprisingly quiet the following morning, and the amount of sweaters worn by girls seemed higher than normal. Ella didn't show up to check her locker or chat before homeroom like she normally did. I felt guilty for criticizing her usage of the word "tits" when our friend was going through something serious, so I was happy to not run into her just yet.

"It's dead in here today," said Benny as he slid his backpack into his locker. "What did I miss in there? That's the last time I go to the bathroom in the middle of a purity conference."

"That's true, considering that was your last purity conference." I could be very literal sometimes.

"Praise Jesus."

"Yeah, I guess the pastors' and teachers' tone was a little aggressive," I said. "I'm really not sure why Rachel and Ella were so upset over it, though."

Benny closed his locker, stood up, and placed his hand on my shoulder. "Oh, honey. Someday maybe you'll learn to understand women."

As he walked down the hall, I responded, "Hey, what's that supposed to mean?"

I followed him into homeroom. As I took my seat, I flashed a small smile at Danielle, the girl that sat behind me. She pulled her arms tight around her sweater.

"Don't look at me!" she sputtered.

Jennifer laughed from the corner. Then, looking at me, she mouthed the words, "told ya so," referencing her cynicism toward the purity conference.

In stumbled Mr. Crumbull, looking a bit more disheveled than usual. He sat in his chair and wiped a drop of sweat off his brow.

From the back row, a boy joked, "Hey, Mr. Crumb! Elevator broken again?"

"Mr. Mason, I am NOT in the mood today."

I sighed, before standing for the pledges.

The rest of the week was extremely quiet, and quite boring. Lunchtime didn't even offer much of a distraction. I sat with Benny most days, but Ella was nowhere to be found on either Thursday or Friday. I wondered if she was avoiding us.

At least rehearsal for *Eden* was guaranteed to bring some fun. The schedule requested the entire ensemble, as we were to block out one of the large group numbers.

The cast and crew slowly trickled in. Andrew, Benny, and I attempted to play a multiplayer game on our handheld Game Boy Advance consoles, but technical issues destroyed those ambitions.

"Okay, everyone," announced Ms. Flannigan. "Seems like we have a few cast members missing today, but let's get started, anyway."

"Sorry, sorry! I'm here!" Ella burst through the doors.

She jogged over and tossed her backpack onto the seat next to us.

Not wanting to sit through two hours of awkwardness, I stood up to get her attention. "Hey, I'm sorry about the other day. I didn't have my priorities straight."

Without making eye contact, Ella assured me, "It's no big deal. Don't worry about it."

Ella followed the small crowd onto the stage. I stayed a few feet behind.

"Okay, you can stand there… and you, please take a few steps to the left." Ms. Flannigan was in the zone. "And Rachel, can you—" Her red hair flipped back and forth as she looked around the theater for a blonde head. "Where the heck is Rachel?"

Ella shrugged when Ms. Flannigan looked at her inquisitively. "I haven't seen her. I just got here."

Ms. Flannigan then turned her gaze to us but we had just as little information to share.

"Mother fudger!" she growled under her breath.

Naturally, the rehearsal wasn't the most productive. We got some rough blocking in, and one of the garden animal cast members read for Eve. We got out thirty minutes early.

Despite accepting my apology, Ella didn't seem interested in being buddy-buddy just yet. She grabbed her backpack silently and walked out the door before anyone else.

*   *   *

Thank God it was a new week. The previous few days had been tense, but it was behind us. The students seemed chipper; the tensions from the purity conference were fading. Ella even said a quick "hi" to me while at our lockers.

The optimism of a brand new week filled me with enough confidence to say hi to a certain someone else in homeroom. "Hey, Jenn. How did last week go for you?"

"Much better than everyone else's, it looks like. Very glad I skipped the purity conference. Do I even wanna know what I missed?"

"Ha ha. I dunno, I thought it was alright."

Bling, bling, blong. The clock TV signaled an announcement.

"All senior students, please report to the *Spóros* ministry room for an emergency assembly. Thank you."

"Okay, Arthur," teased Jennifer. "What did you do this time?"

"Hah…"

All at once, homeroom stood up and migrated to the assembly.

When I arrived, I spotted Ella sitting off to the side.

"Mind if I sit here?" I asked.

"Sure."

Thank goodness, I thought.

I looked around the room for clues to why we were there. "Any idea what this is about?"

"Not another purity conference, I hope."

I chuckled nervously. "Yeah…"

On the stage, behind the podium, were five chairs. Pastor Robbie sat in the second one, and next to him were two adults I didn't recognize. One was a man with a black comb-over and a tucked in button-down with a blue blazer. In his hands, he gripped a notepad, and it appeared to be shaking.

To his left was a thin woman with vibrant blonde hair, wearing a blouse covered in floral patterns, and a frilly skirt. Her hand rested on the man's shoulder.

A fourth person then joined them: Samuel. He exuded noticeably less confidence than I expected from him. He kept his gaze on the ground as he approached the empty chair and sat down. Pastor Robbie patted him on the back.

"Jeez, did somebody die?" asked Ella, half-seriously.

The last chair was then filled by a blonde male student I knew in passing.

"That's weird," I said.

"What's weird?" asked Ella.

Principal Randall stepped up to the pulpit before I could answer. "Hello, students. We have some troubling news to share with you today."

A flurry of whispers filled the room.

"It's best that you hear it from Mr. and Mrs. Bristol. Edgar, Molly, would you like to step up to the pulpit?"

"Oh, shit," said Ella, sitting straight up. "That's Rachel's parents."

"Yeah, and that boy is her brother, Wesley."

All three Bristols approached the pulpit.

Mr. Bristol spoke with a somber tone. "Hi, kids. I know many of you are friends with our beautiful daughter, Rachel. It's with a heavy heart that we bring you the news that, as of this morning, local police have declared her to be a missing person."

Mrs. Bristol raised her hand to her mouth to stifle a cry, as the students in the assembly whispered between one another.

I had never dealt with grief in my short life, though even if I had, I doubt it would've prepared me for the confusion of hearing that my friend had vanished. My heart sank, though it didn't create a feeling of sadness. I felt disoriented and numb, like jolting awake after a nightmare. For a moment, the world seemed fake.

I turned toward Ella, who wore an expression of confusion and shock as she stared at the stage.

Mr. Bristol continued. "We weren't planning on going public with this so soon, but since we have very few leads right now, we're hoping some of you might have some information that could help us find Rachel."

Mrs. Bristol took a deep breath and leaned into the microphone. "Rachel still has such a bright future ahead of her. The way this school transformed her into a beautiful woman of the Lord was so inspiring. We need your help to find her so she can fulfill her God-ordained duty and become a beautiful bride for Samuel."

It seemed Rachel didn't let her parents know she and Samuel were on the fritz.

Ella scoffed and looked away, tears in her eyes.

"We also ask for your prayers," said Mr. Bristol, "for our strength during this difficult time. We met with Pastor Tom this morning, and he shared some biblical wisdom with us. Not exactly a surprise that he knew just what to say, but we feel very blessed to have received just a few minutes of his time. Thanks to his wisdom, we now understand that sometimes God needs to allow tragedy to happen to teach us parents a valuable lesson about resiliency. We welcome this challenge, as it is God's will. I don't think he's here, but thank you again to Pastor Tom for leading this church toward a future brighter than we could ever have imagined. If this heartbreak is part of God's plan for Righteous Christ, we are honored to bear it."

Under her breath, Ella muttered, "Fuuuuuck you…"

I looked around. Pastor Tom was nowhere to be found, little to my surprise.

The Bristols sat down as Samuel approached the pulpit. "I am heartbroken. Rachel makes me a happier man of God than I thought possible. As a child, I always wished I'd end up with the girl next door from the movies, and He blessed me with a bombshell. She's the perfect number two, and she makes me a better man. Rach, I know you're out there, and I will find you." He blew a kiss.

"Well said, son." Pastor Robbie traded places with Samuel. "Rachel is one of the good ones. When I first met her, she was far from the woman of God you see today."

Ella slammed the chair in front of her and stormed out.

After Robbie repeated his problematic anecdote from the purity conference with less of a crass delivery, he said something odd. "The last time I saw Rachel, she was walking into the purity conference. She never went home that night. If anyone saw her in there and knows what happened afterward, please contact the Bristols at the email address on the screen.

That wasn't true. I saw him chase Rachel out of the building, followed by Ella.

Why would he lie? Maybe he just forgot?

I followed Ella out of the room to get to the bottom of it. "Hey. You okay?"

Ella paced back and forth by the bleachers in the gym. "Ya know… just a few weeks in, and it's the same old shit. Even the men of God just take a fucking wrecking ball to the women they cross paths with. Ya know what… actually, it's not the same. I think it might be worse here. At least when the parents of kids at my last school had high expectations, they weren't comparing you to the creator of the goddamn universe."

"Yeah…" Her frustrations didn't entirely click with me, though I sympathized with her shock. "This is kind of crazy."

"That man is a pig. Thinks he's God's gift to the world, and that women are God's gift to him. He really hurt her, ya know? And now she's gone. And I kinda wonder… if I could've done something to help? I thought it was weird when she didn't answer her phone last week, but I figured she just needed some alone time after the purity conference."

"About that. After you left just now, Robbie said that the last time he saw Rachel was before the purity conference."

"HAH. Covering his own ass." Ella sat on the bleachers and stared into nothingness.

I sat next to her. "You don't think it's possible he's involved, do you? I honestly don't know him that well. Pastor Marshall usually ran youth group before this year."

"Ya know," said Ella. "If I found out that man was a kidnapper or murderer, I would not be surprised."

"Jeez, I didn't say that. What about when you followed him and Rachel outside? Did you see what happened?"

Ella glanced at the door. "By the time I got outside, I didn't see either of them."

I stroked my chin. "Hmm… yeah, the conversation wasn't exactly proof of anything."

"Yeah," Ella muttered. "Man… what I wouldn't give to take that guy down."

After a moment, I cleared my throat. "Rachel's bound to turn up, I think. I bet it will be alright. We can always pray for her."

"Right…"

I considered letting Rachel's parents know about Pastor Robbie's lie, but I didn't want to be labeled as the guy who accused one of the head pastors of kidnapping, or worse. For the time being, I would simply process the shocking revelation.

*   *   *

With *Eden* rehearsal canceled for obvious reasons, I had a few hours to kill before my mom expected me home. After scarfing a barbacoa burrito bowl at Chipotle Grill, I found myself pacing around my neighborhood Blockbuster with no goal in mind. I had received just enough weekly allowance to cover one DVD purchase. Even if I didn't stumble upon the perfect film to add to my collection, pacing the rows of sun-bleached plastic cases was never a bad time.

In the new releases section, I picked up a Liam Neeson action flick some friends had recommended: *Taken.* I read the synopsis on the back cover: "When a young girl goes missing…"

No thanks, I thought. *Not what I need right now.*

I hadn't quite processed Rachel's disappearance yet. It hadn't even been a few hours. I'd never experienced anything that serious happening to one of my friends before. Perhaps that's why I found myself trying to use entertainment to lessen the sadness and dread I felt creeping in.

Was Rachel really my friend? I almost never spoke to her until a few weeks ago. It didn't work. *Yeah… she quickly became a beacon of happiness for my friends and me. Dear God, please let her be safe.*

I grabbed a DVD of *Ratatouille* with a holographic cardboard cover, checked out, and headed home. I thought about how it would be the perfect time for some rain to complement the foreboding events of the day. But no; the sweat-soaked Florida sun would set the mood.

I navigated the winding roads leading home with little present thought, since I knew the route like the back of my hand. I hit more red lights than normal, but was too lost in thought for it to bother me.

I pulled into my parking space, grabbed my backpack from the trunk, and opened the front door of the townhouse.

"Honey? That you?" Our rental home was too small to enter without my mom hearing.

"Yeah. Hi."

"How was school? Did you talk to Jennifer today?" She hugged me before I could put my backpack down.

"Ugh." I walked to the snack drawer. "I'm seriously regretting telling you about her."

"Okay, okay. I'll stop now." She followed me to the kitchen, where I was elbow deep in a bag of pretzels. "Anyway, I just got a very disturbing call from the school. They said some girl went missing?"

"Yeah…" I mumbled through a mouth full of pretzels. "Rachel Bristol."

My mom thought for a moment. "Rachel Bristol… I don't think I've met her. Are you two close?"

"Kinda. We've mostly been acquaintances, but she's the lead in the musical this year, so she's been around more."

"Oh, honey. That's so awful. Ya know, when God called us to move to Florida and enroll you in a private school, I thought we'd avoid disturbing events like this. I'm so sorry you have to go through this."

I struck a forced smile. "I'll be fine."

I climbed the stairs to my bedroom, along with the bag of pretzels.

After processing the day's events for a few hours, it felt real. My mind raced.

There's gonna be massive repercussions on the school year if Rachel doesn't turn up soon. The musical, for one. She's the lead! What is Ms. Flannigan gonna do? Not to mention the reality that any day we could get called into an assembly and hear that they found our friend's body.

For the time being, I'd try to put that thought out of my head.

Krr, krr, krr.

PikachuButtcheeks2:

Dude! Are you ok?

Well, that didn't last long. But for Jennifer, I wasn't complaining.

FFXpert89:

Yeah im ok.

PikachuButtcheeks2:

Ive been worried. U have been hanging out with her a lot for the musical, right?

FFXpert89:

Yeah kinda. Definitely disturbing to hear shes missing.

PikachuButtcheeks2:

4 real. Hopefully she turns up soon.

FFXpert89:

I hope so!

PikachuButtcheeks2:

Lemme know if you wanna talk about it or anything.

FFXpert89:

Thats nice. Thx. I appreciate that.

On any other day, attention from my crush would be worthy of a mini dance party in my room.

Ya know what…

I did a little jig, at least as much as I could, while filled to the brim with anxiety and sadness.

After Jennifer logged off, a tempting thought reared its head. *This is all incredibly stressful. I deserve to relax.*

I locked my bedroom door, plugged my headphones into my computer, and opened up Limewire, a popular multimedia browser for downloading pirated content in a pre-streaming world. I entered a search term guaranteed to distract me from the day's anxiety: *big naturals riding.* I downloaded a random video, likely along with a few nasty viruses.

In the heat of the moment, purity culture didn't hold much swaying power.

As long as I put in the effort to not do it again, God will forgive me… right?

After release, my brain returned from its aroused Mr. Hyde mode, and Dr. Jekyll felt a heavy shame sink in.

I'm a sinner. God watched me do that. My dead relatives watched me do that.

"Dear God, please, please forgive me for this terrible sin. I promise I'll try so hard to avoid it going forward. Please grant me the strength to avoid these awful temptations of the flesh. Amen."

To avoid heading to bed full of remorse, I logged onto MySpace to see what my classmates were saying about Rachel. To no surprise, posts expressing fondness for her filled the bulletin section. Some were genuine, and others suggested a superficial desire to hop on the latest social media bandwagon.

I clicked through to Rachel's profile.

Rachel Bristol

Age: 17

Last Online: 4 Days Ago

To uninformed eyes, she appeared to still be dating Samuel. He occupied the number one spot on her "Top Friends" section. Rachel had promoted Ella to number four, behind two cheerleader friends. Samuel also appeared alongside her in her profile picture, which showed them kissing.

I perused her recent bulletin posts, which was thoroughly uneventful. One featured a photo of her family puppy proudly wearing a new collar. Another was announcing her role as Eve in the musical. She had also made a few posts about colleges she planned to apply to.

Pastor Robbie had left cringy comments on a bunch of her posts. "God really outdid Himself when he created you!" made me grimace the hardest.

It was a bust—no clues to her whereabouts. I sighed.

I clicked back to her profile one last time and saw a green circle next to the text *Online Now.*

"Holy cannoli."

I immediately clicked the little envelope icon and typed out, "Where are you?" I hit send and waited.

Five minutes passed. No response, but the green icon remained. I refreshed her profile a few times to see if anything changed, but nothing did.

After ten minutes, I refreshed her profile one last time, and the green icon vanished. *Last Online: Today.*

I wondered if her family had her login, or maybe the police. For the time being, there was no way to know. Something in my gut told me it was her, though. Back then, any flutter in my stomach or intuitive feeling was God. God was telling me she was alright.

I tucked myself into bed and closed my eyes. "Lord, if it's your will for Rachel to stay safe, please protect her. And I pray that Ella and Benny don't take this too hard. Amen."

6. God's Plan

Was it a left turn before or after the train tracks?

Ding, ding, ding. The railroad crossing lights began to flash.

"Guess I'm going left before."

The bent-in-half DirecTV antenna made it easy to spot Benny's place.

"Yessss."

The small wins were worth celebrating in times like those.

"Thanks, train—err, I mean God."

Through the kitchen window of the run-down house, I could see Benny and his mom. The excessive pointing and dramatic facial expressions indicated their conversation was not the most pleasant.

After a moment, Benny noticed my car. He shoved a peeled banana in his mouth and stormed out of the kitchen. A moment later, he was waving with a giant smile, as if nothing had happened.

"Everything okay?" I asked.

"Oh, you saw that, huh? Yeah, it's just Mom being Mom. She just… she was accusing me of being too different after spending time with my dad this summer. 'Too many Broadways on your wall,' she said. Reminds me of Samuel. Graduation cannot come soon enough."

"Does that mean you're definitely going out of state for school?"

Benny nodded aggressively. "Dude, you knew that. There's nothing left for me here. I'm gonna follow where the stage leads me."

I sighed. "I really need to start thinking about college."

Ten minutes later, the enormous Righteous Christ sign welcomed us into the dirt parking lot next to the school building.

As we stepped out of the car, Benny said, "So… horrible elephant in the room."

Looking at my feet, I sighed. "Yeah. I don't even know what to think."

Benny leaned against the passenger door. "Yeah, man. This is messed up. I really hope she's okay. I've really started to love that girl. She's a good one. Have you heard anything? Like from Ella? Maybe she talked to her?"

"As far as I know, she hasn't spoken to her since the purity conference with us. Speaking of which, did you notice that in the assembly Pastor Robbie said—"

Benny jumped up and down. "He lied! He said he didn't see her after the conference!"

My eyes lit up. "I know! Do you think it was deliberate?"

"Maybe," said Benny, grimacing. "He could've just remembered wrong."

"But it's pretty suspicious…" I said. "There's something else, too. Last night, her MySpace said 'online now.' "

"Whaaaaaat??"

"Doesn't really mean anything, though. Could've just been her parents, or the cops, or… someone else."

Benny pointed at me. "Don't you even."

"Okay, you're right. She's… probably fine."

I wasn't convinced.

*   *   *

The school announced during the previous week that the Daily Bread bistro would be available to senior students for lunch starting that Monday, and the promise was indeed fulfilled. It wasn't the liveliest of vibes at the moment—the RCA students eating lunch were quieter than expected, not knowing how to show enthusiasm appropriately during a time of confusion and mourning.

I skimmed the menu. "Do you think if I ask for chips and queso, they can make it?"

"Possible, but unlikely," said Benny. "Might have to branch out a little, Art."

I glanced at one of the empty chairs at our four-seat table. "Ella is joining us, right?"

Benny nodded. "Yep, that's what she said this morning."

As I continued to peruse the menu, I noticed some commotion at the booth next to us. Some students gathered around Wesley

Bristol, Rachel's brother, who was eating personal pizzas with some friends.

"We are SO sorry to hear about your sister," said Jade Parnacle, twirling her dark hair.

"Ugh," I groaned under my breath. I didn't buy the empathy suddenly evident in Rachel's nemesis.

Wesley's eyes seemed permanently half closed, uncomfortably similar to the Blue Steel face from *Zoolander,* but less ridiculous. He brushed his blonde hair out of his face and rested his arm on the booth.

"That's so sweet of you to say. We actually have a donation fund going, so if you wanna contribute to help my family through this difficult time, I'd be personally very grateful. My sister was… is… such a powerful representation of Christ. We want to make sure we have the strength to carry her inspiration forward."

"I would love to, Wes." Jade fetched a five-dollar bill from her purse and handed it to him.

"God thanks you for your loving soul. I'll make sure this goes to good use." He placed the money on the table.

"Have a good day, Wesley. I really hope you find her soon. Well, if it's God's will."

From my left, I heard a voice. "Sorry I'm late." Ella sat down. "Had to call my mom. So, what's good here?"

I replied, "Well, they probably don't have chips and queso."

"I think I'll survive."

"Hi there, kids!" A chipper waitress approached us. "So happy that God brought you to the Daily Bread today. How may I serve you?"

I cleared my throat. "Umm, yeah. Do you have chips and queso?"

"No, I'm so sorry!"

I grunted. "That's okay. I'll get a cheeseburger, and can I replace the fries with whipped potatoes?"

"Great choice, sir."

Benny was next. "I'll have the Caesar salad, please."

"And I'll have…" Ella quickly skimmed the menu. "Pepperoni pizza."

"Wonderful. I'll be back with your food in a jiffy. God bless."

Benny smiled empathetically. "So, how are you holding up, Ella?"

"Umm. I'll be alright, I guess. I mean, this sucks. This royally blows. And I'm so, so angry at like… so many people. And—"

"It's okay. Let it out, girl," encouraged Benny.

"Ugh… never mind. It's all I've been thinking about, and I barely slept. Can we please just live this one hour in delusion? I'm starving."

"You got it," said Benny.

A few minutes later, the scents of melted cheese and beef greeted us.

Ella took a bite. "Wow… that's a good pizza."

I was pleased that Ella wasn't depressed enough to miss out on enjoying the simple things.

"Way better than my old school's 'pizza,' " she said with air quotes. "How's the burger?"

"Really good. I love eating burgers alongside mashed—I mean whipped potatoes. No skins allowed!"

"They do look extremely smooth," added Benny. "Can I try?"

"Me too!" shouted Ella.

Benny and Ella took bites. For that brief moment, we forgot our stresses existed, and took a trip to buttery potato heaven.

"Have a blessed day, Wesley. Best wishes to your family." Our waitress waved goodbye to Rachel's brother and collected the five-dollar tip that had been so conveniently donated to him.

After lunch, I queued up my *Get Crap Done* iPod playlist and dove into my independent study. I had been working on a basic animation of a blocky robot picking up a ball—a project far more Christian-friendly than *Gundam Wing* fan art.

As much as I tried to use the project to distract myself from Rachel's absence, I couldn't help but glance at her empty seat every few minutes. Nobody dared take her spot. On her monitor, a Windows XP screensaver of a colorful morphing object bouncing around the monitor replaced bizarre typing games.

I really hate that screensaver, I thought.

*   *   *

Silence filled the room at the first *Eden* rehearsal since our lead actress vanished. In the corner sat Samuel, sunken and staring at the floor. Jade Parnacle approached him, but he seemed to shrug her off.

Andrew, usually beaming with excitement in every situation, brought with him a cloud of sadness when he sat down next to Benny, Ella, and me.

After staring at the floor for a moment, Andrew sighed and craned his head toward us. "So… do you think Ms. Flannigan will replace Rachel right away?"

"I'm sure they'll at least pick an understudy," I said. "Maybe, if she's found soon, they can swap back."

"Gosh, I hope so. I was actually planning on asking her to prom later this year. Heh…"

Ella chuckled.

"Ah," I said. "Good luck if she comes back. I mean… I'm sure she'll turn up."

"Yeah!" said Andrew. "We've just all gotta pray extra hard, right?"

I smiled. "Yeah!"

Andrew seemed to need to convince himself further. " 'Then you will call on me and come and pray to me, and I will listen to you.' Jeremiah 29:12. I mean… it's gotta be His will that she's found, right?"

Ella swung her neck toward Andrew on a dime. "Was it God's will that she went missing in the first place? What ultimate purpose does that serve?"

Andrew wasn't prepared for Ella's challenges. "I… well, I mean—"

"What about the people that die of cancer? Or starve in third world countries? His will too?"

"I don't think I know what…"

Ella crouched in front of Andrew and stared him down. "You're right. You don't know. You don't know why it was God's will that the Gators won their first football game last week. You don't know why he answered those prayers and not the ones I said for Rachel's safety."

"No human can claim to know the will of God," mumbled Andrew, avoiding eye contact.

"How goddamn convenient."

Andrew suddenly piped up. "I would prefer it if you did not take the Lord's name in vain."

Ella stood up. "THAT'S what your takeaway from this is?! We're talking about the ethics of suffering and our MIA friend, and you care that I used 'goddamn' as a filler word? JESUS, this place needs help…"

It was an uncomfortable encounter to watch from such close proximity, especially since I mostly agreed with Andrew. Thankfully, Ms. Flannigan entered the theater. She walked slowly and silently to the stage and vanished behind the closed curtain. She emerged a moment later, carrying a folding chair. After unfolding it, she sat for a moment, scanning the crowd.

She removed her glasses and placed them in the pocket of her baggy flannel shirt. "This isn't easy. Nobody was more excited for this show to get going than me. I mean, it's my baby! And when Rachel sang *Blackbird* at rehearsal, I almost cried. She embodied Eve so perfectly."

Not a sound could be heard from the crowd. We were on the edge of our seats, waiting for our theatrical future to be revealed.

"I honestly didn't even have a backup Eve in mind. As soon as I saw her sing, the decision made itself. But, as much as it hurts to say, the show must go on. *Eden* is bigger than one person. So, we're going to spend today's rehearsal reading and singing for Eve's part to find a replacement. Since Eve is the only named female role, there shouldn't be any overlap to worry about. For now, let's say it will be an understudy role in case they find Rachel soon, which I know we are all praying for. Also, the faculty has agreed to postpone the performance by two months to allow us time to grieve and regroup."

Ella raised her hand.

"Yes, Miss Kent?"

"Do we have to audition?"

"No, of course not. I know this would be a large burden to bear, especially for you. You seemed very close with Rachel."

Ella let out a sigh of relief. "Cool. Thanks."

"And of course, the boys are free to head out early if they like. As for the girls who are interested, please come sit in the front row and we'll get started."

As five of the girls currently playing background characters prepared for a chance at reluctant stardom, Benny, Ella, and I gathered our belongings and headed out.

"Oh! And please remember, to those of you who qualified for this year's State Thespians competition with your scenes and songs last spring, we leave in one week! I know times are tough, but please continue to workshop your scenes amongst yourselves. Maybe it can be a distraction from all this."

I had totally forgotten about my performance of a scene from a stage adaptation of C.S. Lewis's *Screwtape Letters*. It was a two-person performance with Andrew, for which we received an "excellent" rating, meaning we could perform it at States next week. I wasn't in the headspace to revisit the scene quite yet.

"Don't worry about giving me a ride," Benny told me as we exited the theater. "I'm gonna get some studying done in the library."

I nodded. "All good. See ya tomorrow."

Ella and I walked to the parking lot together.

"You holding up okay?" asked Ella, breaking the awkward silence.

"Oh, yeah. I'm… fine. It's sad and weird, but we weren't close enough that it would derail my whole life. But what about you? I don't think Andrew's perfect parents have ever yelled at him as much as you just did."

"Yeah… I'm just… it's a lot, ya know? First, I'm transferred to this bonkers school where everyone and their mom are trying to fix me…"

I grimaced with guilt.

"And then there's classes, and college, and this musical… Then the only girl in school I feel like I can be myself around goes fucking missing? God's plan my ass."

"That must be tough. Lemme know if there's anything I can do."

"Yeah. Thanks."

"Good evening, Mr. Morton, Miss Kent." Mr. Crumbull had approached us from behind like a mustachioed ninja. "I truly hope you two are doing okay. I spoke with Melinda today—uhh… Ms. Flannigan. She's really taking it hard."

He jiggled his keys into the door of the car next to us.

"Yeah, we'll be alright," I assured.

Ella forced a smile.

"Aww, rats! I forgot my grading rubric inside. You two have a nice evening." He walked back toward the school briskly.

"Alright, Ella, I'll see you tomm—"

I forgot what I was saying when I noticed something odd in the back seat of Mr. Crumbull's clunker of a car.

"Hey, Ella…"

"Yeah?" She stepped toward me and looked through the glass. "What the actual…"

On the floor behind the front passenger seat was a green RCA Gators sweater covered in custom embroidery.

"That's… that's the sweater I stitched for Rachel!"

"I thought it might be. Are you sure it isn't some other sweater?"

"Arthur, I stitched that thing with my own hands. It's the only one like it."

I stroked my chin. "Well… jeez. What the heck is it doing there? Wasn't she wearing it the last time any of us saw her?"

"Yeah, she definitely was."

"Well, what do we do?"

Ella thought for a few seconds before grabbing a nearby rock.

"Hey, we can't break his window!" I said.

Ella stared me down. "And why not?"

"Because he just saw us here. If we want to tell anyone about this, they'll know it was us that broke into his car. Do you really want a potential kidnapper knowing we're on to him, AND that we busted his car window?"

"Okay, fine." Ella dropped the rock. "Ya know what…"

She fiddled with the car windows for a minute. Eventually, one of them budged.

"Yes!" she said.

Using the force of her own body's weight, she got it to roll down just enough to unlock it manually. She grabbed the sweater and dragged the window back up.

"Here." She handed me the sweater.

"What am I supposed to do with it?"

"I'm the new student that everyone thinks is the problem kid. It would mean more coming from you. Just tell someone in charge. And not Robbie."

"Got it." The sweater shook in my nervous hands. "But man… now we're suspecting two of our superiors. This is a bad look if we accuse them without proof."

"Dude. You got this."

"Right, right…"

I speed-walked to my car. I was basically a criminal! When my heart stopped racing, I drove my car home and tried my best not to think about what had just happened. I did not sleep well that night.

7. The World

After days of deliberation, I decided to turn Rachel's sweater over to Principal Randall. The sterile waiting room outside of his office didn't help my anxiety.

His secretary smiled at me. I hoped she didn't see the sweat on my forehead as I flashed a phony smile back.

My mind raced, imagining all the ways the coming conversation could create blowback to my standing with the school.

Ella and I did steal the evidence, and Mr. Crumbull had for sure noticed it had vanished by now. Hopefully, he didn't notice until long after our chat and doesn't associate us with it.

"Ah, Mr. Morton," said Principal Randall. "Please come in! I have lollipops!"

Hmm, creepy, I thought as I entered the small, oddly colorful office. I could hardly see any bare wall between posters featuring animals with cheesy inspirational quotes and Bible verses.

"How may I serve you today?"

He handed me a bowl, out of which I plucked a butterscotch Dum-Dums lollipop.

I gulped nervously as I unwrapped it and stuck it in my mouth. I then reached into my backpack and placed the embroidered sweater on the desk.

"Well, that does seem to be a bit outside of our usual dress code," said Principal Randall, putting his glasses on. "It's like somebody dipped it into Satan's paint bucket! Thank you for retrieving this for me, but next time, let's leave it to the teachers here to confiscate contraband."

"Oh. That's not what this… this is Rachel Bristol's sweater. Ella made it for her. We found it in Mr. Crumbull's… on Mr. Crumbull's car."

"So… you stole this sweater off Mr. Crumbull's car? Like… on top of it?"

"Umm… yes. Well, okay. It was inside it, but the windows were open." My ability to lie was all but non-existent. "Me and Ella just thought it was suspicious. Rachel was wearing this the last time anyone saw her, and—"

"Now, Mr. Morton, what you're saying here is a very serious accusation."

I sat up straight to clarify. "Oh no, I'm not accusing anyone of anything. Just thought it was like… evidence or something."

Principal Randall leaned forward, resting on his elbows. "Tell me, kiddo, how is it you know Mr. Crumbull didn't find this and report it to me?"

"I guess I don't. Did he?"

Principal Randall stared at me for a moment. "No, he did not. I can't say I condone these shenanigans you and Ella have gotten yourselves into, but I'll look into this."

I breathed out an enormous sigh of relief. "Thanks so much. That's all I was asking. Sorry for the trouble!"

"It's fine. But just between us… maybe be more careful with who you spend your time with. It's not always a unanimous decision who we let into our school here…"

"Honestly, I think Ella is a godly person deep down. Was kinda hoping by hanging out with me and Benny that we'd rub off on her. I'll be more careful not to let it happen the other way around."

"That's very optimistic of you," he said. "That was certainly the hope of some of the faculty when we reviewed her father's application."

"Not you, though?"

"Have a blessed day, Arthur."

Luckily, the hardcore theater nerds and I were leaving for the yearly State Thespians competition that afternoon, providing a pleasant distraction from my undercover sleuthing and from the grief we were all feeling. Though first I needed to let Ella know I had handed off the evidence.

As I rounded the corner to find her, I noticed a flier taped to the end of the lockers.

HELP FIND RACHEL BRISTOL!

If we work together and pray hard, we will find her. If you have any information, please send it to findrachel@rca.net.

Also, please consider attending a candlelight vigil this Friday in the Spóros *sanctuary. For any questions, please contact Jade Parnacle at jparnacle@rca.net.*

Beneath the text was a photo of Rachel smiling.

I sighed. *There's no way this is genuine… she hates Rachel. Seems helpful, though. Guess I'll give her the benefit of the doubt.*

"Hey, dude. Sup?" The pep in Ella's voice caught me off guard as I approached her locker.

"Oh, not too much… other than giving Rachel's sweater to Principal Randall just now. He says he's gonna look into it."

"Oh, nice. That's good news. You must've been shitting your pants. Proud of you."

"Yeah… thanks," I said.

I tried to keep my enthusiasm to a minimum, to heed Principal Randall's warning about Ella's influence.

"Hopefully it leads to something," said Ella. "Anyway, sorry to run, but I've got a video editing class to get to."

"Oh, with Mr. Ankler? I heard that's a fun one."

"Yeah, I'm really liking it! I always thought video was something I could get into, but it feels like it's my thing, ya know?"

She's awfully chipper today, I thought.

"That's super cool," I said.

"Thanks, Art. And good luck at States. I'll see ya when you get back!"

"For sure. And let me know how Rachel's vigil goes. I assume you're going?"

Ella looked at her feet. "Oh… right. Been trying not to think about her, for my own sanity. I'll see if I'm feeling up to it."

"Ah, okay," I said. "Gotta take care of yourself first. See ya."

Ella waved. "See ya."

*   *   *

The differences between RCA and public schools were often drastic. School buses, however, were identical to their secular counterparts—yellow tanks that packed children and teens inside with the density of jellybeans, forcing more social interaction than any neurodivergent persons typically desired. When performing arts nerds packed the buses though, good times often followed. At least, they did when they didn't have a missing student on their minds.

I sat next to Andrew, who I would perform a scene with. For the first hour, only whispers filled the bus. After a while, the adrenaline of the trip filled at least some of the hole left in Rachel's absence, and our troupe began singing show tunes, starting with "Be Our Guest" from *Beauty and the Beast.*

"Gotta make one quick stop, kids," announced the bus driver over the racket. "Picking up a late chaperone."

The bus pulled up not to a house, but to a police station.

"Who are we picking up?" asked a student.

The bus driver shrugged.

After a few moments, the bus doors opened. Mr. Crumbull entered the bus.

"Welcome aboard, Jim!" said Ms. Flannigan.

"Happy to be here, everyone! I haven't been to Tampa since my college days."

"What were you doing at the police station?" asked Benny.

"Oh, nothing important, Mr. Bertrand. Don't you worry about it."

I avoided eye contact as he passed my aisle. I didn't notice any signs of stress in his behavior, though I wasn't sure if that was a good sign, or a creepy one.

An hour into the drive, most thespians were worn out from excessive show tune karaoke. A few napped, some caught up on schoolwork, and others counted alligators in the stream next to the highway. Andrew and I studied our scene for a bit.

"Okay, that's enough demons for now," I said.

C.S. Lewis was a little heavy for my current headspace.

"Yeah, we got this," said Andrew. "Hey, uhh… random question. Do you have any advice for dealing with the people of the world this weekend?"

"The people of the world… like the theater troupes from public schools?"

"Yeah."

"I dunno," I said. "God still made them, right? I think a lot of them are good people. We just have to be careful to avoid being influenced by them."

Andrew sighed. "I hope you're right. Except for Regionals, I haven't really spent much time around anyone who isn't Christian. I had to put in some real effort to convince my mom to let me come to States."

"Oh, yikes. What would I have done then? Ha ha. Don't worry though. At the very least, maybe we can spread the word to a few lost sheep."

"That's true! Have you ever converted anyone?"

I thought for a moment. "Ya know, I don't think so. But that's okay. All we can ever really do is plant some seeds, and hope that down the road, they sprout. But yeah, it's hard to share the word when we don't hang out with secular people very often."

"Do you ever think that's a problem? Like, are we too stuck in our RCA bubble? Or do you think exposing ourselves to the influence of the world is too dangerous? First, we go to a worldly college, then a party, and before we know it we're on our way to Hell and—"

"Whoa, whoa," I said. "Slow down. I guess I do think about that sometimes. I bet there's a lot out there we won't experience if we stay in safe circles. As long as we keep each other accountable, we should be safe. So let's start with this trip. To broadening our horizons!"

"Okay, deal. To broadening our horizons… just a smidge."
We fist bumped.

*   *   *

The hotel overflowed with rebellious freedom. Hundreds of students filled the lobby, and show tunes floated through the air.

On the way to my assigned room, I stared at the floor while passing attractive girls in belly shirts. We most certainly weren't in Kansas anymore. Waiting in the room was Benny, my roommate for the weekend.

"Throw that bag on the bed and get changed, Art. We're heading to a mixer with some other schools. Sagan High is gonna be there. You remember them from Regionals, right?"

"Oh, I dunno. I might just take it easy tonight."

The anxiety of social interaction, especially with people of the world, discouraged the potential adventurous spirit in me.

"Dude, no. You are coming. There's no way you're staying in on the one weekend where we get to make some friends from other theater troupes. Plus, we deserve this. Come on, it will help take our minds off Rachel, at least."

"But—"

"Zip it! This is for your own good. Bags down. Let's go."

As it turned out, "mixer" was a chaperone-proof way of saying "hotel party." When Benny and I entered, I felt my brain's social and ethical centers melt into a puddle. The room was packed to the brim with people. Beer bottles filled an ice bucket. Secular music blasted on a boom box. Two boys were making out in the corner— a sight I had never seen before. To young me, it was a den of worldly lions waiting to prey on me; a den quite overwhelming for someone with autism, which heightened sensory experiences in a very negative way.

"Bennayy!" sang a slim boy as he approached us.

Benny flashed a huge, toothy grin. "Oscar, so lovely to see you again."

Oscar kissed Benny on the cheek.

Friendly, I thought.

"It's been too long, Benny. Who's your friend?"

"This is Arthur, my buddy from school. Great actor, too."

I forced a smile. "Hah. Thanks. Nice to meet you."

Oscar definitely noticed my discomfort.

"Do you guys have any sodas?" I asked.

"Hmm, I'm not sure," said Oscar. "There's beer in the bucket there, and there might be some other stuff in the fridge."

"Thanks, I'll take a look."

To my dismay, there was nothing in the fridge—not even water.

Benny seemed deep in conversation with Oscar, and, not wanting to interrupt, I backed up and leaned against the wall.

I noticed the girl standing next to me was wearing a cross necklace. I mustered up some courage. "I like your necklace. Are you a Christian too?"

"I am! I love Jesus. You too?"

"Yeah! I'm Arthur. I go to Righteous Christ Academy."

"Oh, nice. I've never heard of it. I'm Jess. I go to Faraday High. It's not a fancy private school or anything."

"Ah, I see." I wondered how easy it was to stay on the godly path while constantly surrounded by worldly people. "What church do you go to?"

"I go to All Walks Unitarian."

"Oh, I've never heard of it."

I hadn't heard of Unitarian Universalism either—a progressive, Christianity-adjacent religion with fewer problematic beliefs than Evangelicalism.

After an awkward silence, another girl approached us. "Hey, babe," she said, kissing Jess right on the lips.

I had watched far too many lesbian pornos to have any ethical standard in judging, but judge I did. Not wanting to start a scene, I silently walked back across the room, past Benny, who was sipping on a beer, and into the quiet, empty hallway.

I expelled a sigh of relief. I could breathe again.

On the way back to my room, I dwelled on the frustration that my first attempt to find common ground with someone on the trip was such a failure.

I thought the cross meant something, but I guess she wasn't a true *Christian. And Benny? Drinking? What the heck?*

Back in my quiet hotel room, I unpacked my bag and got ready for bed. I stayed up a little bit, hoping Benny would show up, so we could debrief from that party. He never showed up.

My autism meant not getting enough sleep simply wasn't an option, or else I'd feel like ants were crawling all over my body for most of the following day. I turned off the lights and hit the hay.

*　　*　　*

In the morning, there was no sign of Benny. I would've assumed I slept through his arrival, but his bed was still made. I didn't know what to make of that.

After getting ready for the big day, I made my way down to the continental breakfast. I ate a bagel with butter alongside Andrew, who ate nothing but a bowl filled to the brim with whole strawberries. We also ran a few lines from our scene, which we'd perform in just a few hours.

Andrew and I met the rest of the troupe in the hotel lobby as Benny entered through the main doors wearing sunglasses. Without removing them, he approached us and stood next to me.

"Good morning," he said.

"Uh, hey." I furrowed my brow. "Where have you been all night?"

"Just making the most of the trip. It's not every day we get to explore a new city with new friends."

"Aren't you worried that staying up is gonna affect your song today?"

"I'll be fine," he assured me.

"Alright."

Ms. Flannigan stepped to the front of the group. "Alright, actors! Let's hustle! We've got so many performances today, and I know you're all gonna be amazing!"

We walked to a nearby conference hall. Being in a proper downtown city was a fun experience. Skyscrapers surrounded us on all sides, and the fact that theater nerds filled the crowds made me feel welcome. Thankfully, the fall weather wasn't bad as Florida weather goes. A sweaty back wouldn't have had a positive effect on a hypersensitive actor.

With a few hours left before Andrew's and my performance from *Screwtape*, he and I, along with a few other classmates, attended a stage combat workshop. When it was our turn to take part, we acted out a scene from *Star Wars: Revenge of the Sith*, a movie we had seen together. Good times.

An hour before our slot, we rejoined the group and cheered on a few other classmates. Two girls talked about geese while sitting on a bench. They received a "superior" rating—the highest possible result. Benny got top marks for his song as well, proving that sleep was not as important of a contributor to his energy level as it was for me.

After a while, Andrew and I were called up.

"Alright, let's do this," I said. "You ready?"

"Guess I've gotta be," said Andrew before whispering a prayer under his breath.

I did the same as we walked up.

Somehow, small brightly lit rooms with an audience of twenty to thirty semi-serious actors were far more terrifying than massive theaters. It had been a while since I performed in front of anyone, so it took a moment for the butterflies to pass.

"Hi, my name is Arthur Morton."

"And I'm Andrew Plum."

"We'll be performing a scene from *Screwtape*, a play by James Forsyth, based on the book by C.S. Lewis."

"Lovely!" said one judge—a middle-aged woman with a brown ponytail.

The flow state of performing took over my brain quickly, and my natural talent for expressing demonic anger filled the room. I muttered philosophical musings to my demon subordinate, played by Andrew. His demon was far less aggressive.

Before I knew it, the scene was over. We bowed and thanked the judges, and a light round of applause from the conservatively sized audience greeted us. Benny patted me on the back when I sat down.

We remained sitting until the current block of performances passed. Afterward, the judges handed out the scores. Andrew and I received the second-highest possible score, an "excellent"—the same as at regionals. Always the sore loser, I was slightly disappointed.

"That's so amazing! Thank you!" said Andrew, the optimist.

"Thank you," I said.

On the way out, the judge who had expressed enthusiasm at our chosen scene approached our troupe.

"Hi, I just wanted to express how nice it was to see a great Christian group like this here. Jesus would've loved all your performances. Thank you so much for this blessing. I hope to see some of you again next year."

Finally, someone else who loves Jesus, I thought. The weekend in a den of lions had started to wear me down.

*   *   *

Part of the fun of State Thespians was seeing the shows other schools had put on the previous year, which had been selected for encore performances. So far, our school hadn't made the cut.

The festival scheduled the shows for the same time, so we only got to see one. Most of us followed Ms. Flannigan's recommendation: *Spring Awakening,* by one of the most renowned theater magnet schools in Florida. She had seen it locally and had nothing but amazing words to share.

"You sure you wanna see *Spring Awakening,* Artie?" asked Benny, as we changed into our evening outfits.

"Yeah, Ms. Flannigan said it's amazing. Why?"

"Oh, no reason. I'm sure you'll find it… interesting."

"Uh… okay."

In the hotel lobby, Ms. Flannigan looked stunning in a sparkling green dress. She stood next to a mustachioed man in a suit.

"Hello, boys!" he said. "I'm Eddie, the boyfriend, and songwriter for *Eden.* Great to meet you two!"

"Hey there, Eddie! I'm God." Benny chuckled. "I kid, I kid. I'm Benny. Nice to finally meet you."

They shook hands.

"And I'm Arthur. I play the snake."

We shook hands too.

"Ah, I can totally see that!" said Eddie.

I wasn't sure if I should be offended or flattered.

After a few more students joined us, we walked over to a theater that made our multicolored one look like a preschool play area. The color scheme was a far more elegant maroon and silver. It had at least a thousand seats, a balcony section, and even side boxes for VIPs.

When approaching the theater, one more chaperone met us: Mr. Crumbull. He wore a very colorful tie and vibrant red shoes. I barely recognized him.

"Hey everyone! I don't know about y'all, but I am SO excited about this!"

This seems so out of character, I thought.

We took our seats, and I perused the playbill.

Play First Magnet School Presents

Spring Awakening

In late 19th century Germany, students rebel against their oppressive teachers and discover their sexuality.

"Ah, so this is what you meant," I said to Benny.

"Welcome to the world, Art."

The lights dimmed, the curtain rose, and the risqué musical began. Immediately, I could tell it was going to be a conflicting experience for me. The opening song featured a young woman struggling to understand where babies came from because her mother didn't teach her about it. Soon after, characters sang about their longings for physical intimacy.

For obvious reasons, I doubted the message would align with my Christian beliefs. However, being in a new environment, surrounded by theater nerds, I experienced slightly less guilt than I otherwise would have. Since Ms. Flannigan endorsed the play, I felt like I had a free pass to at least try to appreciate it.

The story focused on an older, stricter version of the purity culture I was embedded in. The teachers discouraged the German students from exploring their sexuality, and sometimes they didn't even know what sex was.

Before long, the show took a break for intermission. After using the restroom, I approached Ms. Flannigan and her boyfriend, Eddie, in the lobby. Not knowing how to initiate conversation organically, I simply stood there with my hands behind my back and showed a half-second smile.

Since they weren't exactly introverts, it didn't take long for them to break the silence.

"So," said Eddie, "how have Eden rehearsals been going for you?"

"Oh, not bad. Kinda weird without Rachel, but it's been alright."

Ms. Flannigan placed her hand on her chest.

"Yeah…" said Eddie. "I was heartbroken to hear about her. Melinda shared some recordings of her Eve with me. Simply magnificent. Such authenticity!"

Ms. Flannigan rested her head on Eddie's shoulder. "I do hope she turns up soon. The way that girl lit up onstage gave me the sense that we were on to something special. Fingers crossed."

"Yeah, we just need to keep praying for her," I said.

"Oh, right," said Ms. Flannigan. "Of course."

Eddie smiled.

The second act of *Spring Awakening* went in some unexpectedly dark directions. It tackled abortion, suicide, and ultimately conveyed a cautionary tale about the dangers of the very kinds of institutions in which I spent so much time. Unfortunately, I was in so deep that dissociation prevented me from applying the lesson to my own life. Regardless, it stirred my empathy more than my judgment.

A rousing discussion about the performance accompanied the walk home. When we arrived back at the hotel, Ms. Flannigan and Eddie headed back to what I assumed were two hotel rooms, but, in retrospect, was probably just one. Mr. Crumbull and the rest of the students dispersed as well.

"Well, I'm pooped," said Benny, stretching his arms toward the ceiling of the lobby.

"Yeah, same," I said.

As we walked to the elevator, I heard a cacophony of men's laughter coming from down the hall. I looked toward the sound and saw Mr. Crumbull hugging two middle-aged men in business-casual attire.

"How've ya been?" asked one man as the group walked down the hall.

"I've been so great!" said Mr. Crumbull, as their bodies and voices vanished around the corner.

"What do you ya think that's about?" I asked.

"I dunno," said Benny. "He said he went to college here, right?"

"Yeah… wanna go check it out?"

Benny scrunched his face. "Umm… why?"

"Well, Ella and I may have found Rachel's sweater in his car…"

Benny's eyes widened. "Umm, WHAT? When was this?"

I scratched my cheek. "Like… a week ago or so?"

"And you're just telling me this now? What the heck?"

"Sorry," I said. "It was a need to know basis sort of thing."

"Well… okay. That's pretty big, though, so I see your point. Let's see what this snobby boy is up to."

I nodded. We stealthily inched our way to the end of the hall and poked our heads around the corner.

There was only one door visible before a dead end, and someone had propped it open. We could hear jazz music coming from inside. I couldn't see any people beyond the doorway, so I walked through it.

"Jeez, dude," whispered Benny. "You're really getting into this detective vibe!" He followed me.

The room was a sort of lounge, featuring an elegant bar and small tables. The jazz music came from a live band on a small stage in the corner. At the far end, Mr. Crumbull sat with the other men at a booth, and thankfully, he was facing away from us.

I led Benny to a small, bar-height table at the back, out of obvious sight.

"What do you think they're doing?" I asked.

"Looks like they're gambling," said Benny.

He was right—upon a closer look, I could see piles of colorful chips being doled out to the players.

We couldn't make out what they were saying over the music, but soon, one man waved over a bartender, who poured them each a shot of whiskey.

"Gambling and drunkenness?" I asked. "I can't believe an RCA teacher would take part in something like this. Makes him even more suspicious, right?"

Benny tilted his head. "Oh, come on, Arthur. I'll give you ten bucks if you can point me to one Bible verse that says you can't take a load off with your friends."

"I… well, not directly. But it's pretty obvious this is kind of a sinful lifestyle."

"If you say so," said Benny.

"Shoot," I said. "Hide your face!"

Mr. Crumbull had stood up and was walking toward the exit with his cell phone at his ear. Benny and I turned to face the opposite direction. After a moment, I looked back and saw that he wasn't in the lounge anymore.

"Come on," I said, standing up.

We approached the door and stood just to the side. We could barely make it out, but Mr. Crumbull was having a heated conversation outside the doorway.

"I don't know how that could be… Can you please just… Look, it's probably no big deal… Yes, I'll be there… Yes… Fine."

We heard footsteps approaching and froze in place. Mr. Crumbull walked back into the lounge and right past us.

Benny covered his mouth with his hand to silence his giggles.

Mr. Crumbull flared his arms with frustration as he approached the booth. He patted his friends on the back, likely saying goodbye.

"Oh, shoot!" I whispered. "He's gonna come this way; let's go!"

We slipped through the doorway and hastened to the lobby. We pressed the "up" button by the elevator. After what felt like five minutes, the elevator opened. We entered, I chose our floor, and mashed the "door close" button repeatedly, successfully escaping before Mr. Crumbull caught up to us.

"Woo!" said Benny. "That was a rush!"

I laughed with relief. "It really was… but I don't know if I could handle getting caught."

"Well, good thing we weren't."

I nodded.

The elevator soon arrived at our floor, and we walked toward our room.

"So," I said. "Do you think that call had something to do with Rachel?"

"I suppose it's possible. But I wouldn't read into it. It could've been anything."

"Yeah, I guess. But I still think there's something fishy going on with him. He acts so differently here than when he's in class. It's like he's performing, but I don't know which is the real Mr. Crumbull."

Benny swiped a key card, and we entered the room.

"Honestly, Art, I bet what we just saw was the real one. Teaching ungrateful students all week, every week… it sounds draining. Sometimes ya gotta let yourself breathe a little."

"Yeah… I guess."

"But on the other hand," said Benny. "That sweater is one heck of a clue."

"It sure is," I said. "I guess we'll see what happens."

*   *   *

The bus ride home was far more relaxed than the rowdy trip to Tampa. Burned out from the week in the world, many students spent the ride sleeping, including Andrew next to me. Despite having not slept great the night before, being neurodivergent meant that blocking out the distractions around me was easier said than done. Public sleeping wasn't my forte.

Ms. Flannigan turned around from the seat in front of me. "It's fun to escape our bubble for a while, huh?"

"Oh. Yeah, I guess. Kinda excited to get back home, though. There was so much sin around us this weekend."

"Sin, huh? Like what?"

"Well, for one, Benny and I hung out with some kids from a public school, and two of the guys started kissing. I couldn't believe they'd just do that in front of me."

Ms. Flannigan sat upright. "Come on now, Arthur. There's no wrong way to love."

"Wait, what? The Bible is very clear that—"

"I get it. But listen to me. You are free to live your life however you want, but do you really think Jesus would look down on other people for being different from you?"

I squirmed. "No, I guess not."

"Right. And plus, aren't you and Benny best friends?"

"Yeah."

"Well, then you must be okay with… I mean… I assumed… ya know what, never mind. Just please promise me you'll try to accept our neighbors for who they are. It's okay that not everyone is exactly the same as us."

"Yeah, okay. I promise."

Those ideas didn't exactly sit well with me. I knew our pastors wouldn't approve.

And what exactly was she getting at with Benny? I thought. *Does she think he's gay? Is that possible? What if Samuel was on to something with that rumor about him having a boyfriend in New York? No, no. That's nuts.*

I put those thoughts out of my head for the time being.

While watching palm trees whoosh by my window, it occurred to me that someone who rode in with us was not currently on the bus.

"Hey, what happened to Mr. Crumbull?" I asked.

Ms. Flannigan turned back toward me. "Oh, he had some sort of family emergency. He headed back on his own last night. Took a Greyhound bus, I think."

"Hmm, I see. Weird."

Could this have something to do with that phone call? I wondered.

With no one else to talk to about it, I went back to failing to nap.

8. Drifting Bubble

Ah, the peaceful life. Walking down air conditioned hallways, surrounded by good Christian classmates, none of whom were about to offer me alcohol or act sinfully in front of my eyes. I had missed it.

After basking for a moment, my smile faded. I noticed very few students around me were chatting. Despite a few weeks passing since Rachel's vanishing, things hadn't returned to normal. A thick layer of uncertainty still coated the school, which was slowly turning into mourning.

Rachel's locker was all but covered in notes and flowers. Two cheerleaders approached and added more roses to the pile. Although Benny, myself, and especially Ella were still feeling the repercussions of Rachel's vanishing, many other students had been close to her for much longer. We had gotten to know her during a few weeks of rehearsals, but the cheer squad had spent countless hours practicing with her after school for three years. To them, the last few weeks were likely devastating.

My autism ensured I empathized differently than your average person, but that didn't mean I couldn't feel the pain of others. Observing the sadness left in Rachel's absence dampened my already-lacking positivity as I entered homeroom.

At least the monotony of Mr. Crumbull's routine announcements kicked my brain back into school mode, despite my suspicion of his guilt having increased exponentially lately.

After he finished, the door opened, and in walked Miss Ventura, a guidance counselor who dressed for business.

"So, who in here has their dream college picked out already?!"

Most of the room raised their hands. Miss Ventura's enthusiasm for a topic I wasn't at all ready to think about created an instant pit in my stomach. Yeah, I needed to think about college. And I had some leads on where I might go. But there was so much else distracting me.

"That's great to see. No worries at all if you aren't there yet, though. All this week, the guidance counselors and I will be available each day for one-on-one sessions to discuss your exciting futures for God! There are sign-up sheets outside our offices."

Ugh, fine.

Miss Ventura's office was just as cringy as Principal Randall's, but for different reasons. There were no cheesy posters featuring animals or inspirational quotes in bold lettering. Instead, Jesus-themed artwork covered the walls. Of course he was white in every one, but teenage me wasn't phased.

"So, Arthur. What are we thinking for college?"

"Hmm, probably art school. I think I'd like to major in animation. It seems to be a good hybrid of my passions: art, computers, and acting."

"Oh, that sounds lovely," she said, smiling. "What schools were you thinking?"

"I've heard good things about Barnum Institute of the Arts, GCAD—Georgia College of Art and Design, and—"

"Oh, I don't know about those schools. They're very secular. Have you considered Shield and Sword U? I hear they have a nice art program, and you'd be safe from the influence of the world there, surrounded by good Christian friends every day."

"That does sound nice." *Especially after what I went through at States.* "But a basic art program isn't what I'm looking for. The animation work that comes out of those schools is honestly pretty bad. If I want to break into the industry, I need to go to a school with a reputable animation program."

"Okay, that's fair. All I ask is that you look through these programs." She handed me pamphlets for a few Christian colleges, none of which had proper animation focuses. "We wouldn't want to lose you to the enemy if we don't have to." She flashed a creepy smile.

Was that a threat? I asked myself, semi-seriously.

On the way out of my college interrogation, I heard my name.

"Arthur Morton. How is God moving you today?"

I looked to my right and Pastor Robbie stood in the doorway of the office he occasionally used when called in to perform duties for the school.

"Uh… good?"

"Why don't you join me in my office for a bit…"

Pastor Robbie closed the door behind me. His office wasn't cringy. The blank walls and perfect symmetry of the desk items gave off a sterile, disconcerting vibe.

"So, Arthur. I hear from Principal Randall that you've accused your superior, Mr. Crumbull, of kidnapping."

"Wait, no, I just thought the school should know about some evidence Ella and I found and—"

"It's a very ungodly thing, Arthur, to doubt the authority figures God placed around you."

"I know, but—"

"No buts. This is unacceptable behavior, especially considering the reason Mr. Crumbull had Rachel's sweater was because he found it and was bringing it to the police. He's been cooperating with them on the case, and since you gave Principal Randall reason to doubt him, the police caught wind of this and brought him in for questioning."

Shoot… was his abrupt departure from States my fault?

"Oh. Okay. Well, that's good. I didn't actually think he did anything." I shuffled in my seat, knowing that wasn't entirely true.

"That's beside the point. We hold our students to God's strict authority here at Righteous Christ. I need you to promise me and God that you won't act up like this again."

I felt shut down, but arguing back would play right into the criticisms Robbie was giving me. For my own sake, I put my pride on hold. "Absolutely. I promise."

"You know, Arthur, I think I know of a way to get you back onto the holy path. Have you heard of Cocoon?"

"You mean the movie?"

"No, the church retreat I host in the Florida Keys each year. It's happening over the three-day weekend at the end of the month. It's part of the college ministry, but all that means is that it's eighteen and up."

"Okay, yeah. I have heard of that. And I am eighteen."

"Everyone who has gone has come back with a renewed vigor for God. I think it could be something that really helps you."

"Okay, I'll definitely think about it. Thank you for the encouragement."

"Of course, Arthur. That's what your authority figures are here for—to help guide you. Trusting us unconditionally prepares you for obedience to God, and that's the most important thing. Please make sure you respect us. I'd hate for this to climb up the ladder to Pastor Tom's desk. He'd be so disappointed to find out that this sort of behavior is going on at the school that shares his church's good name."

I gulped. "Thanks. I'll… try to do better."

I thought about confronting him regarding why he lied about not seeing Rachel after the purity conference, but after that lecture about not questioning my elders, it would've been a bad call.

*　　*　　*

Cheesy, meaty goop in a bowl. There was no anxiety that an after-school trip to Chili's couldn't heal.

"Hey guys!" said Ella, as she approached the table where Benny and I sat. "It's so nice to see you! It's been a few."

I was taken aback by her friendliness; she seemed genuinely happy to hang out with us.

She sat next to Benny, who gave her a tight side hug. Feeling like I shouldn't let our friendship get too much closer, per Principal Randall's heeding, I avoided any affectionate greetings.

"So, I have some news," I said. "Today, Pastor Robbie told me the reason Mr. Crumbull had Rachel's sweater was because he had found it and was going to take it to the police."

"Oh. Snap," said Benny.

"Hmm, bummer," said Ella.

I expected more of a reaction from her. *Maybe she's learned to accept all this?*

"In any case," I said, "that's kinda the end of it, assuming Pastor Robbie is telling the truth. No more leads."

"Well," said Benny, "except for when he lied at the assembly about when he last saw Rachel. That means we can't really believe anything he says about her."

I remembered my talk with Robbie from earlier.

"I guess that's true, but I think we should give our authority figures the benefit of the doubt. Speaking of which, he really wants me to go to his Cocoon retreat in two weeks. He thinks it could bring me closer to God. He seems worried about me."

"Ugh, that sounds awful," said Ella.

"I…" Benny paused. "I'm actually going. My mom is making me."

"Oh, nice." At least if Benny was going, I'd have a friend. "I'm on the fence. I think it would be good for me."

Ella shook her head. "Well, count me out. I talked to someone who went last year, and they said it's a straight-up boot camp. Get closer to God through physically grueling obstacle courses and stuff."

"Yeah, that's what I'm worried about," I said. "My Asperger's would probably make that kinda stuff even harder. I'll have to think about it some more. One reason I'm considering it is that spending time with Pastor Robbie might help us figure out if he's hiding something about Rachel."

"Ooh, I like that," said Benny. "Let's play detective in the Keys!"

Ella grimaced. "Ha ha, you two have fun. Lemme know if you find anything. I'd love to take down that dickbag."

Dickbag surprisingly didn't phase me. Ella's nonchalant attitude was definitely normalizing in my mind, for better or worse.

After dinner, I drove the two of them home. First, I dropped off Benny, and then it was Ella's turn. She hopped from the back seat to shotgun and cranked Green Day on the radio as I pulled into the street.

"So, spill the beans, Arthur," Ella said with a smile. "Why have you been acting all weird around me?"

"Huh? What do you mean?"

"Well, you almost never make eye contact, but tonight at dinner was extreme. I won't be mad. Did a teacher put you up to it? They've been talking to me and my parents, too. They see me as a... delinquent." She swiveled her head toward me as she exaggerated her voice. "Do YOU see me as a delinquent, Artie?"

"What? No, definitely not."

"Bull. Shit. You're a terrible liar."

"Yeah... I know."

We laughed.

"Like I mentioned at Chili's, I have Asperger syndrome—a type of autism. Just makes me kinda socially awkward sometimes. Sorry."

"Nothing to be sorry about; I get it. And for the record, I don't generally think you're awkward. You're a good friend and I enjoy hanging with you."

"Thanks," I said. "I feel the same."

"Yeah... you've just been weird super recently, ha ha. I'm honestly not mad, though. I don't know you super well, but it's enough. You have a good heart. I know that once you experience what else the world offers, you'll follow your heart in the right direction."

"Wow. Thanks. That's... very sweet...I think?"

Ella smirked. "That's cause I am very sweet. Didn't you know? At least when I'm not snorting crack out of my backpack and using my devilish femininity to lure weak Christian men into my web."

"Hah. Right. The RCA Gator lurking in the shadows."

"I can't tell if you're joking, but hell yes to that possible compliment. Oh, turn left at that light."

After the turn, we pulled up to a security gate.

"The code is 8873," she said.

I entered the code and drove through.

Enormous houses filled the suburb, a far cry from the community of cramped townhouses my family lived in.

"Wow... these are really nice," I said.

"Ha ha... yeah. That's me on the right with the brick arch."

I pulled the car into the large U-shaped driveway.

"Holy cannoli," I said. "This is your place? It's a fricking mansion!"

"Yeah… I don't really tell people about my rich-ass parents. It's not all it's cracked up to be."

"Well, that pool sure looks like all it's cracked up to be."

"Hah. It's alright. They're buying me a car as an early graduation present, so I'm not complaining. Soon I won't need rides. Thanks for this one, though."

"Any time."

She patted my shoulder and went inside.

Yeah… Principal Randall got this one wrong. Ella's alright.

*   *   *

Entering my home, silence greeted me.

"Anybody home?"

I walked around to the back of the stairs, where my mom sat at the family computer. My dad stood next to her. On the screen was something I did not expect: porn. And not just any porn. It was porn I had definitely seen—not recently, but before I got my own computer. Anime boobs were bouncing in a pixelated Windows Media Player window in front of my parents.

My heart skipped several beats. My mom turned toward me, tears covering her cheeks.

"Van. Now," she said.

I assumed the change in venue was to avoid waking my sleeping sister with what was sure to be a colossal argument.

My dad, my mom, and I made a silent trek to the parking area outside. We stepped into our green Ford Windstar. My mom shut the door behind us as I stared at the ground.

Nobody said anything for at least a minute. My mom was huffing and scowling, but my dad simply stared into the distance, fiddling with his fingers. It was clear who was taking the discovery the hardest.

My mom sniffled. "So. How long has this been going on for?"

"I dunno. A while."

"And who turned you on to this stuff? Do you watch it with your friends?"

"Ew! No. I just stumbled upon it. It's pretty common. They even talked about it in the purity conference. Obviously they don't support it, but my point is this isn't exactly rare. Every guy stumbles into it at some point."

"And that justifies this filth?!"

"I hate myself for this, okay? Every time I look at it, I feel so awful after, and I immediately pray for forgiveness. So far, it just hasn't worked out."

She wiped a tear from her eye. "I'm just so hurt you would watch such vile videos. I thought I raised you better." She turned toward my dad. "Do you not have anything to add?!"

He cleared his throat. "Umm, yeah. Son, if you can, it's definitely best to avoid stuff like this. It's best to save these experiences for your future wife."

"Thanks, you're a big help…" said my mom.

The guilt brought a tear to my eye. "You're right. I'm completely broken. No matter how much I try to stop, I just can't get rid of the temptations. Satan's grasp is strong, I suppose. I do have an idea of something that might help, though. Pastor Robbie has this spiritual retreat coming up. It's in the Keys for a weekend. He already thinks it would do me good to go, and he doesn't even know about the porn. Maybe it could help rid me of these urges, too."

"If you think that will help you stop this," said my mom, "then go for it. Until then, no computer privileges. Maybe none after, too. We'll see."

"That's fair. And I'm sorry. If I knew how to stop, I would."

My mom sighed. "I'll forgive you, eventually. I'm just so disappointed in you. If this retreat doesn't help you, I don't know what I'll do."

She opened the door and went inside. My dad patted me on the shoulder as he left. I sat in silence for a bit, crushed that I let my mom down so much, and determined to fix myself by seeking God.

9. Caterpillar

Two weeks passed without so much as a whisper about Rachel, much to our collective disappointment. Gradually, the missing person fliers on the walls of the school had become less noticeable as students and faculty posted more-recent announcements. Although the student body as a whole was still grieving, the toll it took on our day-to-day lives had lessened.

My guilt over my parents finding my old porn collection hadn't improved. Well, I suppose the guilt wasn't entirely related to being found out. The primary source of guilt was thoughts about disappointing God. I had let Him down, and I didn't know how to stop.

At least the current restrictions on my life made things easier. When home, my parents treated me like a prisoner. School was a temporary freedom, as was church. But two weeks was far too long to go without Chili's queso.

I hoped Pastor Robbie's "spiritual boot camp," Cocoon, would fix me in some way—help show me the strength to ignore the sexual temptations that surrounded me. I wanted to stop feeling so ashamed.

In addition to possibly curing my porn addiction, attending Cocoon could lead to new information about Rachel's whereabouts, though I knew it was a long-shot. With no clues left to tie Mr. Crumbull into the disappearance, Pastor Robbie's lies were the only lead we had left. I was determined to find an opportunity to get to the bottom of things over the next three days.

Two vans drove us to Camp Cocoon in the Florida Keys. The ride was less fun than the bus ride to States and featured far fewer show tunes. The few of us eighteen or older from RCA were the minority. Most of the attendees from Righteous Christ Church's college and young adult ministry were strangers to us. A few people in the van seemed excited and initiated conversations, but the rest of us rode in silence, wondering what we were about to experience. Even Benny and I, who sat next to each other, didn't exchange many words.

Halfway through the ride, the driver handed us paper packets and pens. He explained they were non-disclosure agreements, which would ensure the experience wouldn't be spoiled for potential future campers. It prevented us from sharing the events of the weekend with anyone outside of Cocoon, including our parents. It seemed odd, but I didn't have the patience to read the entire document, or the desire to make a stink about it. We all signed them.

After clearing the mainland, the oceanic scenery was stunning. The highway streamlined itself into a long, thin bridge over the ocean, connecting us to the small scattered islands off the coast. Palm trees dotted the landscape as the waves crashed on the shore.

The unmarked white vans pulled onto a dirt road and drove past patches of forests and one very hungry-looking alligator.

We pulled up to a wooden gate. Other than the word "Cocoon" on the side of a small mailbox, nothing about the location seemed like a church-related property.

We grabbed our bags and stepped out of the van into the brisk beach-adjacent mini-jungle. Samuel stepped out of the second van. Benny and I sighed. Samuel made eye contact with us, scoffed, said "Sup," and entered the gate leading to his father's passion project. We followed a few steps behind.

Inside the camp, it felt like we were detached from the world—equally freeing and unsettling. The only sounds around us were each other's footsteps and the rustling of wildlife in the surrounding trees. It wasn't a large campus, by campground or Righteous Christ standards. There was a decently sized central yard, surrounded by five small homes. At the center was a common area featuring a dried-out fire pit and a few hand-crafted wooden benches supported by rocks. Behind the homes at the rear end of the camp was what looked like an obstacle course, though it was hard to make out from the entrance.

As soon as we entered the common area, Pastor Robbie exited one home and approached us, dressed in his usual getup—a button-down shirt tucked into blue jeans. Following behind him was a small crowd of youth ministers and vaguely familiar faces from the church—former Cocoon attendees, from what I'd heard.

Robbie stood across the unlit fireplace from us, with his followers fanned out around him.

"Welcome, my brothers and sisters in Christ," Robbie said. "I feel very blessed to have you here, for some very important discipleship."

Welp, here we go.

"You all think you're Christians, but some of you are not. Sure, you go to church. Maybe you even share the good word with worldly sinners sometimes. But you see… God asks you to love Him, radically. When I was a boy, my father encouraged me to join my school's ROTC military preparation program. As part of this, I attended a rigorous boot camp. While there, I learned some very important lessons about discipline. Sometimes we have to be pushed out of our comfort zones in order to grow—to become radicalized for God."

I shuffled uncomfortably. Vivid memories of stinging ice buckets swarmed my mind. I shook them off.

This is my chance to toughen up, I thought.

"This type of rigorous discipleship can be observed in the Bible, as well. When God tested Job, do you think he enjoyed it? When his children were killed, do you think he felt no pain? He absolutely did. But he endured it, knowing God had a plan for him. Likewise, Cocoon will test the endurance of each and every one of you."

Robbie stepped toward his son, Samuel, and placed his hand on his shoulder. "You will emerge a more beautiful child of God than ever before." He paced in front of us, his arms crossed behind his back. "For starters, the Cocoon leadership will now collect your personal belongings. You won't be needing them."

The news triggered an increase in my heart rate. I was quite accustomed to the amenities of modern life. To an autistic individual, the thought of losing all of that was horrific.

The adults stepped toward us and began collecting bags, cell phones, and wallets.

As one of the camp counselors approached Lily, the chubby blonde girl to my left, she leaned in and whispered, "Umm… I'm on my period. Can I please keep my—"

The counselor didn't even make eye contact as he grabbed her bag and continued down the row of students, eventually adding my backpack to his collection.

"Please follow me to the dining hall for lunch," said Pastor Robbie.

On our way, I noticed one girl reach into her pocket. She approached Lily quietly and handed her an item.

"Here," she whispered.

"Thanks. You're a lifesaver," said Lily as she stored the pads in her pocket.

The dining room wasn't all that different from a school cafeteria. The smell was especially reminiscent. We all sat at white tables with flat bench seating, all of which were covered in scratches.

Counselors placed paper plates holding one hamburger and one hot dog in front of us. They were about what you'd expect from a church program cooking for thirty people at a time. Personally, I found them to be pretty tasty.

Other than Benny and Lily, I didn't recognize the faces of most of the campers and counselors. One familiar face was Samuel, of course. He sat a few tables over. His hand rested on the thigh of a girl clearly a few years his senior.

"He sure didn't need much time to mourn," said Benny.

When I was hardly three bites in, someone knocked the burger out of my hand, and grabbed my plate. Counselors had swarmed the room, taking everyone's food from them. We all exchanged looks of confusion.

"Okayyyy…" said Benny.

A piercing, high-pitched whistle filled the small cafeteria. My hypersensitivity caused me to cover my ears, along with one or two other students. Pastor Robbie stepped to the front of the room, whistle in mouth.

"Seriously, Dad?" said Samuel.

Robbie ignored him.

"One of the many ways people achieved wisdom in biblical times was through fasting," said Robbie. "Jesus fasted for forty days and forty nights in his human body. I sure hope all of you got a few bites in, because that's the last thing you'll be eating until tomorrow."

Murmurs filled the room. I would've said something if I wasn't so confused by what was happening.

How could anyone at Righteous Christ have approved this? I thought.

"I don't think I've ever gone that long without food in my life," said Lily. "I really think I might pass out."

"Jesus survived much worse," said Robbie. "I think you can handle eighteen hours. Now, to further push your senses to their limits… Cocoon leaders, you may begin."

He nodded to three counselors in the corner, who each held a brown plastic jar in one hand and a spoon in the other. They walked between the tables and began covering each student's head in a smattering of peanut butter.

Expressions of disgust could be heard from the students who were up first. Even Samuel burst out with, "Are you freaking kidding me, Dad?"

This is my Hell, I thought.

I was the kind of neurodivergent person who had a strong aversion to odd physical sensations. I washed my hair every day to avoid oily discomfort. In fact, I never left home without showering. If I didn't feel clean, I could barely function. If I didn't get, at the very least, seven hours of sleep, my whole body would itch. The thought of having my hair smothered in any food gave me anxiety, but peanut butter… nothing could be worse.

At that moment, I regretted so many of the choices that led to my current situation. *Why were Benny and I chosen to give Ella a tour? Why did I help Ella steal Rachel's sweater? Why did I have to look at so much porn? Why was I so stupid to not delete my internet browsing history… on my mom's computer? How did I ever think coming to Cocoon was a good idea? Oh, right… I'm here for God, and for my soul's eternal life. I just need to remember… this is all temporary. It will all be over soon…*

When the counselors reached me, I squinted my eyes and tried to focus on the thought that no matter how uncomfortable the camp experience would be for me, I would get to go back to my regular life in just a few short days—hopefully a changed person.

The sound of the spoon scraping my skull was among the more disturbing sensations that accompanied processed food spreads being slathered on my head. The thirty-second experience was not as horrific as my paranoia prepared me for, but it certainly wasn't fun.

"Thanks," I said, instinctually, as the man finished spreading. The scent of peanuts engulfed me.

Robbie stepped again to the front of the room. "Dear heavenly Father. We come to you this evening, ready for your wisdom to flow through us. May your love and mercy forgive every soul here for their wickedness. May you cleanse us. Amen."

The room hardly participated in the prayer, as our discomforts distracted us.

"Now that you're all prepared to test your limits for God, please follow the counselors outside to get your room assignments. And may God bless you all."

After receiving my assignment, I walked to my cabin in the corner of the campground. I hardly noticed my surroundings, except for a surprising amount of inspirational quote posters featuring cute animals, just like in Principal Randall's office. On them was text that read "Turn my eyes from looking at worthless things; and give me life in your ways." I had no idea what they were for.

As I walked, I focused much of my energy on tuning out the constant itch on my scalp. Brown dust from scratching already covered my hands. I usually put great effort into keeping my hands extremely clean. It wasn't a germ thing; I just hated the feeling of anything on my skin. My misery hit new heights that day.

There wasn't much to do to settle in, considering they had confiscated our belongings. I poked around for a shower to clean off the peanut butter, but there was no water pressure. After some small talk with my bunkmates, we concluded the counselors expected us to deal with our peanut butter hair for the duration of the stay. Regardless, we took turns removing the larger clumps with paper towels and water from the sink. It helped only a little.

I stepped onto the patio to get some fresh air. The starry sky was lovely—a silver lining on a miserable evening. Over a loudspeaker boomed the voice of a counselor. "James Willoughby, please make your way to Pastor Robbie's cabin, 7a, for a personal discipleship lesson. Thank you."

After a few minutes, a college-age student I assumed was James walked past our cabin and toward Pastor Robbie's. Through thin curtains, I watched as he and Robbie had a heart to heart. Every few minutes, some sort of TV screen bathed them in blue light. I wondered what they discussed, and if I was going to be called in later. After about thirty minutes, James exited, shuffling his body across the campground awkwardly.

Over the next hour, two more students were called into Robbie's cabin. One left smiling, and the other left in tears.

If I get called in there, maybe I'll have a chance to look for clues about Rachel, I thought.

While standing there, I spotted Benny on the porch of a distant cabin. We waved at each other through forced smiles.

Over the loudspeaker came the voice of a counselor I didn't recognize. "Attention disciples. Please be aware of the animal posters positioned around the campground. Becoming a radical Christian for Jesus requires focus. Starting tomorrow, if we catch any of you looking at these posters, you will immediately be asked to do forty jumping jacks. The same will happen if we catch any male staring at any female, unless the female is deemed to have been slacking on her dress code, in which case she will do the jumping jacks instead. Good night."

Welp, I thought.

"Hey, we're gonna shut off the lights in here, Arthur," shouted one of my bunkmates.

I headed inside, used the bathroom, and laid down on my bed. Falling asleep was going to be a real challenge, especially since there was no air conditioning, and the nearby beach did little to cool the humid campground.

I couldn't bear to lay my peanut butter-covered head on the pillow. I slid up on the bed so the top of my head hovered off the top edge.

My anxiety held a tight grasp on my heart. It took at least ninety minutes, but I eventually fell into a light sleep.

*   *   *

WEEUU! WEEUU! WEEUU!

There was no chance anyone was still asleep after that unplanned alarm.

"What the... what time is it?" asked one of my cabinmates.

Without our personal items, none of us had watches to check, but given the pitch-black cabin, it was clearly nighttime.

Over the loudspeaker came a voice. "Everyone to the woods! Now!"

We stumbled out of bed and made our way to the woods behind the campground. Many rubbed their eyes along the way. Luckily, the darkness of the night prevented any accidental cat poster glances.

Pastor Robbie awaited at the edge of the forest with a megaphone. "Christians! You are trespassing, and if caught, you will be punished."

Oh… I know this game… it's Underground Church again.

"The undercover Christian has already been chosen. Marco, Stephanie, and Ulga. You are the police; face the campground. Everyone else, hide now!"

I followed the crowd into the dark forest, tripping at least twice before finding a secluded tree to hide behind. Despite the heightened horrors playing in a dark forest brought, I was mostly worried that I'd be asked to stick my hands in ice buckets, like last time.

As the police's flashlights approached my vicinity, I tiptoed around the tree and transitioned to another, successfully avoiding detection. After the lights left, I gradually became more and more aware of every bush rustle and twig snap. My instincts took over, and I sprinted back toward the campground.

As I approached civilization, I hid behind a tree near a commotion. I peeked around the trunk. Through the darkness, I spotted a few glistening whistles around the necks of counselors. I had found the jail.

I scanned the environment. One counselor held a video camera on his shoulder, documenting the happenings. I wondered what they were planning on doing with the footage. I looked at the ground, hoping I wouldn't see any ice buckets. Thankfully, I didn't.

Four Christians were currently in jail. Three of them were blindfolded, squatting on planks like last time. One of them was Benny, and the fourth was Samuel. He was blindfolded, but standing. His hands were behind his back, presumably tied. One counselor walked toward him, holding something in his hands that I couldn't make out from my vantage point. He placed it around Samuel's shoulders and stepped back. It was a large white snake.

Samuel shuddered, and then cried. Through tears, he muttered, "What… what is… what is that? Please, tell me what's happening! Please! Please!"

I had no words. Suddenly, two Christians sprinted into the jail and tagged all the captives, screaming, "Jailbreak!"

With no police present, the counselors had no choice but to unbind the captives, remove the snake, and let them go.

"What the hell?!" Samuel said, tripping while he stepped backward away from the snake, which he was just seeing for the first time.

Benny, almost out of sight, heard Samuel's screams and turned around. He jogged back to jail to see Samuel scurrying backward across the ground.

"Come on, man," said Benny, extending a hand and helping Samuel up. "Let's get out of here."

Once they had vanished into the darkness, the counselor holding the snake said, "Man, that was just getting fun."

They all laughed.

I took the opportunity to sneak away and join the group of Christians who had just escaped jail. After a short jog, I caught up to them, hiding behind some bushes. On the other side were two police with flashlights.

"Hey, Art…" said Benny. "Fun game, huh?"

"Yeah…"

Benny noticed a third flashlight off in the distance. "That must be the undercover Christian," he said. "Let's go."

We snuck past the police, and once out of earshot, we ran. As we approached the spy, we heard twigs cracking and a subtle revving.

"Hurry!" yelled the spy. "Over here!"

As we ran, two golf carts appeared beside us, just behind the trees at the edge of the forest. In the passenger seat of each cart sat a counselor in a ski mask who attempted to shoot us with paintball guns, interspersed with maniacal laughter. Most of us got hit with at least one paintball, though the adrenaline of the situation prevented any significant pain.

We continued to run, jump, and trip toward our goal. At last, we crossed into a clearing with over ten campers and the undercover Christian. Then a whistle blew.

Pastor Robbie stepped into the clearing. "The Christians have won. Well met, soldiers for Christ. Please head back to your cabins."

We didn't move for a while. I needed to catch my breath, as did many others. Some cried. Samuel stared at his dad in disbelief before stomping off to bed. The rest of us trickled back at our own pace. Nobody spoke.

*　　*　　*

I woke to a blaring alarm over loudspeakers, which I mistook for a dream until another camper shook my shoulders. To no surprise, the autistic sensation of ants crawling on my body when I didn't sleep well was very present.

The first thing I noticed after sitting up was the feeling that someone had smeared peanut butter inside my nostrils. I felt around, but they were clean. I stumbled past four peanut butter-covered beds and used the restroom. The sight of the dry shower taunted me, but at least the toilet still functioned.

The lump on my breakfast plate resembled an emptied bag of trash more than an edible meal. I grimaced as I forced a few bites of the mystery concoction into my mouth. About half of it remained when a counselor blew a whistle, ending breakfast. I wasn't even mad.

The counselors led us to the rear of the Cocoon campus. On a dirt field was an obstacle course containing everything you'd expect from a military boot camp. I spotted tires covered in dirt and scuff marks, a climbable rope mesh, monkey bars straight from a children's playground, and various nondescript wooden structures.

Pastor Robbie walked around, checking the integrity of the course. When finished, he and two other counselors spoke to each other while glancing at the sky.

A camper next to me asked another, "Does it look like rain to you?"

After a few minutes, Robbie and the two counselors approached us.

"This event is postponed," said a counselor. "Please return to your cabins and read from the Bibles under your beds for one hour and then report back here when you hear the siren."

I sighed with relief.

As we walked back to our cabins, I felt a drop of rain on my shoulder.

An hour was far too long for an autistic person to ignore a peanut butter-covered head while reading. I re-read the first paragraph of John 1 four times, having repeatedly forgotten to absorb the meaning behind the letters.

My cabinmates and I walked over to the window every few minutes. A light drizzle came and went a few times over the course of the hour, but nothing that would have halted the day's events.

Just as we prepared for the alarm to ring, *sploosh*. Water fell from the sky like a weighted blanket on a mattress. A few campers in my cabin cheered and clapped at the realization that the day's presumably challenging events would inevitably be delayed even further. I smiled bigger than I had in the past twenty-four hours.

Five minutes of tropical storm-level rain later, there it was. *WEEUU! WEEUU! WEEUU!*

"What the heck?" asked a camper. "If they were gonna have us do this nonsense in the rain, they could've had us do it before it… oh."

On the field in the pouring rain, the counselors began handing out tiny water bottles.

"This is your water supply for the obstacle course," said Pastor Robbie. "Jesus fasted without water for weeks. This is nothing. Show God your perseverance today. Make Him proud."

Adrenaline pushed me through the first few obstacles—small hurdles and tire steps. Keeping an eye on the other campers, it seemed only a matter of time before I, too, slipped on a wet surface.

After just five minutes, my heart rate made it readily clear that I was not a golden example of teenage fitness. I nearly salivated thinking about the tiny water bottle in my shorts pocket, but pushed it out of my mind for the time being.

Best to save it, I thought.

After some monkey bars, I reached a flat field where we were instructed to do thirty push-ups. I placed my hands on a carefully chosen chunk of ground, hoping it was sturdy. I winced as my fingers vanished into the mud.

One… two… I counted in my head. I hoped the counselors would ignore my arched back and buckling knees. *So far, so good.*

Every time I lowered myself to the ground, I inhaled a stench of sweat and peanut butter. Pastor Robbie paced in front of us, not even flinching at the rain streaming down his tensed face.

"Note the smell of your unclean bodies. That is the stench of a pitiful human. Repulsive! But here's the amazing thing. God loves you, despite your wretched impurities. Keep pushing, and you will join Him at His side in paradise."

To my left, Lily's plus-size body fell to the ground, submerged in mud. "I… can't do this. Please forgive me, Jesus."

Pastor Robbie stepped toward her. "Lily… what have you done to yourself? 'Their destiny is destruction, their god is their stomach, and their glory is in their shame. Their mind is set on earthly things.' Philippians 3:19. Your body is your temple, and you have defiled it." He placed his muddy boot on Lily's back. "Continue!"

Through tears, Lily somehow summoned the strength to finish her push-ups with the added pressure of Robbie's foot. She stood up and moved on to the next obstacle. I was barely through half of my set when Samuel reached us, plopped down, and put his healthy physique to good use.

He caught up to my twenty in less than a minute, but his father stopped him short of thirty. "That's not good enough, son. Emelia, come over here now!"

The girl Samuel had been flirting with stood up and joined them. "Yes, sir?"

"Lie on Samuel's back," said Robbie.

"Uh… what?"

"Lie on his back. I don't care how you do it. Actually, scratch that. Do it face down and wrap your arms around his stomach."

"Umm… okay." She did as instructed.

"This is really weird, Dad…" said Samuel.

"Thirty push-ups. Now."

Samuel started pushing up and down, his hands sinking into the mud further with each rep. After two push-ups, Emilia slipped off and then climbed back on.

Samuel's arms shook. "Three… f… four…"

"You've disappointed me, son. You can't even focus on Jesus for one weekend. Your drive toward sin is unquenchable."

"Nine… t… t… ten…"

"Emilia, you have committed a sin against God by tempting my son. You are a harlot. You should know God requires you to cover your body more thoroughly. We cannot have you corrupting my son like so many have."

Emilia's tears were visible even through the rain.

"Samuel, as you rise from the mud each time, remember this: The women in your life are burdens, seducing you to stray from the holy path God created you to walk. Do not allow these impure souls to draw your eye any longer."

My self-preservation instinct prevented me from feeling quite as disgusted as I ought to have. I focused on my push-ups.

"I… hate you, Dad…" sputtered Samuel through an unrecognizably hollow voice.

"You may hate me now, but *now* is temporary. Heaven is forever. Through this pain, you will find righteousness."

"Thirty." Emilia slipped off Samuel's back and laid in the mud as Samuel stomped away.

"Good, son. Very good."

I pushed my hands into the mud one last time. "Thirty!" I chugged half of my water bottle as I stumbled away from the few campers still staring at the ground.

After two more routine obstacles, only one remained: a rock climb about twenty feet tall. Soaked bed pillows covered the ground at the foot of the wall in case we slipped on the wet hand and footholds.

My footsteps were slow and heavy, and I was in no rush to reach the wall. Ahead of me, Benny turned around and jogged in the opposite direction, toward a boy on all fours in the mud.

I made my way to them to see what was going on. As I got closer, Samuel's wavy blonde hair was recognizable even through smeared peanut butter. He was sobbing profusely.

Benny kneeled down and placed his hand on his shoulder. Samuel looked up at him and grabbed him. Benny flinched before realizing that it was a hug. He hugged back.

"It's all my fault," said Samuel through tears.

"What is?" asked Benny.

"Rachel is gone because of me. Because of my sin. God must hate me. I just can't control myself, and I don't think I can get better."

"Samuel," said Benny. "I may not love the way you've treated me, but I promise you… God does not hate you. The God I was raised to believe in… He loves you, no matter what."

"But… *sniff*… I've…"

"Samuel. Can you show me one Bible verse that says that God loves you UNLESS?"

"I…"

"No, you can't. You know why? Because if God is love, the buck stops there. If He made you, He made you this way, and He knows your heart."

"I… don't know why you're being so nice to me."

Benny shrugged. "I couldn't live with myself if I just left you there."

"Thank you. I… I can do better. I just can't let my dad find out that… never mind."

I took a step toward Samuel and Benny. "Everything okay?"

"Yeah, we're good," said Benny, pulling Samuel up with his hand. "Let's get the hell out of here."

Samuel and I nodded at each other.

The three of us made our way to the rock wall. I struggled a bit, but with the help of Samuel and Benny, I made it to the top without slipping.

I drank the rest of my water immediately, but I needed more. I held the tiny bottle to the sky until it held about a centimeter of water. It still wasn't enough, but I savored every drop.

10. Butterfly

The chatter that filled the lunchroom was noticeably less than the previous day. Having gone through the mentally and physically draining Underground Church and obstacle course, we collectively occupied a headspace full of dread and a little regret. Most of us ate our slop in silence.

The loudspeaker crackled and hummed. "Arthur Morton, please make your way to Pastor Robbie's cabin for your discipleship session."

I gulped, stood up, and exited the cafeteria.

This could be my chance to find some info on Rachel, I thought. *Gotta keep my eyes peeled.*

The entryway to Pastor Robbie's home away from home featured wood-paneled walls and aging Edison-style light fixtures.

It wasn't an unpleasant vibe after spending the past day and change in such miserable environments.

Through a doorway to the left, the faint white glow of a desktop computer illuminated an office. The yellow and blue colors of AIM were visible on the bulky CRT monitor.

There we go; I'll try to find an excuse to check out his computer later.

In the center of the living room were two chairs facing each other. Robbie sat in one. The only other furniture in the dimly lit room was an old tube TV with a DVD player connected to it, currently paused on some footage of the rainy obstacle course run.

"Have a seat, Arthur," said Robbie, gesturing to the second chair.

My heart rate elevated slightly as I sat down.

"So," said Robbie, "what has God been putting on your heart this weekend?"

My eyes pointed at the ground as my mind jumped all over the place, trying to think of something appropriate to say; I usually drew a blank in response to those kinds of broad questions. Autistic anxiety, maybe.

After what felt like ten seconds, I blurted out the first thing I could think of. "Uh… I've been thinking about how much easier it is to wake up in the morning when you guzzle a glass of cold water."

"Hmm… okay. I meant regarding spiritual battles and the like. Your mother emailed me about your struggles with lustful sins at home. Surely you know what the Bible has to say about this."

I squirmed. "Yeah… I'm praying really hard for the strength to stop. I'm so ashamed."

"That you should be. Remember, all the eyes in Heaven are watching you commit these sins against God. What would they think?"

"Yeah, I know…"

"Your mother tells me you have Asperger syndrome. Is that correct?"

"Yeah."

Robbie thought for a moment. "You know, I'm not sure what those in your life have taught you about it, but mental illness is not simply a condition of the mind. It is a condition of the soul."

My eyes narrowed. "What do you mean?"

"If you look back a few decades, this kinda nonsense didn't really exist. Autism, ADHD, bipolar… you name it. As the world descends into chaos and sin, God's wrath reveals itself. Doctors of the world may tell you it's simply a characteristic of the brain, but they are blind, spreading lies to distract from the truth: we are at war with the agents of Satan himself. You may have heard from some that autism is a side effect of vaccines, and while that may hold some truth, it's not the whole truth. You can cure your autism through a deep, authentic relationship with God the Father. As long as this disease remains a part of you, it's your own fault. Choose God, Arthur."

Pastor Robbie's words made me squirm. Before I could respond, he placed his hand on my shoulder and said, "Let us pray."

I barely absorbed a word of the prayer, as I was lost in thought. *Does Robbie have a point? Is my Asperger's really the result of my own sin?*

I was skeptical, but figured I'd better put in some extra effort into cleansing myself of sin, just in case. I tried to focus on the rest of the prayer, but not much of it registered. I was distracted by how much I didn't enjoy the sensation of his hand sitting on my shoulder, and I normally enjoyed that sort of physical reassurance.

"Amen. God loves you, Arthur. You've shown great promise on this trip. Don't let God down now."

On the way out, I felt grateful that Robbie didn't feel the need to lambast me over my obstacle course performance while forcing me to watch footage of myself. I thought about what he said about mental illness. I was shocked because I really didn't believe any of it.

Lost in thought, I walked right into Benny.

"Whoa there, Artie. Heavy lesson in there?"

"Oh… yeah, I guess. You up next?"

"I am, indeed."

"Good luck," I said. "Lemme know how it goes."

"Will do." Benny glanced toward the open office where Robbie's computer sat, still screensaverless. "Ya know, there's no rush for you to get back to your cabin… might wanna see what you can find in there."

"Oh… yeah, I was gonna. Guess I got distracted."

"You got this," said Benny.

Benny walked into Robbie's prayer room and shut the door. After peeking out the front window to make sure nobody was approaching, I entered the office and sat down at Pastor Robbie's computer desk as my heart rate increased.

What's gotten into me? Stealing a sweater, stalking Mr. Crumbull at States, and now snooping on my pastor's computer? I guess if it's in the name of finding a missing friend…

Since the camp counselors had confiscated our belongings, I didn't have a flash drive to store any files on. I opened Microsoft Internet Explorer and logged onto *aol.com*.

I jumped every time I heard Pastor Robbie's or Benny's voice. Quickly, I downloaded chat history for all of Robbie's recent AIM chats, as well as his emails, and emailed them to myself.

The volume of Robbie's voice increased as his session with Benny continued. The words were muffled through the walls, but he sounded angry compared to his meeting with me.

What could he possibly be upset with Benny about?

Having learned an important lesson from my mother's recent sleuthing, I deleted all my downloads, emptied the recycle bin, and cleared the internet browsing history.

I stepped softly toward the doorway, but before I could complete my exit, I heard a door open. I jumped back behind the desk and lowered my head.

Benny stepped into the hallway. His face lacked life. He walked slowly past the office without even glancing in. The sound of the front door opening and closing followed. A moment later, Pastor Robbie walked past the office and exited the building, too.

After peeking out the office window to make sure he was out of sight, I exited the building and speed-walked to the cabins. My heart had never raced so much.

Did I seriously just do that? I thought as I zipped across the campus.

Under my breath, I muttered, "Dear God, please forgive me for doubting my pastor, and for… breaking the law. I hope you understand it was for a good reason. Wait, of course you do… you're omnipresent. Amen."

Before bedtime, I swung by Benny's cabin to touch base on what had just happened. I sat next to him on his bed. He was expressionless.

"Something happen in there?" I asked.

"It's fine," said Benny without making eye contact.

"Uh… okay. You good?"

Benny nodded.

"I emailed myself a bunch of messages and emails from his computer," I whispered. "I'm so scared I'm gonna get arrested for this."

Benny nodded again.

"I'll read them when we get back to civilization. Maybe something's in there that can help find Rachel."

"Sounds good," said Benny. "I'm gonna get some sleep."

"Oh… you don't wanna hang out for a while or something?"

"I'm good. Just tired."

"Hmm," I said. "Alright. Hope everything's okay with you."

Benny flashed a phony smile and tucked himself into bed.

*   *   *

By day three, the peanut butter in my hair had hardened into a web of rocks, despite the previous day's downpour.

The morning brought with it the running of laps and jumping jacks for whoever the counselors caught staring at the cute posters. A welcome step up from the previous day's endurance test.

After lunch, we had more than a few hours of private Bible study. A pretty slow day so far, but I knew better than to let my guard down.

Once we had eaten dinner, the counselors asked us to put blindfolds on. My spine stiffened slightly.

They blindly corralled us into lines and told us to walk forward. When the ground under my feet changed from grass to dirt, I knew we were leaving the premises.

"Watch your step," said a counselor as she guided me into what I discerned was the back of an empty van.

After a ten-minute ride in darkness, the van came to a stop, and we emptied out. I could hear waves crashing on the shore. I shivered in the cold night air.

"You may now remove your blindfolds," said a counselor.

As the edge of the fabric rose across my eyes like a transitional screen wipe from *Star Wars*, more darkness greeted us. The private beach had no artificial sources of light, and the crescent moon did little to illuminate the surroundings.

After my eyes adjusted, I could faintly see the area. In front of us, the counselors laid out backpacks. Despite the stressful situation, the dark waves crashing on the shore brought a peaceful tone to the night.

I could make out a small light a ways down the beach—presumably from a bonfire. We whispered amongst ourselves, wondering what was in store for us.

"This is your final test," said Pastor Robbie. "To truly seek The Lord, you must push past your petty human responses. Rise and endure, just as Jesus endured the cross for you. Trust in Him, and He will deliver you to salvation. Trust in Him, and He will reveal himself to you."

Against the silent wind and the crashing of waves, his voice carried a commanding resonance. The finish line was literally in sight, and I didn't doubt my ability to finish the fight.

"In front of you are backpacks. Put them on and make your way to the burning bush. God is waiting for you."

I grabbed a backpack strap and lifted. My shoulder rolled forward, pulled down by what felt like one of the heaviest bags I'd ever lifted. A sound of rattling filled the beach; the counselors had filled the bags with rocks. I tensed my core and hoisted the bag onto my back.

I lifted my foot and took a step, followed by another. After a few moments, I had a rhythm going, as did most of the other campers.

This isn't so bad, I thought.

Suddenly, I felt a sting on my shoulder. The odd sensation drifted down my arm. It felt wet. In front of me, a red blur flew through the air and hit Benny.

"Ouch!" he yelled.

The counselors were throwing water balloons at us.

A second balloon hit me in the chest. The freezing water exploded all over my neck, arms, and belly. A little got in my mouth. It tasted of salt and seaweed.

I spat it out. "Are you kidding me right now?!"

A third balloon hit my hip. My shorts were drenched, making it hard to walk through the sand. I hated sand as it was. It would always get everywhere, taking up so much of my attention, and was such a pain to walk through, causing me anxiety. Normally, I'd focus on how annoying it was, but the freezing wet clothes made that phobia seem almost irrelevant.

The bonfire seemed to have doubled in size.

Okay, halfway there. I can do this.

VROOM! VROOM!

Two counselors approached with leaf blowers and aimed them right at us. Sand blasted into our clothes and faces. I blocked my eyes with my arm, preventing some of it from hitting me.

Seriously? This is insane…

My walk had slowed significantly. I was taking one step every two or three seconds. The fire was so close, I could almost feel it. That thought helped to quicken my pace.

As I approached, I heard slow acoustic music. It was Samuel, wearing dry clothes, and sitting on a log around the inviting fire. I didn't even have the energy to scoff at the nepotism. I dropped the bag of rocks, sat on a log next to a few classmates, and joined them in rubbing our hands near the flame.

As the rest of the campers arrived, shivering, we heard a single slow clap from beyond the fire. The silhouette of a tall man approached.

"Well done, my children," he said.

I knew that voice. We were in rarified air. It was Pastor Tom, the head pastor at our branch of Righteous Christ Church. As he stepped closer, the cufflinks on his jacket sparkled in the firelight. For a beach campfire evening, he was dressed surprisingly dapper. Even his designer shoes displayed not a speck of sand, against all odds.

"I am so proud of every one of you. It's easy to talk the talk, but you have shown this weekend that you can walk the walk."

His voice brought with it a sense of fatherly comfort and validation. At last, the pain of Cocoon was fading away. We had survived.

Camp counselors passed out cups of water, which we ravenously guzzled. Then they brought out a large, beautiful white cake. As they sliced it, Pastor Tom continued to share his wisdom and Samuel's guitar shifted from ambient to cathartic.

"You know, I wasn't always the man of God you see before you today. When I was a young man, I fell down a path rife with sin. I worked at the clubs in Miami. I fornicated with women of the night frequently. It wasn't until I found the forgiveness of the Holy Spirit that I could leave that life behind and find peace."

I took a bite of cake. My eyes closed in ecstasy, and I may have moaned.

"You have all shown this week that you have what it takes to be genuine men and women of God. You too have overcome temptations of the flesh. You have persevered and suffered for Him, and He will repay you tenfold."

As Pastor Tom's passion grew, I noticed rays of light emanating around the fire behind him. My eyes welled up. I felt the presence of God.

"I want you all to repeat after me," said Pastor Tom. "Lord, I know that I am broken."

"I know that I am broken," I said through tears.

"I know that I am only made whole through you."

I repeated.

"I devote my life to you, and to spreading the good word, so that if we believe, we will be saved from eternal damnation."

"Amen," said Pastor Tom after I, and the rest of the campers, echoed his emotional words.

As everyone mingled and recovered, I waited in line to meet Pastor Tom for the first time. After roughly ten minutes, I reached out my hand and shook his.

"S-so nice to finally meet you, Pastor. I've gone to hear you in the main service plenty of times now that I'm eighteen. I just wanna say that—"

"Arthur, right? Yeah, I've seen you in a few plays. Good stuff."

"Wow, really?" I asked. "That's so cool. Thanks!"

"You were close with Rachel Bristol, right? Shame what happened to her."

"Uh… yeah, I was."

"Yeah, Pastor Robbie told me about the incident with the sweater. Probably best to let the adults handle the detective work, hmm? Could be dangerous. Wouldn't want any other students to disappear."

"Oh," I said. "Yeah, definitely, definitely… thanks for that advice… and thanks again for the inspiring words before."

"No, my boy." He smirked. "Thank God. I'm merely His messenger."

When we returned to the campground, flashing red and blue lights awaited us.

"Please return to your cabins, disciples," said Pastor Robbie as he approached the police officers. "What seems to be the trouble?"

As we walked past them to our cabins, I made out just a few words: "vans," "blindfolds," and "kids." As I rounded the corner, Pastor Robbie shook the hands of the police. That was the last we heard about any of it. I figured a local must have seen us getting into the van blindfolded and thought we were being kidnapped.

A few minutes after collapsing on my bed, I heard a shout from the bathroom. "Water! We've got water!"

I'll never forget that shower. It was the most satisfying of my life. I washed my hair repeatedly, removing as much of the dried peanut butter as possible. I cried multiple times, as I just stood there, letting the hot water pour over me. If I hadn't been the last in line, I'm sure someone would've gotten annoyed with me.

After drying myself, I noticed a change of fresh sheets next to my bed. It was a pleasure to replace the peanut butter-covered ones. We all slept well that night.

*　　*　　*

The drive home the next morning was mostly silent. Everyone seemed lost in thought, not really knowing how to react to the weekend we had just experienced.

I fished through my backpack, which the counselors had returned to me prior to the drive, trying to find something to entertain myself with. I found the pamphlets for Shield and Sword U, the Christian college my guidance counselor had recommended to me.

Part of me felt compelled to continue my journey toward godliness, but after that weekend, it wasn't my most active desire. Regardless, I perused the pamphlets.

Very pretty campus, I thought. *I'll apply to all my prospects when I get home.*

When we arrived at the church, I drove Benny home. During the ride, I asked him, "So… what did you think?"

"Oh… uh… I dunno, man. That was a lot."

"Yeah… it was. But we made it, right? And I really felt God at that campfire."

Benny scratched his head. "Uh… you sure it wasn't just the cake they were giving us after literally beating us? Or the fire and the music?"

"Oh yeah, this was different. I saw rays of light surrounding Pastor Tom. I think that was God."

"Sorry to burst your bubble, Art, but that's what happens when car headlights hit fire. Pastor Tom's Jaguar was parked off to the side."

"Oh… I see."

Benny got out of the car. "Have a good night, Arthur."

He walked to his front door.

"Yeah… you too."

I put my car in drive, but I remembered something. "Oh, do you wanna get together and look at what I downloaded from Robbie's—"

Benny had already entered his house.

11. Evil Pool Party

I was never a patient person. Even in a world before smartphones and red notification bubbles, the desire to accomplish tasks quickly and efficiently often blanketed my day-to-day.

Weeks had passed, yet I still hadn't read the conversations I stole from Pastor Robbie's Cocoon office. To do so would mean confronting my guilt over committing a crime. The files also just weren't a landmark in the wasteland that was my post-Cocoon subconscious. I wasn't aware of it at the time, but that trip melted a portion of my mind that would never fully reform.

I mentioned my detective work to Ella, who understood my hesitancy and told me to take my time. She was more worried about the emotional strife Benny and I went through at Cocoon. Ella also mentioned that the vigil Jade threw for Rachel didn't lead to any new information, which disappointed me.

"It was all for show," said Ella, confirming my skepticism about Jade's authenticity.

When discussing Rachel, I was taken aback by Ella's lack of urgency. Maybe she'd accepted that Rachel might not turn up at all. Or maybe she was hiding something.

Could Ella actually be involved with Rachel's disappearance? She sure has moved on fast…

The gaping hole Rachel left in the musical was slowly but surely shrinking into a small crack. Ms. Flannigan cast Jade Parnacle as the new Eve, and much gossip could be overheard during rehearsals about how the newcomer couldn't quite live up to Rachel's soul, but still gave a solid performance. At least Jade and Samuel didn't have a dramatic history, which allowed for more organic chemistry. In any case, we only rehearsed a few times before everyone split for winter break. We'd get a better taste of where things were heading in January.

Perhaps as a defense mechanism, I spent a lot of my free time during the first week of winter break memorizing lines for *Eden*, which provided a much-needed distraction from the stresses of the year. I even got Benny to practice lines with me once or twice, but I caught him staring off into the distance frequently. He didn't seem interested in sharing what Pastor Robbie said to him at Cocoon, but it shook him. It even affected his performance of God in our practice sessions, though he showed some signs of renewed energy after a while.

The days passed with little drama, aside from arguments with my mom about post-porn computer privileges, which she had since come around on.

I had received acceptance letters to both Shield and Sword U and Georgia College of Art, just a few weeks after applying. I hadn't thought too heavily about whether I'd attend either of them, since I was still waiting for the letter from the most prestigious program I had applied for: Barnum.

To avoid incrimination, I transferred Robbie's emails and messages to a flash drive and deleted the emails from my AOL account. Sometimes I'd skim the filenames, but I never opened or read anything.

"You've got mail!" chirped the AOL man on my parental control-laden computer. It was an invitation to a pool party. From… Ella?

That seems out of character, I thought.

"To me and… FIFTY THREE other addresses? Even weirder."

I poked through the email addresses included. There it was: *PikachuButtcheeks2@aol.com.*

I'm definitely not missing what might be my only chance to see Jennifer over the break.

*   *   *

"Are you sure this is the right address?" asked Benny from my passenger seat as we pulled up to Ella's family's enormous mini-mansion.

"Yeah, I dropped her off once," I said. "She tries to keep it on the DL."

Benny scoffed. "I'm a little offended she never invited me over before. The GALL!"

"I wonder what made her want to throw any party, let alone one with the entire class. I mean, honestly… this seems like the last thing she'd ever do. She's been acting kinda weird lately, if you ask me."

"Well, I'm not complaining!" said Benny as he exited the car and skipped to the enormous front door.

In the foyer (yes, she had a foyer), Ella greeted some parents of classmates. I'm sure they thought she was entirely pleasant, but Benny and I knew her well-enough to spot a fake smile easily. She wore a large t-shirt over a bathing suit, seen poking out by her shoulder. She seemed fully dry; not much time for a host to swim, I supposed.

"Hey, guys," said Ella, dryly. "Welcome… to my home…" She gestured with hokey enthusiasm. "My lame parents threw this lame party as a way for me to fit in better at school or something."

"Ohhh," said Benny, sarcastically. "Okay, okay. I bet you are loving this, huh?"

"Shut it," said Ella.

From behind me, a boy's voice interrupted. "It's okay, everyone! It's okay! You can start the party now. I've arrived." Samuel laughed at his own lack of shame as Pastor Robbie shut the door behind them.

"I didn't create the guest list…" muttered Ella.

"Hey, Samuel," said Benny.

"Uh, hey."

Samuel jogged to the pool while removing his shirt. Before entering the backyard, he turned around and blew a kiss to Ella.

She retched.

Pastor Robbie approached Ella, who folded her arms.

"Ella, your parents have a lovely home. And this party seems like an epic win. Gotta be careful with pool parties, though. Lots of room for temptation. Hope you're not wearing a skimpy two-piece under there."

Ella raised her already-folded arms to cover her chest.

"You know, it's been quite some time since Rachel vanished," continued Robbie. "I think Samuel has moved on. Wouldn't it be so fun if, after I helped you get into RCA, my son ended up with you? God works in mysterious ways. Just something to think about."

So, Principal Randall voted no on Ella's enrollment, but Pastor Robbie voted yes. Weird.

Robbie patted Ella's shoulder and headed to the door.

He glanced at us and nodded on the way out. "Boys."

We forced smiles. We weren't thrilled to see him so soon after he basically tortured us at Cocoon.

Ella stormed away, saying nothing else.

The backyard would put your average home to shame. The large pool was shaped like a pear, with an elevated hot tub on the side big enough to fit upward of ten people.

"Look out below!" yelled a boy as he cannonballed from a stone structure atop a cascading waterfall. His theatrics splashed at least three girls in the pool, who screamed and leaped away through the shallow water.

I walked around the lovely yard to get the lay of the land. Extravagant South Florida homes didn't end at a white fence; they instead transitioned from grass to wooden docks hanging over the roughly one-hundred-foot-wide canal that led directly to the ocean.

On the canal sat many family-sized boats, including one that must have belonged to Ella's parents.

Perusing the far side of the pool, I encountered Ella with her video camera.

"B-roll for my video class," she said. "Get out of the shot!"

"Ah, sorry."

"Hey, Arthur!" came a familiar girl's voice from my left.

My heart fluttered. Jennifer was waving me over from the hot tub.

As I walked over, she got out and gave me a big, wet hug. My usual autistic aversion to wet clothes wasn't present, since purity culture had inadvertently conditioned me to focus on the young woman's half-naked body currently pressed against me. Or maybe that's just being a teenage boy.

"Hey," I said.

"It's so nice to see you! How is your break so far?"

"Pretty good."

She probably expected more details, but wasn't gonna get them from someone as shy, or as detached from typical social behavior as I was.

"So, you gonna join me in the tub?" she asked.

"Oh, uh… sure!"

I hopped in, shirt and all. Jennifer giggled.

She held up her red Solo cup. "You wanna try my drink?"

"What is it?"

She leaned in and whispered, "It's a vodka soda. Don't tell."

I then noticed her slightly wobbly body language. "Oh, umm… I'm okay. Thanks."

"Oh, come on, you party pooper! Have some fun with me!"

She placed her hand on my knee, causing me to flinch.

I looked around to make sure no adults were watching. "Okay, fine."

I took the cup and sniffed it. It smelled like a doctor's office. I winced.

"Oh my god, just try it!"

I took a sip, swallowed, and retched with disgust.

Jennifer laughed loudly. "Very cute," she said.

A commotion stirred in the house. A few boys ran past the pool, whispering, "Chaperones! The school sent us babysitters!"

Jennifer grabbed her drink back from my hand, chugged the remaining few sips, rinsed out the cup in the hot tub, and placed it next to the ledge.

I looked over my shoulder and saw Mr. Crumbull entering the backyard.

"Your breath smells like vodka, Artie," said Jennifer. "You scared?"

I really was. I couldn't bear the thought of my godly image being ruined. I imagined the worst-case scenarios—of not being let back into RCA for the rest of the year, and having to take public summer school, where, according to my mother, they'd eat me alive.

Without a word, I leaped out of the hot tub and speed-walked to my towel.

"Hey, I was just kidding!" said Jennifer. "Dork!"

I dried myself off and entered the house. The air conditioning was freezing against my wet shirt. I wondered if I could get drunk from one sip of vodka, since my tolerance was likely quite low. I decided to eat some snacks to soak it up, just in case.

I placed my towel on the couch and sat down with a bowl of potato chips. I avoided plenty of opportunities to join conversations in the room, as per my usual. I simply people-watched and thought introspectively about my social awkwardness.

On the coffee table in front of the couch were a few scattered snack plates and some cell phones. As I was chomping down on a particularly oily chip, one phone rang—a cream-colored Motorola Pebl phone. On the top in tiny letters it read: "Rachel Calling."

Could it be? There's no way. I think Ella has a Pebl, but I don't remember what color it was. Plus, it's such a popular phone these days.

"Umm… is that anyone's phone?" I asked.

No response from the room. I figured it must belong to someone currently swimming.

Out of the corner of my eye, I spotted a gaggle of unfamiliar teens and Ella heading down a hallway while whispering.

I looked back at the phone, which had stopped ringing.

It's probably not her, I thought.

I followed Ella and the strangers down the hall.

Past a few family portraits, two bedrooms, and one extravagant bathroom, I heard giggling behind a half-closed door. I peeked in and saw a group of teens in what I could tell by the grungy decor was Ella's room. A hazy smoke filled the room, and I noticed a scent of skunk.

"I can see you, Arthur," said Ella.

I pushed the door open. "Heyyy…"

"These are friends from my old school."

"Sup," said a boy in baggy clothes.

Ella sighed. "You can come in. Just shut the door."

"I'm okay. Have fun." I closed the door and left.

As I walked down the hall, I heard the door open again.

"Hey, wait up," said Ella. "You're not gonna go run and tell our babysitters now, are you?"

"I just don't understand why you need to do that stuff."

Ella rolled her eyes. "It's just weed, Art. Never killed anyone."

"But it's a gateway drug," I said.

"Arthur, there's more to the world than what Christian propaganda videos tell you. Sometimes it's good to just take the edge off. Plus, I saw you with Jennifer out there. You're not so innocent. Alcohol actually has killed people, by the way."

I avoided eye contact. "I guess." A moment passed. "I just wish you could see that if you need drugs to find happiness, it's a sign of a bigger missing piece only Jesus can—"

"Jesus is not a magic pill that fixes all mental health issues. You really think that every TRUE Christian is completely free of all depression? You think Rachel's parents aren't grieving?"

I shook my head. "I didn't say that… it's just, I don't want you to end up in Hell."

"Okay, well, that's an entirely different point, and if fear of Hell is your biggest reason for doing or not doing something, this isn't even a topic of ethics anymore. Anyway, that's enough evangelizing for you. Go flirt with Jennifer some more or whatever."

"Sorry… maybe I'm drunk."

"You're not drunk, you innocent child. Now skedaddle."

Ella turned and walked back to her room.

"Hey, about Rachel," I said. "I saw caller ID on a Pebl phone in the living room say Rachel. Was that your phone? You don't think it could be her, do you?"

"No, it's not. And Rachel is a very common name, Art. Maybe you are drunk."

"Yeah, you're probably right."

Unsure if Ella was joking about my potential drunkenness, I stopped by the fancy bathroom before returning to the party. I stared at myself in the mirror, trying to figure out if I was inebriated.

When I got back to the living room, the phone was gone.

It was probably nothing.

I returned to the pool and tried to take my mind off things. I played a round of pool volleyball with Benny and Samuel on my team. They got along well. Even I didn't feel disdain for Samuel at the moment. Maybe Cocoon had softened him.

Jennifer was on the other team, but didn't go out of her way to chat with me much. After the game, she answered a phone call and headed out. We exchanged a brief wave from a distance.

Oh well.

As the sun set, I changed into dry clothes and beckoned Benny to join me, as it was time to leave.

By the entryway, Ella was having a mildly heated conversation with a middle-aged woman with two young children beside them.

"Next time, can you please give me a heads up first?" said a frustrated Ella.

"Of course, I'm so sorry. I called Mr. and Mrs. Kent but they didn't answer. I just had an emergency and had to bring the kids back right away. My mother is at the hospital, and I—"

"It's fine. Don't worry about it. It's my parents' fault, as usual."

"Okay, thank you so much, Ella."

Ella took the hands of her siblings and led them to the hall. "They force me to throw this party, don't even come themselves, and then dump me with these two. Classic."

"Sorry, Ella," I said. "We're heading out. See you in the new year."

"Bye, Ella!" said Benny.

"See you guys."

*   *   *

Holiday breaks weren't particularly exciting for my lower-middle class family. The little money we had went toward RCA tuition, meaning travel was incredibly rare. My extended family wasn't exactly on talking terms most of the time, so usually we did Christmas and New Year's at home with little fanfare.

After a very filling Christmas dinner, I spent the evening playing video games on my computer in my room, but even that had gotten monotonous over the past few weeks.

Ya know what… it's time.

I inserted my 128-megabyte flash drive into a free USB port and stared at the temporary "Drive E" icon for more than a few seconds. I took a deep breath and double clicked.

There were a LOT of files to sort through. The AIM conversations were broken up by screen name, so finding Pastor Robbie's chat with Rachel was easy enough.

The chat history wasn't very long, despite spanning many months, so I read through it all. Most of it concerned simple logistics of plans with Samuel, carpools, etc. At one point she had lost an earring at youth service, and asked if he had seen it.

"Blah, blah, blah…" I scrolled and skimmed, scrolled and skimmed, until one chat session from about a month before Rachel's vanishing caught my attention.

MasterPastor1:

Rachel, I hear you and Samuel have been having some troubles. Maybe you and I should schedule a private ministry session to work on this?

cheer4jesus23:

omg that would be so helpful. thx!

They scheduled a session. The following day, the chat continued.

MasterPastor1:

Rachel, I am sorry if my behavior upset you yesterday. Remember, God works in mysterious ways. You're a very special young woman, and I look forward to getting to know you better.

He followed up the next day.

MasterPastor1:

Hey Rachel, just following up. Let me know when you'd like to have another session. Looking forward to it.

Rachel never responded. A week before her vanishing, Robbie sent one last message.

MasterPastor1:

Rachel, we need to talk. I think you know what about. And no, Samuel doesn't know. Please come to my office during school hours tomorrow. We can handle this. There's no need to be afraid.

A few hours later, Rachel responded.

cheer4jesus23:

k

I didn't know what to make of all that. It sounded bad, but it was unclear what they were talking about, and none of my business.

My naïve mind gave Robbie the benefit of the doubt, and I moved on to the emails. I downloaded software that would allow me to search their contents for Rachel's email address. There were no results, so I searched for her name instead. One email thread contained her name in its body, exchanged between Pastor Robbie and Pastor Tom.

From Pastor Tom:
So, do you have any updates on our Rachel situation?
From Pastor Robbie:
It's taken care of. She won't be a problem.

And that was it. There was no way I could weasel my way around the sinister implications of those emails. But it also didn't prove much, specifically. They would expel me in a heartbeat if I brought it up without hard proof of anything. Plus, I'd be accusing two of the most powerful men in the entire South Florida branch of Righteous Christ Church itself.

My heart pounded. I always ran in the opposite direction when anxiety at that level took over. There's just no sanity amid a panic attack.

I should've seriously pondered my next steps, but instead I entered a panic-induced delusion, putting all of it out of my mind. I should've at least mentioned the messages and emails to Ella, but I closed the browser window and removed the flash drive without even hitting "safely eject" first (the horror).

I took a shower and laid in bed with the lights on for a while. Despite what I had read, I still found ways to give the Righteous Christ pastors the benefit of the doubt.

After all, I thought, *God works in mysterious ways…*

I turned off the lights and went to sleep, though I wouldn't wake well rested.

12. Nuggets and Honey

Even while successfully compartmentalizing the info I read on Robbie, there was little time for relaxation once school started back up in the new year. Classes jumped back into full swing, and I still hadn't heard from Barnum Institute.

At least *Eden* rehearsals after school allowed me to take my mind off the rest of the senior year stresses. Jade Parnacle was taking to the role of Eve nicely, though we could still feel Rachel's lingering presence during rehearsal. Ms. Flannigan showed occasional enthusiasm, but it was clear she still mourned for Rachel's Eve. Regardless, the show was starting to feel like it could turn out pretty cool. It was fun, but it was also hard work.

None of those stresses sat at the forefront of my mind during the first week back, though. Something much more stressful was looming: prom.

It's not much of a stretch to say school dances lie outside of the comfort zones of most neurodivergent individuals. The loud music, embarrassing rhythmic wiggling, and worst of all, the plus one. Naturally, I thought about asking Jennifer, but we hadn't spoken since the pool party, where I missed my chance to make a move.

"Ya know, Art, it's really not that complicated," said Andrew at our lockers. "You just walk up and ask her. It's only ever flattering to be asked out."

"I don't buy that. What if she panics, says yes, and then cancels later, like Alice Newton did to Jake last year? Ugh. So awkward for both of them. I don't wanna put Jenn in that situation."

"Dude, I promise you she wouldn't think about it even one tenth as much as you are. Worse case, she says no, but is impressed by your cah-hourage," said Andrew, imitating the lion from *The Wizard of Oz*.

"Eh… maybe."

"Hey, Jennifer!" screamed Andrew at the top of his lungs. "Arthur wants to ask you something!"

He sprinted away, laughing, as I turned blue.

Jennifer approached me. "Hey, what's up?"

I gulped. "Uhh… I was just wondering… if you wanted… to go to prom with me." I made zero eye contact.

"Oh, I'm so sorry, Arthur. I'm already going with Randy Mandible."

"Oh, that's no big deal," I said breathily. "I just thought I'd ask. No big deal. All good."

"Okay, good. Sorry again. Thanks for asking, though. That's very sweet."

"Yeah…"

The distance to class after one of my first ever rejections felt like a mile.

At lunch, I had a feeling everyone was staring at me, but I'm pretty sure I was just being paranoid. Benny sat down next to me. His exuberant personality still hadn't fully returned to its pre-Cocoon heyday, but he was friendly enough.

"Hey, Artie. What's up?"

"Not much. Just eatin'."

"Hah… I can see that much. Get up to anything interesting since the pool party?"

I thought about sharing the information I got from Robbie's emails, but abstained. "Eh, not much. Started replaying *Final Fantasy X*. Oh… and I asked Jenn to prom today…"

His eyes widened. "And?"

"She's already going with Randy Mandible," I said while rolling my eyes.

"Ah bummer. He is pretty hot, though…"

"Oh… umm… okay."

Benny cleared his throat and shuffled in his seat. "Have you seen Ella around? I didn't get to catch up with her much at her party."

"Nah, just the few minutes she had rehearsal with us a few days ago. I caught her smoking weed with her old public school friends during the party, by the way."

"Hah, nice."

"I don't think so," I said. "I thought I was gonna rub off on her, make her more Christian. I don't even know if she'd get into Heaven right now."

"Hey man, just let her live her life. It's really none of our business."

"I guess." I sighed. "I kinda miss when we'd all hang out, though."

"Yeah, me too."

*   *   *

On Wednesday night, I opted to attend the adult church service instead of Pastor Robbie's youth group, as Cocoon was still an unpleasant recent memory. Although it seemed Pastor Tom could also be involved in Rachel's vanishing somehow, the evidence was less direct.

"I want to thank each one of you for being here tonight," said Tom. "We are truly living in the end times, and it takes true courage to remain on the straight and narrow path. Lewd images on the TV, and even on our cell phones, assault us and our children every day. Temptation to stray from God's plan is everywhere. As a former heathen, I know temptation. God saved me from my wickedness, and he, too, can save you."

The music team performed, carrying a cathartic cadence.

"But it's simply not enough to accept his mercy and carry on with our lives. As Christians, we are called to spread the good word to one and all. It is through us they will find salvation."

I thought about Ella and how I had failed to convey a compelling example of life with God to her thus far.

"It's not an easy task, my friends. The devil is a powerful foe— the most powerful there is. It's easy to see our failures and retreat out of shame. But Paul said in Romans, 'For I am not ashamed of the gospel, because it is the power of God that brings salvation to everyone who believes.' "

Maybe it wasn't too late. There were still a few months left to show Ella the light.

"Believe, my friends, and God will guide your hand."

*   *   *

Blue lights and bubbles danced around the hotel ballroom that RCA hosted our prom in. A large sign on the wall read "Praise the Roof." I rolled my eyes.

The boys all wore tucked-in shirts with ties, including me. I wore a royal blue shirt and a sky-blue tie with a diamond pattern, and black slacks.

The girls wore all kinds of dresses—some extravagant, some simple. RCA teachers and faculty didn't seem to enforce the rule about how much knee girls could show that night, as that would result in half the girls being kicked out.

I heard footsteps approaching.

"My boy cleans up nice!" said Benny, placing a hand on my shoulder.

"Thanks," I said. "You look nice, too."

Benny's pink patterned shirt and bow tie made me look like a businessman by contrast.

I shifted my weight back and forth. "I never know what to do with myself at things like this."

"Well, I'm not gonna lie to you, Art. Alcohol helps." Benny chuckled and placed his index finger on his mouth.

"Oh… hah. Hey, I don't know how long I'm gonna stay. When we get bored later, do you wanna come over and play *Halo*?"

"So sorry, Artie! I can't. I promised I'd help my mom with something tonight. Next time!"

"Yeah. For sure."

Benny headed to the dance floor, and I explored the snack table. The virgin punch was delicious.

Every few minutes, various chaperones would peruse the dance floor. When they saw a couple dancing too closely together, they would place a hand on one of each of their shoulders and push them to stand one foot apart.

"Leave room for Jesus!" yelled Mr. Crumbull over the music while pushing a clearly drunk Samuel away from his date.

After Mr. Crumbull left, Samuel pulled his date back in, smooshing her chest against his. She then slapped him across the face and stormed off.

Plenty of room for Jesus now, I thought.

To my surprise, Pastor Tom was in attendance. He didn't have a high school-aged child, so it didn't really make sense that he was there. Over the course of the night, he spoke to a few students and faculty, but didn't speak with me. I noticed that whenever he'd speak with a girl, he'd place his hand on the small of her back.

After micro-dancing to "Every Time We Touch" by Cascada with Andrew in the corner of the dance floor, I felt the punch moving through me. The timing was convenient since the loud music and bustle of the crowd had me craving an introvert battery recharge break.

I sat on the toilet even though I didn't have to, and ended up doing some people watching through the surprisingly large crack in the stall door. First up was Principal Randall, who made a terrible dad joke about washing hands and the washing away of sins, to the boy at the sink next to him.

As they exited the bathroom, Benny entered, exchanging a nod with them. His shirt was sweaty from dancing. As he washed his face at the sink, Samuel stumbled in.

"This freaking place," Samuel mumbled to himself before noticing his bathroom company. "Benny!"

"Heyyy, Sam."

"Ya know what… hiccup… Benny?"

"What's that, big boy?"

"Sometems," slurred Samuel, "I wish I… wasn't 'ere."

"Hah, what's that supposed to mean?"

"Oh, not like… here with youuuu… in this bethrum. Here like, the big here. Well, not that big. Just like… I just wunna run away! No dad. No school. Tooo much preshuh. Not everyone can be like you, Benny boy."

He took a step toward Benny.

"I… get that," said Benny. "Is there anything I can do to help?"

"I… maybe. Yes."

Samuel grabbed Benny's face with both hands, pulled it to him, and kissed him right on the lips.

I gasped, but they didn't hear me. I expected Benny to pull back, but instead, he lingered there.

Suddenly, the bathroom door swung open, and Randy Mandible, a handsome football player and Jennifer's date, walked in. Samuel pulled away from Benny immediately. Randy froze in his step, turned around, and exited.

"Oh, shit, shit, shit," said Samuel, running out of the bathroom.

Benny laughed in disbelief and exited.

I felt conflicted. On one hand, seeing Samuel and Benny get along was a welcome sight after years of horrendous bullying. On the other hand, they just engaged in a sin that God absolutely hated.

Benny didn't even look upset, I thought. *What's gotten into him?*

I washed my hands and exited the bathroom. Samuel and Randy were nowhere in sight. Benny was right back on the dance floor as if nothing had happened.

"Hey, kid," said Ella from behind me.

She wore a black dress with some custom blue floral stitching.

"Oh, hey! I didn't know you were coming."

"Yeah, I figured I'd stop by. Did I miss anything exciting?"

"Umm… kind of."

Ella looked over my shoulder. "Hey, uh… you've got a visitor."

She smiled and walked away.

I turned around to see Jennifer approaching me, wearing a lovely sky-blue strapless dress. "Hey, Arthur. Would you like to dance?"

My heart skipped a beat. "Oh, uh… what happened to Randy?"

"He and Samuel just walked out, arguing. They're probably fighting in the parking lot or something. He was kind of a jerk, anyway."

"In that case, sure," I said. "I'd like that."

Holy crap, holy crap, I thought.

She took my hand and led me to the dance floor as "Because of You" by Kelly Clarkson started to play.

I placed my hands on her hips, and she draped her arms around my neck. My heart was beating embarrassingly fast.

"You can look me in the eyes, you know," she said.

"Oh, right. Sorry. I'm weird about that."

I looked her in the eyes and smiled. She smiled back.

We swayed back and forth for a while.

"This is nice," I said.

"Yeah, it is."

"So," I said. "Do you know where you're going to college yet?"

"Maybe. I'm thinking of staying with some relatives in Mexico City and studying there."

"Oh, wow. That's a big change."

"Yeah, it is. Where are you gonna go?"

"I applied to a few; I got into one Christian college's art program, and one proper art school's animation program. Still waiting to hear from a second art school, which is my top pick. We'll see what happens."

"That's so cool! I hope I get to see your name in the movie credits someday."

"Hah. That would be cool."

My eye contact drifted again.

"It's hard to believe these are our last months, huh?" said Jennifer.

"It's been a good few years, mostly."

"There were some good moments. Right now isn't so bad."

She stepped closer and rested her head on my shoulder.

I blushed and looked around the room. "Aren't you worried the teachers are gonna—"

"Oh, just be in the moment for once, ya dummy."

We continued to sway until the song ended. The chaperones didn't push us apart.

"Thanks for the dance, Arthur."

"Yeah. You too. See ya around."

Jennifer waved with her fingertips and vanished into the crowded dance floor. I headed to the snack table for some water, my cheeks still rosy.

Across the room, I spotted Benny and Ella talking into each other's ears, presumably so they could hear their words over Usher's "Yeah!" blasting.

I was about to head over to them when Ella pointed at the exit and headed out. About twenty seconds later, Benny looked back and forth suspiciously, then exited the same way.

I followed Ella and Benny outside and saw Ella get into the driver's seat of her new car, a purple PT Cruiser. Benny got into the passenger side.

What the heck are they up to? And why didn't they invite me?

As a wave of paranoia crept into my stomach, Ella started the car, and drove herself and Benny out of the parking lot.

I got into my car and followed them.

*　　*　　*

My wipers did a passable job keeping the drizzling rain off the windshield, but just barely. Ella's car headed down familiar roads for a while, but soon we were further out of our immediate town than I'd usually venture. I kept my distance, which was luckily fairly easy with the lack of late-night traffic.

After about fifteen minutes of driving, they went through a McDonald's drive-through. I parked in the lot so as not to get too close, though I was tempted to get a McFlurry.

After I followed their car out of the fast-food joint's parking lot, the drizzle expanded into a downpour.

A few minutes of driving later, Ella and Benny pulled into the parking lot of a small two-story motel. I parked on the street so as not to be noticed and watched through thick wisps of rain as Benny and Ella entered a second-story room.

What on earth? Would they seriously ditch me to go to some after-prom party that I'm not cool enough to be invited to? And at a sketchy motel?

Weemp, wump, weemp, wump went my wipers.

After a few minutes, I quietly made my way up the stairs to the door.

I pressed my ear up against it and heard laughter. The voices were too muffled to hear what they were talking about.

I took out my cell phone and called Benny. I could hear it ringing through the door.

"Hey, bud," said Benny.

"Hey, where did you go?"

"Uh, my mom called. She needed my help sooner than expected. I'm in a taxi right now."

I used my free hand to knock on the door, which I could hear echo through the phone call. "How can you be in a taxi if someone is knocking on your door?"

The door opened, revealing a scowling Benny, who snapped his flip phone shut.

Ella joined him in the entryway. "Arthur… what are you doing here? This is creepy."

"I could say the same thing."

"I think you should leave," she continued. "This doesn't concern—"

"It's fine, Ella," said another voice. "I don't mind."

Out from the bathroom stepped a blonde girl in a pink prom dress. It took me a second to register who was standing there since it had been a while, but there was no denying it—Rachel Bristol stood right in front of me.

My mouth fell open. "What the heck?"

She wore her hair in a curled ponytail, similar to her cheerleading look, but far more extravagant. Her makeup was also pushed to a heightened level for whatever special occasion I'd just stumbled into. I'm not sure I would've recognized her in passing on the street, but regardless, she looked healthy, and very much alive.

"Hey, Arthur," said Rachel. "It's nice to see you."

"Uhh…yeah. You too."

Rachel, Ella, Benny, and I exchanged silent glances, not sure exactly what to say next. I had so many questions, the most obvious of which was why Rachel was there. And then, as was entirely in character for me, I found myself confused and a little angry, wondering why all my close friends were in on a secret while keeping me in the dark.

Do they not trust me? Or worse, are they starting to not like me?

"So, elephant in the room," said Rachel. "Why am I… in a prom dress?"

"Ah yes," I said, sarcastically. "That's… exactly what I was wondering."

"I figured I'd bring the prom to her," said Ella, picking up a McDonald's bag off a table and handing it to Rachel. "Chicken McNuggets with two sides of honey."

"My favorite," said Rachel, smiling.

"Good choice," I said, dryly, disoriented by why we were talking about McDonalds at a time like that.

I sat on a chair by the window and stared out at the rain for a moment. "So… is anyone gonna clue me in on what's going on?"

Rachel sat down on the bed and ate a honey-dipped nugget.

"Well," she said through a full mouth. "RCA… broke me, and I didn't appreciate that. I needed some space. It's as simple as that."

"Broke you?" I asked. "What does that mean? Like, I'm sure some people there aren't perfect, but to blame the entire school…"

"Oh, come off it, Arthur," said Ella. "You should know by now that there's some dark shit going on at RCA."

"It's fine, Ella," said Rachel. "It's fine."

"Was this about what happened at the purity conference?" I asked. "Cause, like yeah, I'll admit, Pastor Robbie isn't exactly a saint, and he shouldn't have said that stuff in there, and—"

Ella interrupted. "Arthur, you don't even know what they said to us in the girls' conference. Like, this is so much more layered than you know, and that's not even your fault, so like, I'm sorry if I'm a little snippy. It's just… UGH. It's…"

"What did they say in there?" asked Benny, leaning back against the door.

"Well," said Rachel, "the first thing that made me feel a little ill was when they described a woman's virginity as a rose. They said that every time we have sex, a petal falls off. And what kind of gift is a rose with a bunch of missing petals? They also described it as a wrapped gift. Once you unwrap it, you can never re-wrap it with the same paper and bow. I'm guessing they didn't say anything like that in the guy's conference?"

"Definitely not," said Benny.

"They taught us that adultery is a sin," I said, "no matter if it's boys or girls. I'm not sure I see the issue."

Ella stood up. "THE ISSUE—"

"The issue," interrupted Rachel, "is that for guys, there's no irreparable consequence. You just say you're sorry to God and all is forgiven. For women, if we mess up, we're painted as sluts forever, and what man of God would want to marry used goods? It brought great shame to my life when… Samuel and I first stumbled. And that shame didn't go away when I prayed to God for repentance, because, according to Pastor Robbie, 'I would bear the scars of these transgressions forever.' "

I felt a tinge of judgment toward her, but swallowed it. "That's rough. I'm sorry."

"Thank you."

"Ya know guys," said Ella, "those aren't the only hurtful things they said to us in the conference. For one, they said Eve's betrayal of God is the reason women feel pain during childbirth." She paced. "And I'm sure this one isn't a surprise to you, but Righteous Christ seems to think men are the only gender capable of making good leadership decisions. No woman pastors, principals… and in the purity conference they really hammered down on how important it is to follow our husbands' examples. They kept using that word: husband. Save yourself for your husband, keep your husband satisfied, never question the male leadership God has put in your life, blah, blah, blah. As if men are one hundred percent flawless in every situation. The whole thing is basically that men are God's perfect superheroes, and women are their sexy sidekicks, literally created for their pleasure."

"I don't see the big deal," I said. "If God designed us to fill these roles, who are we to question it? Plus, when women get PMS they—"

"HAH!" squealed Benny. "OH MY GOD, Arthur."

"What?"

"Like… you know what it's like to be a horny dude, right? You're telling me that when you're in THE MOOD, it doesn't compromise your judgment?"

"Thank you, Benny!" said Ella.

"Arthur," said Rachel, calmly. "I understand some of this is difficult to hear. I wasn't raised in the church like you were, but I'm definitely going through some shock trying to wrap my head around this kinda stuff." She turned toward the others. "It would mean a lot to me if I can finish the story without the yelling. Okay, everyone?"

"Yeah, okay," said Ella.

Benny nodded.

"Thanks. So, a few months into dating Samuel, I realized it was unlike any relationship I had been in before. The role his parents played in it was so… present. They'd lavish me with love, and say God chose me to build Samuel up into an amazing leader for God. It was all very encouraging to hear. It was like I had a purpose for once."

"Ugh," groaned Ella, sitting down next to Rachel.

"Eventually," Rachel continued, "I felt stressed, and I wasn't sure why. Things were going great with Samuel, and it led to many opportunities with the church and school. But there were just so many eyes on me. I couldn't make any missteps, or everyone might hate me. And then when Samuel and I slept together… the fear of

Robbie finding out… what he might do to me… and then the purity conference catcalling…"

"Did Robbie find out you slept with Samuel?" I asked.

"Later he did, yeah. When the stress got to be so much I didn't even feel like myself anymore, I called things off with Samuel. A few days later, Robbie offered me personal counseling, and I accepted, not knowing what else I could do. He kinda suspected we had been intimate, and I confirmed that to him. He promised to keep my secret… but then things got weird."

"Weird how?" asked Benny.

"He… pulled his chair really close to mine. He put his hands on my knees to pray for me, but then they kept sliding higher. He didn't… get all the way there… but I was extremely uncomfortable and asked him to stop, which he did, eventually. He later reminded me he was going to keep my secret… which kinda felt like he was making sure I would keep his."

I cleared my throat. "That… I mean… I'm sure he—"

"He's done this before, Arthur," said Ella. "There are a few rumors going around about him acting inappropriately with a few girls."

"I haven't heard of any."

"Well, yeah," Ella continued. "It doesn't affect the guys, so why would y'all bother gossiping about it?"

"I guess," I said. "So, Rachel, was that it? Robbie didn't do anything else to you? He wasn't involved with your disappearance?"

"No, that was all me. A while after he touched me, he reached back out about something I was going through… but—"

"It's not important," interrupted Ella before Rachel could finish.

That's a little suspicious, I thought.

"Yeah, I don't feel comfortable sharing anything else, but it's over. I ran away right after all this. I just couldn't take it anymore. I felt so betrayed by those closest to me, and I needed to calm down. My heart felt so tight for so long. I just needed it to end. So, I snuck away and stayed with an old friend for a few days. I thought about reaching out to my cheerleader friends, but I decided it was too risky to trust them to not rat me out. Then I reached out to Ella, who let me stay in her pool house for a while, but that was a little risky. So, then Ella used some of her early graduation money to get me motel rooms—a different one every week. Thank goodness she turned eighteen this year or it would've been a bigger issue. Thank you so much, again, Ella…"

"Wasn't even a question," said Ella.

"And yeah," said Rachel. "I've just been cooped up, working on college essays… not that they'd accept me if I never finish high school. Hanging out with Ella, lots of books and TV. Occasionally, I'd put on some glasses and a hat, and go for a walk. But yeah… now you're all caught up."

"Wow," said Benny. "That's an insane story, Rach. I'm so sorry you went through all that."

"Thanks, Benny."

I was relieved that Rachel was okay, but couldn't help but feel a little lied to.

"Yeah… that sounds really rough," I said. "I'm glad you're not dead, but wow… that's a lot. I'm still processing it."

"I'm glad I'm not dead, too," chuckled Rachel.

"Ya know, Art," said Ella, "I only told Benny about this like half a day ago. We were gonna tell you soon. Just thought it was risky to tell you both at once. Needed to keep it tight-lipped."

I smiled with relief. "My lips are sealed."

"So," said Benny, "what's the plan now? Do you think you'd ever go back to RCA to finish up the year?"

"Maybe. I'm feeling a little better now, and seeing you all here has made me so happy. I miss everyone, and living in a motel room… it's not ideal. But to have to see Samuel and Robbie around again… I don't know. I wish I could tell people what Robbie did… expose his hypocrisy so I could finish the year without him, but I don't think anyone would believe me."

"True that," said Ella.

I reached into my pocket. "Well… what if you had evidence?" I pulled out my thumb drive.

Ella perked up. "You finally read it, huh?"

"Yeah… it's not much, but there's some fairly incriminating bits on here. Maybe you can find some more too; I only skimmed it."

Rachel stood up and hugged me.

"Thank you so much, Arthur. Maybe this can help me."

"Hah… you're welcome."

Benny clapped his hands a single time. "Well, we're all dressed to the nines with some grub. These hips ain't gonna wiggle themselves!"

"Dancing?" I asked. "Now? I'm like… still reeling from all this."

"Arthur," said Rachel. "I know this is a lot, but can we please put all the drama on hold? I'd really love to have a moment of fun with my friends for the first time in a very long while."

I smiled. "Yeah… of course."

Rachel connected her iPod to a nearby boom box and blasted "Poker Face" by Lady Gaga. I brought back my micro dances while the others turned the room into a dance floor that rivaled the real prom—debatably better because we got to eat chicken nuggets.

Benny and Ella had a small dance-off while Rachel attempted to drag me into a proper dance. She barely succeeded.

As "Mr. Brightside" by The Killers came on, Rachel and Ella danced together. They swung their arms around wildly while head banging. There was lots of flailing.

When the song ended, Benny and I both thought to grab some more nuggets at the same time. A slower song, "I Miss You" by Blink-182, started playing. Ella and Rachel stepped closer to each other. They both draped their arms over the other's shoulders and swayed back and forth.

"This is so weird," I said to Benny.

"Yeah," he said. "But good weird, right?"

I sighed. "Yeah… good weird. Not sure what all this is gonna mean tomorrow. I have so many questions, and—"

"Just be in the moment, Arthur. Tomorrow can wait."

"Yeah," I said, watching Ella and Rachel sway back and forth to the passionate song. "It's a nice moment."

"I'm so happy right now," said Rachel, pulling Ella in tighter. "Why are you the best?"

Ella smiled. "You make it easy, cause you're the best."

They giggled and rubbed noses together.

"Hey, come on," I said.

Ella spun her head toward me, smooshing her cheek against Rachel's. "And what exactly is your problem?"

"I mean… I know you're not gay, but still… you don't have to act like it…"

Ella folded her arms and scrunched her face. She stared at the ground for a moment before looking sharply at me.

"And what if I am gay, Arthur?" she said. "What would you think of that?"

I gulped. "I… I mean… you're a Christian, I think. And homosexuality is a sin to Christians. I'd try to share information with you about what God thinks of that; maybe convince you to change."

Ella wiped a small tear from her face. "So, that's what you really think of me? That who I am is a crime against the creator of the goddamn universe? Arthur, do you not realize just how hurtful that is?"

Rachel turned off the music. She stepped closer to Ella and placed her hands on her arm.

"No, no!" I said. "Okay, I'm sorry. Let me rephrase. I don't think any less of you. I don't hate you, and neither does God. He loves the sinner. He just hates the sin."

Ella laughed through her tears. "Arthur, you really need to stop acting like everything our pastors say to you is flawless wisdom! Hasn't learning about Robbie the molester taught you anything? See, this is why we didn't tell you about Rachel. You're in too deep. You can't see the forest through the trees. Real people with actual feelings are getting hurt, and all you care about is whether we're perfectly following arbitrary rules set by one specific version of one specific god, as interpreted from a collection of poorly translated books by men at one particular point in time! It's fucking ridiculous!"

Benny stepped to the girls' side of the room. "People don't choose who they love, Arthur. Could you choose to be gay?"

"I don't know, cause I would never choose to go against God's will. He knows everything, so why would I question Him?"

Ella groaned. "Because nobody has actually talked to God, Arthur! You're not questioning God, you're questioning a flawed man's interpretation of God, which can always be wrong."

"I talk to God all the time…"

"Sure, just like followers of other gods talk to them all the time. You can't all be right. You say a prayer and then interpret butterflies in your stomach and feelings in your heart as the god you already believe in. It's a fucking self-fulfilling prophecy."

Rachel added her calm demeanor to the confrontation. "Arthur, powerful men taught your idea of God to you within an enormous organization called Righteous Christ. It's all you know. But what if you're wrong? What if another church that interprets the Bible differently is right? What about another religion? Surely you don't think it's worth it to hurt your friends in the name of something that might not be true, right?"

I squirmed, uncomfortable with the thought of questioning the authority figures in my life. "I… don't…"

Rachel continued. "I know people with autism sometimes have a strong sense of moral justice, and that's admirable. But this is more complicated than a set of rules. Your real-life friends are standing in front of you, telling you your actions are hurting them, and you seem focused on checking boxes in an instruction manual instead. Context matters, Arthur."

I fidgeted with my fingers and stared at the floor.

"Listen, Arthur," said Benny. "I'm sure you've suspected it, but… I'm attracted to men."

I wasn't surprised to hear it. I had noticed the obvious signs, but, viewing homosexuality as one of the darkest corners the mind can wander to, I always gave my friends the benefit of the doubt.

Benny continued, "Ya know, while we're getting all this out in the open… it really hasn't felt great when you've avoided hugging me, out of fear that someone will think you're gay."

He looked at me with wide eyes, as if hoping for a sympathetic response.

"Hrmm," I grunted, still looking down.

In moments like those, a part deep inside me knew I was in the wrong, but in the heat of the moment, I was like a stubborn deer in the ethical headlights.

Benny sighed and shook his head. "I have tried so hard… to be… normal. It just doesn't work. This is why Pastor Robbie was yelling at me in his cabin at Cocoon. He had heard a rumor I was gay, and that was all he needed to hear. The things he said to me in there… screaming, while pointing at recorded footage of me acting too feminine… there's no way any god of love would condone that. Soon after that, I realized… God made me gay. And if He's real, and if He loves me… He'd want me to be happy. He wouldn't want me to hide who I am. He wouldn't want me to be miserable, or to live a life without love."

"I just… don't understand why this matters!" I said. "Haven't you all taken our apologetics classes? We know the Bible is true, and that God condemns homosexuality. If you choose to engage in the homosexual lifestyle, that's on you, even if it's hard."

"How do you know it's true?" asked Ella. "Have you ever even talked to someone outside your little Christian bubble about this? Maybe a Muslim? A Jew? Hindu? Cause guess what. They use the same faith-based reasons as you, and come to completely different conclusions. Diversity is a good thing, Arthur! Christian, atheist, gay, straight, Black, White… everyone is doing their best to get by and find love and passion during this tiny speck of a blip we happen to be alive for. And then people like you just mess everything up!"

I prepared to spout some canned Christian talking points. "Well—"

Ella didn't even let me begin. "You spend your whole life stuck in a tiny room with NO ONE that challenges your beliefs. This goddamn echo chamber is destroying you! We're not hurting you, so why do you give a shit about changing us?! Stop being so GODDAMN AUTISTIC and have some FUCKING EMPATHY!"

Benny's jaw dropped, and all expression vanished from my face. Nobody had ever insulted my autism so directly before. For it to come from a friend made the gut punch hurt so much more.

Nobody said anything for a while.

Ella rubbed her face, exhaled, and looked toward me, avoiding eye contact. "Look, Arthur… I'm… sorry. I didn't mean that. I just—"

"It's fine," I said.

I walked to the door and opened it to the roar of rain smashing into concrete. "I hear you, but I just can't throw away everything God has done for me in favor of not hurting your feelings. He created us and knows what's best for us. I hope you can see that someday."

I shut the door and walked down the stairs. It was hard to tell because of the rain, but I was crying. I drove home and had one of the worst sleeps of my life.

13. The Crossroads of Faith and Compassion

I always hated brushing my teeth. Any activity we do solely to avoid potential future unpleasantry was so monotonous to me. In that way, I suppose I was a rather "in the moment" sort of autistic. I'd always rather be doing something that benefited me right away. Chores like those were even more grueling in the weeks following my confrontation with Ella, Benny, and Rachel. My day to day was so filled with sadness that any slight frustration was salt to the wound.

School was packed with awkward moments passing Ella and Benny in hallways, though at least we didn't presently share any classes together, aside from homeroom with Benny.

I longed for moments of escapism, which I could rarely find during school hours. Improving my animation skills in my year-long independent study provided an adequate distraction, but only for a few hours a week.

I thought the smiley-shaped French fries with nacho cheese dip would brighten up my lunch break, but no. I suppose I had indulged in them one-too-many times.

I sat a few rows over from my usual lunch table, where Ella and Benny continued sitting, facing the other direction to avoid unnecessary eye contact. I didn't say much to the students that sat at my new table, but I partook in plenty of unintentional eavesdropping, which provided a welcome distraction from my inner thoughts.

A girl whispered to her friend, "Oh. My. God. Did you hear Daniel VanBrunt got to second base with Sara Calhoon in the northeast stairwell?"

"No way," responded her friend. "Sara told me they just kissed!"

I rolled my eyes.

At the table behind me, I heard a familiar voice going on about something else. "Yeah, they haven't told many people yet, but it's true. She's supposed to come back on Monday."

"That's so special, Wesley," responded Jade Parnacle. "I'm so happy she's okay."

"Yeah, me too," said Rachel's brother. "I really didn't think I was gonna see her again. It's… weird."

"That's so hard. Lemme know if you need someone to talk to after school. My shoulder is always available."

"Totally, babe. I'll give ya a ring."

I guess my flash drive was enough to give Rachel the confidence to return.

I caught myself smiling and quickly inverted it.

From my right came a voice. "Hey, Arthur." Andrew joined me at my table. "How ya been?"

"Eh, I'm fine. Honestly, things have been a little… complicated lately."

"Yeah, seriously. I just got back from my guidance counselor's office, and I overheard some teachers talking. They said RCA asked Pastor Robbie to take a leave of absence while they look into some… accusations of some sort."

"Oh… dang. I wonder what that could be about…"

My heart rate increased as I realized Rachel had likely come forward. Whether anonymously or not, I wasn't sure.

Over the loudspeaker came Principal Randall's voice. "All senior students, please report to the *Spóros* sanctuary for an emergency assembly after lunch. Thank you."

"Wonder what that's about," said Andrew.

"No clue," I said, dishonestly.

Grabbing my backpack from my locker, I felt bad I wasn't exclusively happy for Rachel's apparently imminent return. *That's one more person I need to avoid,* I thought.

I felt a tap on my shoulder.

"Hey, stranger," said Jennifer.

I turned around. "Hey."

"You doing okay? You look kinda sad this week."

"You sure that's not just my face?" I asked.

"No, you usually look at least a bit happier," she giggled.

"Yeah," I said. "I guess I'm pretty bad at putting on a smile when I'm not happy."

"Walk with me to the assembly and tell me about it?"

"Sure."

We walked for a minute or two without speaking. I stepped up to the side of a bridge connecting two buildings and leaned on the railing. The view of the grassy football field was pretty.

"Question for you," I said.

"Shoot," said Jennifer, joining me.

"Let's say you have a close friend who loves… eating pasta. Like, it's their life's purpose. If you somehow found out this person had a virus that guarantees they will die at age thirty if they don't stop eating pasta soon, would you ask that person to stop eating pasta?"

Jennifer raised an eyebrow. "Well… I don't know what you're talking about, but I'll play along. My first question is… how do I know for sure this virus is real, and that the friend has it? Did I do the research myself?"

"Umm… I dunno, I guess the people around you—really well-respected people—told you it's true, and you trust them."

"Are there other people in the world who are also respected, who have differing opinions on the dreaded virus, Alfredo 549?"

"Yeah," I said. "I suppose."

"So, how do you know if… ya know what, this metaphor is losing me. Just be straight with me?"

"Okay…" I leaned in and lowered my voice a little. "I have some… I have a friend who told me they're gay. Obviously, that's a sin, and I don't want them to end up in Hell. We had a huge fight because I told them that."

"That's… intense. I can't say I love to hear you have such a problem with that, but given where we go to school, I guess I can't be surprised."

I looked away. "Oh… sorry."

"It's fine. So, what did they say to you?"

"They're mad at me for hurting them, and I get that… but also, I kinda don't? I don't get why it's offensive for me to not like their lifestyle. It's like someone not liking that I think *Return of the King* is the best *Lord of the Rings* movie. It's not essential to who I am as a person."

"Okay," said Jennifer. "First off, the best *Lord of the Rings* movie is definitely *Fellowship,* and two, that's not even in the same ballpark. Imagine living in a world where if you're public about your love for the second-best *Lord of the Rings* movie, almost every one of your parents, teachers, pastors, government, and, heck—random citizens of the world, will devote time and effort to telling you that you are going to burn in a pit of fire, simply for being yourself. They'll call you sick. They'll try to put you in therapy where they play the final thirty-minutes of *Return of the King* on repeat for hours until you beg them to stop. The government even outlaws watching it at parties, and they give tax breaks to anyone who vows to never watch it again. Plus, you came out of the womb humming 'Into the West,' so it's basically burned into your DNA. You never had a choice, and the world has decided that's just not okay."

"Okay, okay. I get it. It wouldn't be fun. But what are temporary feelings when compared to eternal happiness? A little pain now is a small price to pay, right?"

"Sure. But like, no offense… I just don't think the science, logic, or whatever, for any of these claims, is as strong as you think it is. Like, why are you so sure you have all the answers to the universe's biggest questions?"

"Well," I said. "If I'm right, I go to Heaven. If I'm wrong, no big deal."

"Hurting your friends isn't a big deal? What if you keep doing that your whole life? Isn't that kind of a waste of what might be your only life?"

"Okay, fair point. But if THEY'RE wrong, they spend an eternity in Hell. Pretty big caveat. I feel like 'better safe than sorry' is my only option here."

"I get you grew up around Christianity, but there's a lot more out there. Do you spend your time stressed about going to the hells of all the other religions? Like the ones with punishments for not believing?"

I shook my head. "No, because we know that they're wrong."

"And they know you're wrong," said Jennifer. "See the problem? Faith can be nice, but it doesn't get you all the way to truth. By the way, have you ever read the Quran or The Book of Mormon?"

"Uh… no."

"See? If everyone just assumes they got lucky enough to be born in the right place at the right time, how could we ever know who's right? And on a smaller scope, let's limit it to just Abrahamic religions. What if Southern Baptists are the ones who got it right? Or Catholics? Or Orthodox Jews?"

"I'm not very familiar with—"

"Ya know what… one more metaphor. You're acting like buying a lottery ticket has two outcomes: you either win or you lose; a fifty-fifty shot. But it's not. It's a one in hundreds of millions kind of shot. And are you really willing to blow your life savings on that one ticket? Or to be extremely literal, since I know you like that, do you think being hurtful to your friends is a fair price to pay for a guess at a single salvation hypothesis out of who knows how many?"

"I… don't know."

"Right!" said Jennifer, staring at me intensely. "Nobody does. Also, I'm sorry if that was… a lot. I've been watching a lot of YouTube lately."

"It's fine. I appreciate your honesty."

"Good. I appreciate my honesty, too."

I sighed. "Ya know, I sure do find myself surrounded by worldly advice these days. Our pastors would say you're a bad influence."

Jennifer smiled. "Good thing you're into bad influences, huh?"

"Ha ha. I guess."

"Come on, let's head to the assembly."

As students packed into the youth sanctuary, I smiled, knowing for once, everyone was there to receive good news. Jennifer and I sat together toward the back. I breathed a sigh of relief when Benny and Ella sat far away.

"Please be seated, everyone," said Principal Randall. "I'll just cut right to the chase. I have wonderful news. After months of uncertainty, Rachel Bristol has been located, and will rejoin us starting Monday to finish out the school year."

The crowd whispered amongst themselves. Some clapped, and a few cheered. A few cried tears of joy.

"Settle down, please. Now, her parents have asked us not to disclose any details about her recent experiences, but rest assured, she is in good health, and nothing sinister was afoot. Please be respectful as she rejoins us, and give her the space to heal that she needs."

Jennifer turned to me. "That's so great! Did you know about this?"

I shrugged.

"Now, besides this great news, we have something unrelated and rather serious to discuss. Pastor Robbie, we're ready for you."

Robbie approached the pulpit, appearing slightly more disheveled than usual.

I guess Andrew heard wrong, I thought.

Pastor Robbie cleared his throat. "As you all know very well, God commands you to obey your elders. God has chosen each one of us pastors and teachers to guide you toward a more spiritual life, but if you don't trust us, how are we supposed to do that?"

"What's this about?" whispered Jennifer.

Robbie continued. "In the coming weeks, some of you may hear some rumors about the leadership at RCA, including myself."

I sunk into my seat.

"I am here to tell you, as a chosen disciple of God the Father, that whoever is the source of this slander is simply trying to drive a plank between the members of our strong community. Even if they truly think I—uh, we… are capable of such sinful actions… remember, Satan can use even the purest of us to plant seeds of unholiness. This is what happens when you follow the temptations of the world. It blinds you to the example of God standing right in front of you."

Students around me whispered to each other, unsure of what rumors Pastor Robbie was referring to.

"If we hear anyone among you spreading these or any other harmful words toward your faculty, we will deal them with in a manner that is appropriate. And don't worry; no matter what weapons of spiritual warfare they use against us, we will not falter. I'm not going anywhere."

I felt a heat creep up my neck as my teeth clenched, knowing the man standing before me was, at least in some ways, a fraud. I felt a desire to expose his lies to the world, but thoughts like that don't stick around for long in the mind of someone conditioned to never question authority. I shook those thoughts from my head.

*   *   *

Monday before homeroom, I was at my locker when I heard a commotion. I walked down the hall to see what, or who, quite a few students were gathered around. I had a pretty good hunch what the answer was.

"It's so nice to have you back," said one boy.

"Happy to be back," said Rachel, exchanging hugs with a few students.

Jade Parnacle approached her, flipped her dark hair over her shoulder, and said, "I'm so glad you're okay, Rach. I was so worried."

I groaned to myself.

Rachel forced a smile. "Yeah… thanks, Jade."

"Don't you get any ideas about reclaiming the role of Eve, though," said Jade, folding her arms. "That ship has sailed."

"Oh, I wouldn't dream of it," said Rachel. "I've got too much school to catch up on, anyway."

I kept my distance for the time being. I headed to homeroom, looking back over my shoulder at a nice moment I should have been a part of.

Rehearsal that afternoon wasn't the usual one or two scene practice we'd grown used to. It was a full run-through of *Eden*, with the entire cast present. That meant waiting to pick a seat until I saw where Benny and Ella sat to avoid any awkward encounters.

"This is so exciting!" said Ms. Flannigan, flailing her arms above her head in excitement. "Our first complete rehearsal of *Eden*. I can't wait to see all your hard work on the stage today. First up, a few announcements. As I'm sure you've all heard by now, our prayers have been answered, and our dear Rachel Bristol has returned to us unharmed. Welcome back, Rachel!"

I hadn't even noticed Rachel enter. Ms. Flannigan initiated a clap, and the cast followed suit. Rachel smiled coyly as Ella beamed with happiness in the seat next to her.

"Welcome back, Rach," said Samuel, surprisingly respectfully.

Rachel flashed a brief smile at him.

Ms. Flannigan continued, "We have welcomed Rachel back into the cast in the low-pressure role of another garden animal."

I could feel the room's disappointment that Rachel wouldn't be reprising her role of Eve, but Jade sure was smiling wide.

"Second," continued Ms. Flannigan, "Pastor Robbie will watch this performance. Everybody say hi!"

She looked at the back of the theater and waved energetically. Pastor Robbie nodded from many rows behind the cast.

"Fingers crossed he loves it and helps get the word out to the Righteous Christ congregation!"

I looked over at Ella, who seemed predictably sour at the information. Rachel wore a blank expression on her face and held her arms close to her chest.

"Alright, everyone," said Ms. Flannigan. "Let's get this party started!"

The cast and I took to the stage and began to perform the show. My scenes with Benny were a little awkward, but luckily, he didn't directly interact with me since he played a detached voice of God.

Ella played a generic garden animal character along with Rachel, so I didn't have to act with them directly, either. They didn't seem entirely in the moment when onstage. They constantly exchanged playful nudges and whispers, like they were in their own little world. It irked me a little.

Despite the tensions in the air from my personal dramas, and the seething gaze of Pastor Robbie, the run-through was a ton of fun. For the first time, we really got a feel for the overall flow of the show, and the emotions came through effectively. Even Jade Parnacle's performance of Eve impressed us all with its gravitas.

The stage kiss between Samuel and Jade earned a few "whoops" and "owws!" from the small audience. I also felt I performed my song rather well.

There were, of course, some quirks and forgotten lines throughout the cast, but overall, Ms. Flannigan's vision of an empowered Eve struggling to find her identity shone through rather emotionally.

As Jade belted out the final lyrics of the show, Ms. Flannigan stood up and applauded vigorously. The cast not involved in the final scene of the show clapped as well, myself included. Ms.

Flannigan turned around to gauge Robbie's reaction to the show. He simply sat there, arms folded and expressionless.

"Great job, everyone," said Ms. Flannigan. "Get some rest and I'll see some of you tomorrow for some scene polishing."

As I gathered my belongings, Ms. Flannigan headed to the back of the theater to talk to Pastor Robbie. They shook hands and conversed. After a few moments, Ms. Flannigan threw her arms up in the air. Their voices carried, although I couldn't make out their exact words. They were clearly arguing about something. I wondered what it could be as I exited the theater and headed home.

The following day, I was scheduled for rehearsal, along with a few other cast members. Ms. Flannigan was running ten minutes late, which was unusual. When she arrived, her usual energy and smile were absent.

She took a seat on the ledge of the stage. "So… umm, I don't even know how to say this. Inviting Pastor Robbie to sit in on our run-through yesterday was… a HUGE mistake. He, uh… he's forcing us to make changes."

"What kind of changes?" asked Jade.

"Big ones. Well, kind of. Basically, the church finds the show to contain some… problematic material. They don't think our portrayal of Eve is biblically accurate. So, pretty much everything about Eve finding her strength… we've got to cut it. The kiss is gone, too. I spent most of today adjusting and rewriting. The bones are the same, but I have trimmed some scenes down, and a few lines and lyrics needed altering. And, as much as it breaks my heart… I cut Eve's *I want* song entirely."

"Are you serious?!" asked Jade, standing up. "That's the most important song!"

"Believe me, I fought this, but they gave me no wiggle room. We're lucky they didn't can the show completely. They even wanted me to recast God with a White student, but I talked them out of that, at least. I don't think there's any need to burden Benny with that information, though."

"This is all so messed up," I said.

"Yeah… I know. Ya try to be an artist, to do something good… Leave it up to self-righteous men to silence anyone trying to empower women, right?" She cleared her throat. "Anyway, we're gonna go through some of these changes today. I'll make a posting in the hall about this afterward. We'll make the most of this, okay?"

The few cast members in attendance and I were silent, unsure of what to say.

After running through the changes, which luckily didn't affect my lines or song too much, Ms. Flannigan ended our rehearsal fifteen minutes early. Morale was understandably low.

As we collected our things, Ms. Flannigan said, "Oh! One more thing. Robbie asked me to share these flyers around. They're looking for some performing arts students to help the *Spóros* youth ministry put on some sort of Hell-themed haunted house experience. So, if you're inclined to take on even more responsibility in addition to learning the new changes to *Eden*, be my guest."

Needing something to take my mind off the stresses of recent days, I took a flyer.

When I got home, I looked it over. It was in Comic Sans and Papyrus fonts, because, of course.

The Fall in February Hell House

Seeking actors to volunteer. Be part of a spooky experience that is a force of change for Christ.

I heard a knock at my bedroom door.

"Hi, honey," said my mom. "There's mail here for you. It's from Barnum Institute."

"Thanks."

After she exited my bedroom, I opened it. It was a single letter.

Dear Arthur Morton,

We regret to inform you that we cannot accept you into the animation program at Barnum Institute at this time.

We have reviewed your portfolio and think you have potential. Please feel free to reapply next year with an improved emphasis on life drawing skills.

Thank you.

I tossed the letter to the side. GCAD had already accepted me, but they accepted almost everyone.

Maybe this is God telling me to go to Shield and Sword U, I thought.

I'd need to think about it for a while before making a choice, and luckily, there was no rush. It also wasn't quite my highest priority at the moment; there was too much else going on.

*   *   *

Sitting in a church service by myself reminded me of a time before Rachel and before Ella. Those times were simpler, but I wouldn't have traded their friendships for it. I longed for our strained relationships to be mended.

The bombastic worship music present in the adult service provided a fun rock vibe. It was basically a full-blown concert with a light show. The sensory overload was a nice distraction, and thankfully, wasn't loud enough to overwhelm my hypersensitive ears.

As Pastor Tom took to the pulpit for the Saturday night service, I sighed. Righteous Christ used to be a place of peace for me, but recently the church's various leaders represented something sinister at worst, and questionable at best. Seeing as how my usual teammates were all missing from my life for the moment, I chose to give Tom the benefit of the doubt. Surely he had some godly wisdom in store that could provide me with some encouragement?

"When we think of God," said Pastor Tom, "what do you think of? His love? His wisdom? Those are fair answers. But one trait I think we often overlook is his goodness. There are those in the world who think they can somehow find morality in their sinful passions, but they don't know God. God is good, and good is God. You cannot separate them from each other. If a man comes to his own conclusions about what is good, he's simply saying he likes to sin, and will justify it through any means necessary. He has no authority to say that it is TRULY good."

I focused intently on Tom's words, trying to understand this philosophical idea.

"Morality is not relative. God is the author of right and wrong. Either something parallels God's character, or it does not."

I scrunched my face. Something about the message didn't sit right with me. I found myself lost in my head for a moment.

But if God decides what is right and what is wrong... how do we know He's the good guy? I guess maybe He knows what's in our best interest... and we just gotta have faith...?

Tom continued. "When someone calls themself your friend but questions your loyalty to God's perfect wisdom, I implore you to challenge them. Who are they to question God the creator?"

Something Ella said to me bounced around my head. *Nobody has talked to God. Nobody knows His will. Mankind's interpretation of the Bible can be flawed.*

After church, while lying in bed, I called Jennifer with some questions.

"Arthur," said Jennifer, "haven't you ever seen a movie or played a video game where you root for the heroes fighting against a bigger power?"

"Like what?"

"Well, how about *Star Wars*? Just because the evil empire has more resources, education, money, and firepower than the scrappy rebels, does that mean they know what's in their best interest?"

"I wouldn't really say a powerful government is the same as a god that created you."

"Sure," continued Jennifer. "But think of it this way. What's in our best interest is what *we* want for ourselves, our family, and our friends. Whatever God wants to do for, or to, us… we can still say 'no thank you.'"

"But He's omnipresent. He knows everything—about today, the past, and the future. He knows our eternity is at stake, and He wants more than anything to prevent us from being cast into Hell."

"So, I'm no expert on this stuff, as you know… so correct me if I'm wrong. Didn't God create Hell? Or at least the rules that determine who He saves from it?"

I thought for a moment. "I've heard conflicting things about if He created it, and I'm pretty sure Heaven has concrete qualifications for entering."

"What are those qualifications?"

"Just to believe."

"Just believe? Artie, belief isn't really a choice. If I told you I'd give you a million dollars if you could genuinely believe you could fly like Superman, and to believe it for the rest of your life… could you?"

"Hmm… probably not."

"Right," said Jennifer. "It's basically impossible. So, you have this all-powerful, supposedly all-loving God who wants to save as many people as possible from Hell. And yet, instead of just choosing to save everyone, He says you have to believe He exists first."

"Sure."

"But there's so many people out there that genuinely just aren't convinced. Like, how about me? Do you think I deserve to go to Hell, just for not finding the apologetics Righteous Christ teaches compelling? Is whether I find some proposed evidence convincing really the ultimate test for whether I'm a good person?"

"I… guess not."

"Right. Like, is getting into Heaven really just about whether you were lucky enough to be born in the right place at the right time, and lucky enough to be surrounded by the right people?"

"Hmm…" I said. "That doesn't sound like a fair system. But God says everyone has the opportunity to come to Him, so it's our fault if we ignore it."

"So, every non-Christian on their deathbed that has said they don't believe in the Christian God is lying, or prideful? All, however-many billions of them? Don't you think that's a little irrational?"

I stroked my chin. "I see your point. Maybe… I dunno. I'm not sure what I think anymore."

"This is good, Arthur. I'm proud of you for asking the big questions. This is a big step. And don't get me wrong, I think there might be something greater than us out there. I just really think the way Righteous Christ pitches it is pretty flawed. Lots of holes in there. Like, if there's a Hell, I definitely don't wanna go! But I can't just pretend I believe, ya know? God would know I was faking, anyway. If He's real, I just hope He someday shows me some evidence that He knows I'd be able to believe."

"Yeah, that's fair."

"And, tying this back to your conundrum… if you agree with me that at the very least there's some inconsistencies here… maybe it's not worth it to throw away your friendships over it?"

I felt a tinge of guilt creep in. *Am I actually doubting the very core of my beliefs?*

I rubbed my face. "I don't know… you might be right. Thanks for the talk. Lots to think about."

"Always here, Art. Good night."

"Good night."

Those deep talks with Jennifer were too stimulating for me to sleep yet, so I headed to the kitchen to get some water. Halfway down the stairs, I heard my mom's voice.

"You know, Madeline," she said to her friend, presumably on the phone. "I worry about our kids at that school… Uh huh. Yes, exactly. They teach them these ideas, and push them away. I don't know what they expect."

I crouched to make sure the stairs didn't creak.

"Yes, I heard that Billy's parents pulled him from the school? Yep, if RCA doesn't… Mmhmm… Right, they've got to find better ways to teach them the Bible or they're gonna end up sending all these kids to Hell!"

I gulped. *Is she really worried that I'm gonna end up in Hell? Maybe she overheard me talking to Jenn…*

"Yes, okay, dear. Have a nice night. Buh-bye."

After my mom entered the bathroom and closed the door, I walked into the kitchen. On the table was a half-empty bottle of red wine, and a used glass. I took a pitcher of water out of the fridge and poured myself a cup before heading back to bed.

Lying in bed sipping my water, my chest tightened. *Even my mom is worried I'm gonna drift away from God…*

I had heard of students whose parents kicked them out of the house when they fell away from the faith. The thought was too much to bear. I took a deep breath, shut the lights, and closed my eyes.

I need to get back to the righteous path, and quick, I thought as I laid there, unable to sleep. *Maybe volunteering for the Hell House will help.*

14. Walking Through Fire

I pulled my collar away from my neck and let it snap back, allowing a small gust of air to swoop in and cool my chest. I repeated this many times throughout the morning ride to school on the city bus—RCA didn't do the school bus thing outside of off-campus trips. My car hadn't started that morning, though luckily my dad said he'd have it fixed by the following day.

Public transit wasn't my favorite way to get around, because of the many unpredictable variables relating to comfort. Aside from the lack of climate control consistency, there was the personal space anxiety when someone sat next to me, and long drive times. If a stranger tried to make small talk with me, it would just ruin my day. Thankfully, the ride was quiet and uneventful, if quite sweaty.

After the bus dropped me off at one of its regular stops, I walked the few remaining blocks toward the school.

While crossing a small bridge, I leaned on the railing and peered into the flowing stream. The babbling sound soothed me as the breeze cooled me off.

Part of the reason I was procrastinating finishing my commute was that my feelings toward Righteous Christ had become so conflicted lately. Watching the water flow over pebbles distracted me from the hard stuff, if only for a moment.

Quack, quack.

A family of three ducks made a commotion a ways down. They splashed around, presumably playing. It made me smile.

Right underneath where I stood, a fourth duck sat, using its beak to clean its wings. It appeared to be the runt of the family. Occasionally, it would look downstream at the other ducks frolicking around.

As a sinking feeling cramped my stomach, something dark caught my eye across the stream. On the bank sat a small, black alligator. I detected no movement on its ominous facade. It stared at the lone duck, who didn't seem to notice it.

"Hey!" I said, looking at the alligator. "Get lost!"

It didn't budge. After about a minute of no development, I checked my phone. School was starting in just ten minutes.

I stared down the alligator. "Don't you do it," I said before jogging the last block to school—back to real life.

The following few days of *Eden* rehearsals went about as smoothly as you'd expect. The fun vibe present in the run-through had vanished—replaced with arguments, rushed practice sessions, and general stress.

Ms. Flannigan no longer showed signs of passion and artistry. She instead spent her time barking orders, rubbing her forehead, and occasionally popping pills I deduced to be anti-anxiety meds.

The changes made to the script weren't so colossal that we'd have to delay the show, but it was devoid of almost all the meaning and pride we used to see in it. Yet still, we weren't going to leave it in the dust. We had come too far for that.

Rehearsal on Friday transitioned right into the only dry run for the Hell House, which we would perform in full that evening. Ms. Flannigan was involved, mostly to consult on costumes and makeup. A small team of youth pastors took on creative direction.

The Hell House was, in essence, a Hell-themed haunted house. Righteous Christ by no means endorsed Halloween, which some churches viewed as "the Devil's holiday." They didn't go quite that far, but they never had proper Halloween-themed parties either. Each October, they seemed pretty okay with students showing up at school in costumes. Why they put on a haunted house in February, though, was anyone's guess.

The entire *Spóros* youth ministry room served as the host for the spooky experience. The ministers had stacked all the chairs into piles that, when draped with black sheets, created a path that would guide attendees through various themed sets, featuring live actors, music, and lighting effects.

As preparations unfolded, I noticed Pastor Robbie pacing the room. The youth pastors directing the Hell House would report to him occasionally. It occurred to me he was likely the brains behind the operation, which soured my expectations a bit.

"Howdy, Arthur," he said, walking past me. "Keeping your urges in check, I hope."

"Ha ha… yeah."

As soon as he looked away, my smile reversed.

Ms. Flannigan, who was visibly irked to be involved at all, handed me a black robe and a prop whip. I was to play the role of a demon. She and the ministers in charge gave other demonic actors and actresses similar robes, and other weapons such as pitchforks and scythes. Ms. Flannigan also came around to give us some evil makeup.

The ministers cast some students in human Hell-dweller roles, wearing tattered modern-day clothes. One of them voiced concern that their clothes appeared too clean, which led to them raiding a nearby refrigerator, and dousing their clothes and hair with chocolate syrup and ground coffee beans. I was very glad to not have to do that.

The ministers also instructed a few select students to play living humans in a scene at the entrance of the experience. Each section rehearsed their parts with a different supervisor because of the tight same-day schedule. Because of that, nobody was entirely sure what the complete narrative to the experience was.

They divided us into two groups to perform in alternating shifts rather than marathon the entire hour-long block.

As we rehearsed, a tech crew put together some very basic sets. In the area where I was instructed to perform, they placed cardboard cutouts with stands painted to look like fire. There were also some red and yellow lights that spun around when plugged in.

"Okay, Arthur," said a youth pastor whose name I didn't know. "You're going to pretend to whip this human here."

He gestured to Andrew.

"Hey, Arthur. Can't wait for you to torture me." Andrew laughed.

"Yeah…" I said. "Can't wait…"

Andrew kneeled and placed his hands on the ground, facing away from me.

The youth pastor used his hands to direct us into position. "So, Arthur, you're going to whip just to the side of him, and improv some lines you think a demon would say while torturing someone. You think you can handle that?"

"I'm always cast as the villains here, so…should be fine."

"Okay, great. I'll leave you to practice. I've got a few more demons to set up. God bless!"

After a few minutes of awkward practicing, they gave us the fifteen-minute warning. "Use the bathroom now if you gotta! First shift starts soon!"

I did have to use the bathroom.

After doing my business and washing my hands, I stopped by The Link, the youth ministry's cafe, to grab a bottle of water. At one of the round tables in the seating area were a few familiar faces I did not expect to see that night.

"Hey, Arthur," said Ella. "Nice outfit."

Rachel and Benny smiled and waved.

"Oh… hey," I said.

I walked over to them, fidgeting with my hair and avoiding direct eye contact.

"So," said Benny. "How have you been?"

"I'm okay, I guess."

I took a second to think of a conversation topic that didn't include our drama.

"Been trying to figure out which college to go to lately," I said. "I got into GCAD and Shield and Sword U, but I didn't get into Barnum."

"Ah, I'm sorry, Arthur," said Rachel.

"It's okay. I'm kinda thinking I should go to Shield and Sword, anyway."

"Oh," said Benny. "I thought you said they didn't have a great animation program? And what about Georgia Art?"

"Yeah, but… I dunno. I'm not sure if I wanna surround myself with non-Christians."

I could tell by their blank stares and insincere nods that they disapproved.

"So…" I said. "What happened with Robbie? I heard that cryptic warning in the assembly. Did that mean you submitted the… stuff, Rachel?"

"I leaked it anonymously to a few parents, yeah. I also dug up some… other stuff. Luckily, at least one parent seems to have come forward. But the bad news is that so far, it doesn't seem to have done what we hoped. Robbie is just so respected here; I don't think many people believed it. Plus, like you said, all the evidence was fairly circumstantial and vague."

"Oh darn," I said. "That's not good. How are you feeling about it?"

"I'm okay. Honestly, I'm glad to be around friends again, even though it's really annoying avoiding Robbie all the time."

"I'm glad too," I said.

After a moment of silence, I scratched my nose and said, "Ya know, I didn't expect to see y'all here."

"Yeah," said Benny. "I didn't expect to come either. It was Ella's idea."

Ella cleared her throat. "Yeah… I just wanted to say… about the other night… some of the stuff you said to us was very not okay… but I said some messed up stuff, too, and I am sorry for that. I don't think any of it is worth ending our friendship over. At least, I hope we can work it out."

Benny and Rachel nodded in agreement.

"Yeah… me too," I said.

Ella leaned forward, stared at me, and raised her eyebrows. "So… do you have anything to say to us?"

I shifted my weight back and forth and scratched the back of my neck. "Umm… no, I don't think so."

"Ahh," she said, sitting back in her seat. "Got it."

I really wanted to reconcile our differences, but there was no denying the remaining ethical impasse between us, and so, the conviction to apologize evaded me.

Nobody said anything for a few seconds.

"I uh… gotta get back. The Hell House is about to start. I'll see y'all in there?"

"Super ready to be spooked," said Benny, holding back on his usual enthusiasm.

Ella folded her arms and grunted.

I smiled, waved, grabbed a water bottle, and headed back, slightly disappointed that the air between my friends and me remained foggy.

As I pulled back the curtain to the entrance of the Hell House, the ambiance struck me. Seeing it with the recessed lights turned off for the first time was very immersive.

Everything was pitch black except for the few tableaus where actors were featured. Dry ice machines pumped smoke across the entire room, which sold the spooky vibe. Over the loudspeakers came ghoulish music. It was impossible to tell it was the same room I had attended so many youth ministry services in.

I made my way through a sea of actors and crew members scurrying to their positions as the youth ministers counted down the final few minutes until showtime.

"You ready?" asked Andrew, plopping down onto the dark floor.

"As I'll ever be."

"Action!" yelled a voice over the loudspeaker.

The demons around me sprung into character, growling, spitting, and spewing insults at those they were torturing. The sudden immersion caused me to flinch. We had created a truly disturbing immersive experience.

"Hey!" whispered Andrew. "You gonna torture me or what?"

"Oh. Yeah, sorry."

A few adults and a teenager walked around the corner, following the Hell House's guided trail. The lighting made it hard to see their faces, but I could tell I didn't know them. As they approached us, I jumped into character.

"Uh… you wretched filth!" I snarled and accessed a guttural voice for my intimidations. "This is what you deserve! Just try to worship your God now!"

I slammed the whip into the ground next to Andrew every few seconds.

"Bow to your God!" I screamed.

After every few lines, I had to clear my throat, which wasn't used to that sort of abuse. I eventually rolled it into my character as an exaggerated quirk. I could tell the Hell House would be a grueling acting experience, and it had only been a minute or two.

"OWW!" screamed Andrew after my whip accidentally hit his back.

"Sorry!" I whispered.

A tall boy stumbled around the bend. I couldn't tell who it was at first, but when a light caught a golden glimmer on his full head of hair, I knew it was Samuel.

His body language confused me. He didn't quite seem in control of his movements. As he got closer, he appeared to be shaking.

As he passed me, I could hear him muttering, "No… no, no… I can't… I don't want…"

He continued stumbling and mumbling to the exit.

What's up with him? I wondered, before snapping back into character.

As the first twenty-minute shift approached its halfway point, my whip smacked Andrew's back again.

"Uahhhh! That really hurts!" It was hard to tell where Andrew's actual pain ended and his character's began.

"You disgusting, wretched sinner! Bow down and repent and maybe the agony will stop! Oh wait, it won't! Because this is FOREVER!"

I fell out of character for a few seconds, shocked at how disturbed I made myself.

Just a few more minutes, I told myself as sweat covered my back.

The silhouette of a girl I immediately recognized came walking slowly around the bend. It was Jennifer. I summoned my strength and dove right back into character.

"Bow to your God, you scum of the Earth! Beg for forgiveness!"

I could see that Jennifer's arms were folded, clutching her torso. As far as I could tell, she didn't recognize me. Just as she passed my station, she suddenly changed pace and sprinted for the exit.

What on Earth was that? was all I could think during the final minute of my first shift.

"Shift break!" said a voice over the loudspeaker.

Andrew immediately headed for the exit, saying nothing. I followed him, though my main goal was to find out what had happened to Jennifer.

As I exited the dark room, I needed to squint to get used to the brighter lighting, even though the exit room was dimly lit for a relaxing ambiance. White, translucent drapes hung from the walls, and an acoustic musician played quiet melodies in the corner. There were a few small tables in the room, with a pastor seated at each one.

I looked around, but didn't see Andrew or Jennifer anywhere. Walking further into the room, I approached a table full of tracts, small pamphlets containing brief summaries of faith-based concepts, usually of the "good news" variety.

I picked one up entitled "Prayer." Inside was a series of comic-style illustrations telling a very simple story. In it, a young girl prays for her big brother's high school football team to win their big game. Because she asks so sincerely, and because she loves God, He answers her prayer.

Immediately, I had concerns about the idea—a reaction I didn't expect. I had said countless prayers in my life, and the idea of prayer always made sense to me. But upon viewing this comic, my thoughts became cynical.

What about all the prayers God doesn't answer? How could a good God let children die overseas, and yet intervene for a silly football game? Wouldn't an all-powerful God grant both prayers? How could we celebrate His football gift as answered prayer, and then say that not answering a much more important prayer is simply God working in mysterious ways?

I noticed that my thoughts were subconsciously delivered in Ella's voice, which made me chuckle.

I put the tract down and noticed Jennifer at the back of the room. She didn't look well. A woman assisting with the Hell House handed her a small bottle of water, which she drank.

I approached her. "Everything okay?"

Jennifer shook her head as I sat down next to her, still wearing my demonic getup.

She stumbled over her words a few times before finding herself. "This… is wrong, Arthur. This is so wrong."

Deep down, I knew something about that night was off. I felt dirty, but I wasn't sure why.

"What do you mean?" I asked.

"Arthur, look around. See that old man talking to Pastor Robbie over there? Why do you think he's crying like that?"

"I'm… not sure."

"He's crying because he just walked through a simulator that showed, in immersive detail, exactly how all his dead loved ones are being tortured right now. His parents, his friends, maybe his wife, or a sibling…"

"Oh… I hadn't thought of that."

Jennifer's eyes welled up. "They designed this whole thing to scare people into coming to Jesus, Arthur. It's a literal fear-based marketing campaign. They activate a very real trauma response in these innocent people and then prey on that to grow their church's numbers. Do you really think this is how Jesus wanted to spread his word?"

"No… no, I don't. I see your point. But I really don't think the pastors here are the con artists you're painting them as. They genuinely believe they're doing God's work for the greater good."

"You may be right. They may think they're the good guys, just like I know you do. But like I keep asking you. Is it worth it? Is your gamble that you're in with the right crowd really worth the absolute anguish that you're causing people?"

I remained silent.

"Have you gone through the whole Hell House yet?" asked Jennifer.

"No, but I'm about to, now that my shift is over."

"When you do, I want you to think about Rachel, and how you think she'd react to the narrative they chose for this thing."

"What do you mean?" I asked.

"The whole thing is an abortion story, Arthur. The girl in the first scene gets an abortion, goes to Hell for it, and is tortured forever. I'm sure you think abortion is murder because that's what you've been taught your whole life, but think for a second what kind of trauma something like this can do to someone who just went through that devastating experience."

"Wait… Rachel got an abortion?"

"Everyone's been talking about it at school this week. I figured you heard. The documents that got leaked about Pastor Robbie's behavior. In there was a medical receipt for Rachel from an abortion clinic, and the credit card it was charged to… it was Pastor Robbie's. He has everyone convinced it was fabricated, but I think you know that's not true."

"I-I had no…"

I remembered the cryptic email I found between Pastor Tom and Pastor Robbie.

It's taken care of. She won't be a problem.

Suddenly, everything made sense. First, Rachel was brought into Robbie and Samuel's family and given insurmountable expectations. Then Robbie violated her physical boundaries. After that, she tried to back away, but realized her time with Samuel had unforeseen, long-lasting repercussions: she was pregnant. Pastor Robbie couldn't risk his son's premarital relations soiling his image, so he ignored everything he preached from the pulpit and took action.

My world flipped in an instant. I realized Rachel had been through so much, and that my worst fears about those I used to look up to were true. Even if I had learned plenty of great life lessons from the Righteous Christ pastors over the years, the corruption ran deep. They were, at best, hypocrites.

My mind bounced from shock to guilt, then to denial, and finally to sadness. My heroes were villains, and those I lambasted with biblical scorn were their victims.

On the other hand, I thought, *I can't believe Rachel got an abortion. That goes against so much of what I know.*

I began to think out loud. "I can't believe—"

"Just… don't," interrupted Jennifer. "I'm sure you've got plenty of reasons you think abortion is wrong. I don't love it myself, but sometimes it's necessary. Becoming pregnant can completely derail, and sometimes end, someone's life. You don't have to like it, but you're not her. You don't know what went into the absolutely grueling emotional decision she had to make. It probably devastated her. Please, just respect that this wasn't easy for her, and that publicizing those documents is probably causing her more anguish than you can imagine."

"I—"

"Please. Just please, Arthur. Just say 'okay.' "

As Jennifer stared into my eyes, longing for relief from the hell I had helped Righteous Christ put her through, my mind raced.

Everything is spinning. Morals I once saw as universal laws have been turned on their heads. Up is down, and wrong is right. Is there a chance there's more to learn here? Maybe I should take a beat and give my friends the benefit of the doubt when they tell me they're in pain…

I looked at Jennifer's tear-covered face for a few seconds before saying, "Okay."

Jennifer smiled. "Thank you."

"I'm gonna go walk through the Hell House now," I said. "I think you should get out of here."

"Thanks, Arthur. Good luck."

Outside, a line of people waited to enter the Hell House. I spotted Ella, Rachel, and Benny about halfway down. As a cast member on break, I could cut the line and head right in.

I pushed the heavy black curtain out of the way as I entered the dark, smoke-filled room. The ominous music I had grown quite accustomed to sounded exactly the same from the entryway.

The first scene took place in a very low-budget recreation of a doctor's office. A teenage girl with pillows under her shirt sat on the examination table, and a boy stood next to her. A doctor faced them.

"God loves our baby," said the boy, placing his hand on his wife's pillow-filled stomach. "I beg you to reconsider, Martha."

"I have too much left I want to do," said Martha. "The baby is just gonna get in the way."

The boy continued. "God has a plan for this baby. Do you really wanna get in the way of God's plan? If you really wanted to avoid this, you shouldn't have seduced me…"

I walked around the bend to the next scene, in which there were no actors. A cardboard cutout resembling a car was positioned next to a tree, with a mannequin made to resemble Martha stuck between them.

The first batch of demonic torture differed from my section. There was only one demon, using a pitchfork to scratch the back of a girl with hair and clothes identical to the girl playing Martha in the doctor scene.

The demon screeched and shouted. "This is your own fault, you slut! God had a plan for that baby and you spat in His face!"

The tableau churned my stomach. Nothing about any of it lined up with the God of love I thought I knew.

Around the final bend, there was my station. The lighting was extremely dark, and whoever was playing my second-shift equivalent had a very similar body type to me. The human currently being tortured resembled Andrew from a distance as well.

The euphoric experience created by the atmosphere prevented me from seeing the two actors in front of me. Instead, I saw myself standing above the helpless Andrew, whipping his bloody back while he begged for mercy.

"Bow to your God!" I saw myself scream.

I watched myself kneel on his neck, hunch down and whisper in his ear, "This… is God's love. This is what is good. This is what you deserve."

I sprinted to the exit, knocking over a light in the process. I flung the black curtain out of my way and ran past the dozens of people crying with pastors in the heavenly conversion room.

Outside, I made a beeline straight to the Hell House entrance.

"Rachel!" I screamed. "Benny! Ella!"

My friends turned around just as they were about to enter.

I bent over, catching my breath. "Don't… go in there."

"What the heck?" said Benny, as they all stepped out of the line. "You okay, buddy?"

"I'm… good. Yeah… yeah. I'm good. I think I got some things very, very wrong. I don't know exactly what, or how… but I wanna make things right, whatever that means. From here on out, your happiness makes me happy. I'm so sorry for my behavior."

"Heyyy, heyyy," said Ella, placing her hand on my shoulder. "It's okay. I forgive you."

Benny and Rachel joined in for a group hug.

"I've never seen this side of you, Arthur," said Rachel. "I like it."

"I missed you, Art," said Benny.

"Me too, me too," I said. "But yeah, don't go in there. It's not what any of you need right now. Let's just finish out the year and bid this place good riddance."

"Hear, hear," said Rachel.

Our group hug stumbled out of the gym.

"Ya know what?" I said. "Maybe I will go to Georgia Art for college, after all. Screw Shield and Sword U."

"That's what I'm talkin' about!" said Benny, squeezing my shoulder.

As we opened the youth building's front door, we heard voices.

"Get the hell away from me!" said Samuel, pushing away Pastor Marshall.

"Jeez, okay, okay. I'm going." Marshall walked back to the building. "Be glad I'm not calling the cops, you drunk fool!"

Benny jogged over to Samuel, and we followed behind. "Hey, buddy! What's goin' on?"

"No!" screamed Samuel, pointing at Benny. "Not you! This is all your fault!"

"Hey, hey, hey, hey," Benny said softly. "What happened?"

"I… shouldn't…"

"Samuel," said Benny, "I want to help you, but I can't unless you tell me what's going on. Do you think you can do that?"

Samuel collapsed to the ground, leaning against a pole. "I… can you just… not look at me while I say this?"

Benny looked to the side.

"Okay… I told my dad that I've been having… thoughts. G-gay thoughts. And they only ever started because of… you…"

Samuel's eyes welled up.

Benny looked at him, kneeled down, and placed his hand in his.

"Hey. That is extremely flattering. Any man would be honored to have you."

"No… don't say that. My dad says he's gonna send me away to the army if I can't get my urges under control. Also, I really don't wanna go to… it sounds so silly…" Samuel made brief eye contact with me, and then looked away. "I don't wanna go to Hell…"

I wiped some demon makeup off my face, as if it would erase the part I played in the Hell House.

Samuel looked toward the three of us standing behind Benny. "What are you staring at, losers?"

"Nothing, Sam," said Rachel, approaching him. "It really hurts me to see you like this." She sat down next to him. "Your dad really hurt us both. I promise… I just want you to be happy."

Ella stepped forward, too. "Yeah… you are kind of the worst. But given who your dad is, it's a miracle you didn't turn out way worse."

Sam wiped his nose with the top of his hand and looked directly at me. "And what about you, brown-noser? What do you think of my dad?"

"What do I think?"

I thought for a moment while looking at my friends, all of whom had been severely hurt by one man who claimed to be a messenger of the god of love. They looked at me, longing for support, and smiling with cautious optimism.

I smiled. "I think… fuck Pastor Robbie."

"Oooh hoo hooo!" howled Benny. "My BOY with the f-bomb!"

Ella guffawed. "Yes, Arthur! I fucking love that!"

Rachel whooped and clapped with enthusiasm.

Samuel stood up and walked over to me, and the rest of the gang joined us.

"Fuck Pastor Robbieeeee!" screamed Samuel at the moon.

We all screamed, "Fuck Pastor Robbie!"

We laughed intensely as a massive weight lifted from my chest.

"So…" said Rachel. "What are we gonna do about him?"

"I've been working on something," said Ella. "But I'm gonna need some help."

"Count me in," said Benny.

Samuel nodded.

I smiled. "Let's burn his reputation to the ground."

15. Animals

With my friendships back to normal and the Righteous Christ chapter of my life on its way out, I found it much easier to enjoy simple hobbies such as video games. In other words, the low effort "it's basically over" state of mind called senioritis had set in.

"The shotgun AGAIN?!" whined Benny as an enemy player killed him in an online match of *Halo 3*.

"You just ain't good enough, I guess," I said.

A knock came from my bedroom door as it creaked open. "Arthur, honey," said my mom. "Can I talk to you for a sec?"

"Can't right now, Mom."

She put her hands on her hips. "Can't you just save your game?"

"It's online, Mom. Can't save. Can't pause."

"Okay, well, can you please come downstairs to talk when you can?"

"Yeah, yeah. Fine."

My relationship with my mom still hadn't fully mended since the porn fiasco, but at least she gave me my privileges back. I'd been avoiding direct interaction with her whenever possible, as I worried that if she suspected I'd been doubting the teachings of Righteous Christ, she'd have a meltdown like when she found my porn.

After the match, I told Benny I'd be right back, and hopped downstairs.

"What is it?" I asked my mom, who was cooking us baked mac and cheese in the kitchen.

She turned toward me. "So… I got a concerning email from one mom at RCA. Do you know something about a Hell Run?"

"The Hell House?" I sat down at the kitchen table. "Yeah, I acted in it."

"I thought I heard you mention that before. I'm hearing some VERY disturbing things, Arthur. That people would go through it and be so disturbed they'd come out crying? And the pastors would then use that as an opportunity to evangelize to them?"

"Yeah, that's pretty accurate. I'm kind of surprised you're concerned about that. I was actually pretty disturbed by what I saw there, too."

"Oh, honey." She sat down next to me and put her hand on my arm. "I'm so relieved to hear that. I always knew you had a good head on your shoulders."

Hmm. Maybe she's less gung ho about Christianity than I thought… Maybe I can trust her.

"Can I tell you something?" I asked.

"Of course."

"I wasn't planning on telling you this, but… I don't even know if I believe what RCA teaches anymore."

"Honey. I wasn't gonna tell you this either… but neither do I. I haven't for a while. Don't get me wrong… RCA, and particularly a few pastors there, have been incredibly helpful to you and our family. We wouldn't have been able to cover your tuition if it weren't for their generosity. But some of the stuff I've heard come out of their mouths over the years… I can't even repeat."

"Wait, but I overheard you on the phone. You were worried that if RCA didn't get their act together, we'd start to drift away from God."

"Ha! Oh, honey, no. Madeline and I were having a laugh about how backward we think some of their teachings are. If you or the other students drift away, well… maybe that's for the best."

"Oh, okay," I said. "That's a relief."

"I am sorry, by the way. About my reaction to finding your porn. I still find it repulsive, but I think Righteous Christ may have colored my perception a little bit."

"Oh, wow. Thanks." I flashed a smile. "And yeah, I think there's a lot of darkness in how they teach purity culture. My friends helped me see that recently."

She smiled, and her eyes darted across my face with compassion. "I had a feeling you'd pick up on that darkness eventually."

"Yeah…"

"Did I ever tell you the story of the first time I met you after I gave birth?"

"Yes, many—"

"You looked me right in the eyes with such seriousness. No baby had ever looked at me like that, and in that moment, I knew… this one's a thinker."

"Yeah, I know…"

She smiled. "I'm very proud of the man you've become."

"Thanks, Mom."

*   *   *

The energy in the theater on the night of the *Eden* dress rehearsal resembled when you order a fast-food cheeseburger based on the menu photo. It's not a bad burger for two bucks… but it's a far cry from what you thought you signed up for. RCA had drained *Eden* of its magic, but the adrenaline that pumps through a theater nerd when the production finally comes together was in full force, nonetheless.

Ms. Flannigan directed the massive group with as much precision as any RCA show she had helmed. "Look alive, people! Thirty minutes until showtime!"

The cast and crew hustled across the stage and through the dressing rooms. Stage managers spoke aggressively into headsets while they fiddled with electronics hooked to their black pants. Sets were wheeled on and off the stage as lighting artists bathed the once-blank slab of concrete with life.

"You wanna get a selfie?" I asked Andrew, showing off my shiny green snake costume with some flowing hand gestures.

"Yeah… sure."

Andrew, dressed like a creepy bipedal horse, still seemed a little sour from my overacting in the Hell House.

I held out the disposable camera and snapped a photo while we smiled. There was no way to know how it turned out until I got them developed at the photo store later. Afterward, he sat next to Jade Parnacle in the theater, who promptly twirled her black hair with her fingers.

I spent the next few minutes of downtime pacing around the theater, taking a gander at all the costumes, and getting selfies with various friends.

"Ella! Benny! Rachel! We gotta get one!"

I jogged over to my friends, who sat in the orchestra section in full costume.

"You know we do, brother," said Benny, standing up and waltzing over in a flowing white robe with a gold sash.

"Ugh," said Ella the raccoon, as Rachel the giraffe dragged her over by the hand.

"Cheese!" I said. I could tell it was a good one as I pressed the button. "Our last show… hard to believe."

"And their first show!" said Benny, gesturing at Ella and Rachel.

"Kill me now," said Ella, sitting back down.

"Oh my God," said Rachel, "you are such an Eeyore! It's gonna be so fun." She sat next to Ella and tickled her side.

"Stop… hehehe… stop that! You know I can't… ahhhh… handle tickles there!"

Benny and I sat in the row in front of them. Other than us, and various cast and crew members dilly dallying, students and faculty filled a few random theater seats. Toward the back, Pastor Robbie entered and sat down, looking stern. The energy in the room lessened as the four of us noted his presence.

Rachel noticed him soon after me. "Ugh. Way to kill the vibe, asshole."

"Okay," said Ella, "so I was at my locker today and I heard some kids talking about Samuel. I think word's going around that he's… ya know. Let's say… super over Rachel."

Rachel scrunched her face into a smile and stuck her tongue out at Ella.

"Damn…" said Benny. "You think he's doing okay?"

I looked at the stage where Samuel, covered with leafy garments along with Jade, rehearsed one of their scenes.

"I think he's lucky this is such a busy week," I said. "Hopefully he's staying distracted."

"Yeah…" said Rachel. "I hope so."

She looked toward the distant Robbie and raised her middle finger below her waist, low enough that nobody of note could see. Then she looked at Ella.

"So, how's the Fuck Pastor Robbie plan coming along?"

"Shh!" said Ella. "It's coming. I'll have it ready for graduation."

"Niiiice," said Benny.

Mr. Crumbull then walked by us, as if out of nowhere. "Howdy, kids," he said as he continued by.

We simply smiled and nodded.

I felt a little guilty, knowing how much time I had spent thinking he was a criminal.

"So," I said. "How are you feeling, Rachel? Been back a few weeks now. Everything back to normal?"

"Ugh. Not exactly. School is mostly fine, and Robbie has kept his distance. I assume he knows I was the one who leaked everything, but so far, no issues."

"That's good," I said.

"Yeah. My parents have basically disowned me, though. I've been grounded this whole time. And I think they're coming to the show tomorrow… just to make sure I don't embarrass them even more."

Benny plopped into the seat next to her and gave her a squeeze. "Well, we're all so happy you're back. Screw your parents. They don't deserve you."

"Thanks, Benny," said Rachel, leaning into the hug.

"Okay, everyone!" said Ms. Flannigan over the sound system. "We're starting in five minutes, so let's have a quick huddle at the stage."

The cast and crew who weren't sitting near us already soon joined.

Ms. Flannigan took a seat at the front of the stage. She turned her mic off so those toward the back of the theater, including you know who, couldn't hear, which made me chuckle.

She sat there silently for a few seconds, looking at us while smiling.

She cleared her throat. "I know this goes without saying, but… this show isn't exactly what I promised you all. But even so… I am so proud of what each one of you has accomplished. I want you to give this show your all tonight and tomorrow, and I want you to have fun! That's why we're here."

"Woo!" shouted a cast member.

A few more cast and crew clapped.

"It's been the pleasure of my life to help each one of you find your inner artist. I wish I could keep doing that for years to come, but due to… some reasons… I won't be able to continue working at Righteous Christ Academy after this year."

Whispers filled the crowd. "No!" said a few students. We seniors wouldn't be missing out on any quality time with Ms. Flannigan, but it was still surprising to hear.

I looked back at Pastor Robbie, wondering if he had fired her. He remained stoic.

"I wanted to tell you this tonight so that it wouldn't be on your mind during the show tomorrow. I'm repeating myself now, but I really love you kids, and if I've impacted your lives in any tiny way, then I have no regrets. It's a big, big universe out there. I hope you all spread your wings and experience its adventure and its love."

"We love you, Ms. Flannigan!" shouted Benny.

The entire crowd echoed his words and applauded. A few stood up and ran up to the stage to hug her. Most of the rest of us soon joined in, turning it into the biggest group hug of my life. I ignored the sensory overload and soaked up the bittersweet feels.

The dress rehearsal went about as well as I expected. It was a mostly functional performance, give or take a few technical hiccups and scene restarts. I missed a few notes in my song, but I had the next night to nail it since I was by then accustomed to hearing my voice through the theater speakers.

All things considered, we had fun that night. It wasn't the explosion of progressive passion Ms. Flannigan set out to make; in fact, the show was quite bland, and a little bad. But it still had a few infectious songs, and was an excuse to tap into our hammy sides on a giant stage with our close friends, and that was always a win.

*   *   *

The day of *Eden's* performance wasn't my most diligent school day. I practiced my song in my mind frequently, to the dismay of my teachers.

I did, however, wrap up my robot animation in my independent study. Simple as it was, seeing my creation come to life was a cathartic experience.

After Mr. Snirdley left our daily check-in, I smirked. I opened a file I hadn't worked on in a while: the "satanic" gundam. Using the experience I gained through the independent study, I beefed up the model, and even added some metallic surface detail.

Perfection, I thought.

The hour leading to *Eden* was similar to the dress rehearsal in many ways. We wore the same costumes. We prepared to perform the same show. Ms. Flannigan barked similar orders. But pacing around backstage while you can hear hundreds of audience members filing into the theater, ready to judge every move that we'd make… that's some anxiety.

Ella, Benny, Rachel, and I huddled up.

"Y'all ready for this?" asked Benny.

"Yeah," said Ella. "What the hell. Let's make a memory."

"That's what I'm talkin' about!" said Rachel.

I smiled, and we all high fived each other.

Over the theater speakers, we heard that unmistakable rising hum of an orchestra preparing to deliver a spectacle to an audience.

"Places, everyone!" said Ms. Flannigan. "Break a leg!"

We took our places onstage for the opening number, and prepared for the curtain to rise, but instead, we heard a strange noise.

Thump, thump went a hand on a microphone.

"This thing on? Okay, there we go. Greetings… disciples of Jesus Christ."

Despite standing behind a curtain in almost total darkness, we all recognized the voice booming around the theater. Pastor Robbie was introducing the show he basically destroyed. I couldn't see their faces very well, but I could just feel that my friends and I were exchanging furious glances.

"Thank you all for being here tonight to celebrate the amazing God-given talents the wonderful RCA teachers have stoked in our amazing children. You'll laugh, you'll cry, and maybe you'll leave feeling a little closer to God than you did before. But before that, I wanted to address some concerns so many of you parents have reached out to me and my colleagues about recently. It seems that because of a select few weeds in our garden, the Devil's wickedness has been… running a bit more rampant than usual lately. There have been some unpleasant rumors circling about myself and the Righteous Christ staff, spread by students who intend to divide our spiritual family. But it won't work. Some of these heretics have also been spreading sympathy for the mental illness known as homosexuality."

My eyes had adjusted to the darkness a little by then. I could just barely see Samuel staring at the ground, tapping his foot rapidly. Benny walked over and put a hand on his shoulder.

"I believe God has blessed some of us with the test of raising children who have developed these tendencies. I believe that, in the end, helping our children overcome these struggles will strengthen us. We must be vigilant. The Lord may allow Satan to infiltrate our borders for the sake of strengthening our resolve, but it's a narrow tightrope, my friends. They may say we hate them, but we know better. We don't hate anyone. We love the sinner. We simply hate the sin."

I tensed as Robbie spoke that harmful phrase I had used many times prior. Rage entirely replaced my stage fright.

"The show you are about to watch, dear congregation, is a lesson about obedience. As we at RCA crack down on the delinquents that threaten our community, we must remember we can do all things through Christ Jesus, who strengthens us. Now, please enjoy… *Eden.*"

As the curtain parted and the stage lights illuminated us in emulated sunshine, my friends and I exchanged glances. I could tell we were all thinking the same thing: *How are we supposed to perform when we're this mad?*

Rachel, in particular, was scowling hard.

Brummppp!

Trumpets heralded the start of the show. Then came the flutes. Soon, we all flowed across the stage to *Eden's* catchy orchestrations, which remained safe from Robbie's editing mandates.

Contorting my upper body, I slithered through the garden animals that spread out according to Ms. Flannigan's precise choreography. Spotlights spiraled around, giving the show its distinct rock opera vibe.

"In the garden, one perfect garden," we sang. "No hate, no misery. In the garden, the lush, lush garden. There was but one forbidden tree."

Was it always this corny? I wondered.

Before long, the ensemble introductory song hit its final notes, and the lights dropped. The audience applauded moderately.

Watching the show unfold from the wings of the stage was always a fun experience, teasing the edge of the wing curtains to the very limit, or else the audience might see us waiting for our scenes to arrive.

"From your rib," said Benny as God in a scene with Samuel's Adam, "I shall create for you a perfect companion. Treat her with love and respect, and lead her toward wisdom, for she is unlikely to find it on her own." He struggled to get those words out without breaking character.

Ella and Rachel rolled their eyes backstage in perfect unison.

Soon it was time for my solo, and it went… okay.

"Hissss… There's more to life than God's love," I sang.

The recently changed lyrics rang very hollow. I still missed a few notes and felt like a failure as I exited stage right.

"That was SO good," said Benny. "I'm so proud of you."

I smiled. "Thanks, bud."

In what felt like the blink of an eye, we were all back on stage for the finale. Benny and I stood at the back, and Ella and Rachel huddled together by a prop tree sitting stage left. They giggled and whispered to each other, clearly VERY over all of it.

"And thus," said Benny in his commanding God voice, "I cast them out of Eden, for they were no longer worthy."

"I'm going to miss this place," said Jade Parnacle as Eve.

"We had some good times," said Samuel as Adam.

One of the biggest changes to the script was the removal of the kiss between Adam and Eve in the finale. It left in its place a bizarre dance number where garden animals, in pairs of two, filtered toward the front of the stage and then split toward the sides.

As animals began flowing across the stage, I people-watched the audience. I thought I spotted my mom, but it was hard to tell.

A moment later, I saw Pastor Robbie sitting in the front row, arms folded. It made the entire experience feel so surreal, and a bit meaningless.

As the music crescendoed, Ella and Rachel looked directly at me and Benny and smiled. Rachel even winked at me.

What are they up to?

They clasped hands and ran along their choreographed path toward the front of the stage. Instead of splitting apart like the rest of the animals, they stopped right at the front of the stage and faced each other.

Rachel used her upstage arm to grab Ella's face, and Ella used her downstage arm to grab Rachel's thigh, pulling her leg to her as it bent. Ella dipped Rachel down and laid on her the biggest smooch I had ever seen in my short life.

The audience erupted into a sea of gasps and conversations. A few of them instantly stood and stormed to the exit.

I leaned over to Benny and whispered, "Now that's some serious PDA."

Benny laughed and clapped. I joined in, as did one or two other cast members, and a few audience members.

"Hell yeah!" yelled Samuel. "Get some, Rach!"

Jade folded her arms and stomped offstage, furious that her performance of Eve had been upstaged.

I looked at Pastor Robbie. His face reminded me of Willem Dafoe playing The Green Goblin from *Spider-Man,* with his angled brows, wide-open eyes, grinding teeth, and gripped fists. He stood up, stomped up the stage stairs, and up to Ella and Rachel, who were still putting on a show.

As he stormed up to them, he screamed, "You harlots! What is wrong with you?! How dare you desecrate the house of God with your FILTH?!"

They released each other and sprinted into the wings of the stage while both giving Robbie the middle finger.

Benny and I looked at each other and burst into laughter.

Pastor Robbie grabbed the microphone from the side of the stage. As the curtain closed, he brushed his hair out of his face and yelled, "This show is over! We will deal with this sinful behavior swiftly; you have my word."

Benny and I jogged into the wings and found Ella and Rachel laughing hysterically in their dressing room.

"You two are a RIOT!" said Benny.

"That was kind of awesome," I said. "Aren't you worried you're gonna get kicked out of school?"

Ella shook her head. "There's only a few weeks left, Art. I'd like to see them try."

"Ha ha. I guess."

"Sooo," said Benny. "How was Ella's kissing, Rach?"

Ella groaned. "Oh my God…"

Rachel twirled her hair with her finger. "Umm, it was like… super hot. Can't say I'm surprised, though."

"Yeah," said Ella. "It was, wasn't it?"

Pastor Robbie's voice echoed down the backstage hallway. "I think they went this way. Out of my way."

"Shit!" said Ella. "Let's sneak out the back before he finds us."

Ella and Rachel grabbed some green cloaks from a costume rack and threw them over their heads. As Pastor Robbie and two other youth pastors entered the dressing room corridor, we slipped out the stage door.

"That was close!" said Benny. "And now we need to celebrate."

My eyes widened. "I'll drive us to Chili's? We can eat queso and talk details about… Operation Fuck Pas—" I leaned in and whispered, "Operation FPR."

Rachel threw her hands in the air. "Fucking perfect."

16. Seniors Trippin'

Benny and I speed-walked down the hall and into the waiting area outside the offices of the RCA higher-ups. Ella and Rachel sat on chairs outside of Principal Randall's office, staring so intently at nothing in particular they didn't even notice us walking up to them.

"Hey," I said. "Andrew told us you two got called to the principal's office in the middle of Spanish class?"

"Accurate," said Ella, as I sat down next to her.

Benny tiptoed over to the office and peeked in. Muffled voices could be heard, and not of a friendly tone.

"Benny, what are you doing?" asked Rachel.

"Mr. Bertrand, please stay seated or see yourself out." The receptionist wasn't playing around.

Benny sat down with us. "So, I have some intel. Mr. Crumbull is in there, of all people. They're in the middle of a pretty heated argument, by the looks of it."

"No shit," said Ella.

"Miss Kent!" said the receptionist. "I do NOT think you're in a position to be pushing your chances of finishing the year any further."

"Yeah, whatever." Ella leaned toward us and lowered her voice a smidge. "They've been in there for like ten minutes."

"Why Mr. Crumbull?" I asked.

"I have no idea," said Rachel.

After another minute or so, the door opened. Mr. Crumbull exited the office, leaving the door open, and walked up to Rachel and Ella.

"Everything's going to be okay," he said in an indoor voice. "Just… please don't push him any further."

"Uh… okay," said Rachel.

Ella's eyes followed him out of the room. "What the hell…"

Principal Randall stood up at his desk in his office. "Miss Kent, Miss Bristol. Please join me, and shut the door behind you." He turned his eyes toward Benny and I. "This doesn't concern the rest of you, kay?"

Rachel entered the principal's office, followed by Ella, who shut the door almost all the way. She made eye contact with us through the crack as she turned around and joined Rachel in the two chairs facing Principal Randall.

"You two," we could hear Principal Randall say through the cracked-open door. "What did we ever do to you to deserve this humiliation?"

Rachel and Ella remained silent.

He continued, "You know, we have seriously been considering expelling both of you, regardless of how soon you graduate. Rachel, I'm especially disappointed in you. You used to show so much promise, and now you gallivant around with this…"

Rachel sat upright. "I really—"

"Ya know what? Let's keep this short. I don't know why he bothered defending you two, but Mr. Crumbull made a compelling argument for why there's no way to end your enrollment at RCA, so close to graduation, without it turning into a PR issue even worse than that awful kiss of yours. So, once you graduate, we will bid you good riddance, and sincerely hope someone else can share God's good news with you in a way that clicks, because we sure failed."

"Gee, thanks," said Ella.

"Yeah…" said Rachel. "Thank you."

"Now get the heck outta here. Please."

Rachel and Ella exited the office, and we all swiftly walked to the hall.

"Well," said Benny. "I say we take that as a win."

Rachel blew air out of her mouth in relief. "Yeah… I really thought we were done for."

"Yeah," said Ella. "I guess we owe Mr. Crumbull a thank you."

"More like Mr. Stays-in-one-piece," I said.

Nobody laughed.

*   *   *

"I just don't understand why I need any new clothes for this," I said. "It's all gonna be hidden under the graduation gown, anyway."

Benny picked up a pair of navy dress shoes with brown leather accents from the department store's shoe rack. "Arthur, my boy, we are going out in style, whether you like it or not. Now, try these bad boys on."

I put the shoes on and took a few steps. "So, how do they look?"

Benny clapped, slowly. "Uh. May. Zing."

"Yeah?" I said. "Well, they feel awful."

"Oh my god, Arthur. That's like the fifth pair! You're so goddamn picky!"

I shrugged, not even noticing that Benny took God's name in vain.

"Well," said Benny. "You get whatever you want. You KNOW which pair I'm getting."

He jiggled a pair of bombastically blue sequined dress shoes in front of him.

"They sure are something," I said.

We got in line to check out. Benny carried the shoes and a pink dress shirt, and I carried nothing, because clothes shopping is hard!

On the shelf next to us sat a plethora of gifts and knick-knacks, from pins to mugs to candy.

I picked up a mug with the text "I Graduated!"

Benny sighed. "It's crazy how fast we got here, huh?"

"Yeah," I said.

Benny picked up a rainbow pin from the shelf. "Just a little while longer, and we're home free. We can live how we want, be who we want, and love who we want."

I looked at the rainbow in his hand. Thanks to eighteen years of conditioning, my gut reaction was to show disapproval, but the pain in Benny's eyes reminded me I could do better. I felt my heart sink, overcome with regret. Benny was living a lie, and I had played a small role in that oppression, at least.

"I'm so sorry, Benny… I feel so awful that I made you feel like you couldn't be yourself."

Benny placed the pin back on the shelf and turned toward me. "Hey. No. Don't do that."

"But I—"

"No," continued Benny, placing a hand on my shoulder. "Listen to me, Arthur. You are not a bad person. None of us can control what situations we're born into, and by what we are influenced. We're barely adults here. We're all just doing our best to be good people, and right now, your best is to recognize where you can improve… and that's exactly what you've done. It's all just baby steps. I forgive you, completely."

I wiped a tear from my eye. "I-I mean… thanks."

Benny smiled.

"Ya know," I said. "I don't think you have to wait any longer to live your life without shame." I picked up the rainbow pin from the shelf and handed it to Benny. "Just start now."

Benny looked at the pin and smiled. "Arthur… I can't believe you, of all people, are suggesting I stick it to the man. Aren't you afraid I'll get expelled?"

"Nah… if Ella and Rachel can get away with kissing on stage, I think you can afford to show some pride. I'm pretty sure you can't get expelled during graduation, anyway. Plus, it's just a baby step."

Benny smiled. "Thanks, Art."

I broke eye contact, opened my arms, and gently beckoned with my hands.

Benny gasped. "No. Way. For real?"

I sighed and nodded.

Benny hugged me. "I'm proud of you."

I squeezed him back. "Thanks, bud."

Benny grabbed a second rainbow pin off the shelf. "Ya know, I think there's one more heretic who will join me."

*   *   *

Throughout my years at Righteous Christ Academy, I never attended any class trips. Generally, it was because my parents couldn't afford the costs. Most of RCA's end of the year excursions had been mission trips, where students would travel to an impoverished area, usually in Mexico or the Bahamas, to share the word of God with those who likely hadn't heard it. Often it would coincide with some sort of minor construction project. Conveniently, the vibe those trips usually struck was never in my comfort zone. Talking to strangers and hard labor were never my forte, so I rarely felt like I missed much.

For senior year, the chosen trip was far more leisure-focused, which I was VERY okay with. We'd head to a quaint, beachside hotel an hour outside of town, and just chill. Even Ella and Rachel were excited for the trip, having had a few weeks to distance themselves from the targets painted on their backs by principals, pastors, and most teachers.

We sat together on the bus ride, playing games like Twenty Questions, and that one where you draw a spiral on paper and learn who you're going to marry. Ella would marry Jade Parnacle, apparently, much to Rachel's dismay.

The hotel was very cute. The paneling on the building was all white, with just a hint of erosion around the corners. The sound of seagulls and waves crashing cascaded over us, washing away the stresses of the year from Hell, which was finally almost entirely behind us.

After dropping our belongings off in our rooms, we ate a delicious buffet lunch together. The French fries were particularly tasty, and Rachel couldn't get over the hibiscus agua fresca.

"Okay, everyone," said Mr. Crumbull, sporting a tie dye tank top and white swim trunks. "When you're finished eating, head out to the beach and split yourselves into teams of six for beach volleyball. It's tournament style, and the winning team gets this basket of goodies to take to your rooms tonight. See you on the court!"

"Ugh, I hate making our own teams," I said.

"Nonsense, my dude," said Benny. "You've got us."

Rachel rubbed my back as she headed to the white double doors with Ella. "Yeah, come on Artie! We gotta win that basket!"

"You guys are the best. Let's do it."

As the first game played out, I gathered on the sand with Benny, Ella, Rachel, and our newest team member, Andrew.

"We still need a sixth," said Rachel.

Benny stood on his tiptoes and looked around. "I… don't see anyone by themselves. Maybe we have an odd number of people on the trip?"

"I think I know who to ask," said Ella.

She walked through the sand toward the chaperones, and we followed.

"Hey, Mr. Crumbull," she said. "We need a sixth teammate. You game?"

Two of the chaperones crossed their arms and furrowed their brows. Mr. Crumbull blushed and placed his hand on his heart.

"Why, Miss Kent, I would be delighted."

Our team of six made our way back to the courts and waited our turn.

Ella folded her arms and tilted her head toward Mr. Crumbull, playfully. "So, Mr. Dress Code Police. Why are you the only one who doesn't hate me and Rachel right now, huh?"

"Heh," chuckled Mr. Crumbull while twiddling his fingers. "I guess I just don't always agree with everything that… I mean, sometimes Pastor Robbie and Principal Randall, they…"

We stared intently as he stumbled over his words.

"I love my job, and I will always strive to do what is asked of me within that, whether it be enforcing the dress code or teaching approved curriculum. But my primary job description is to make sure the kids I teach leave me better than they arrived. And sometimes ya need to stick it to the man to get that done."

"Right on," said Benny.

"Ya know," continued Mr. Crumbull, getting quite expressive with his hands. "My parents raised me to believe God is love. It's as simple as that. It's why I'm a Christian to this day. And when someone like Pastor Robbie treats MY kids with such hatred? Naw. Not a chance in heck I'm gonna stand by and let him beat the love outta ya."

He pointed at the sky with force. "It's love that I work for. Not that walking pile of mung beans they call a preacher. And if that gets me fired someday, so be it."

Ella smiled. "Thank you, Mr. Crumbull. You're alright."

"Aww," he said. "I try."

To nobody's surprise, we lost our volleyball match to a team of football players, but we went down swinging. I did score one point, and it felt really good.

After dinner, a few of us played some card games in the lobby before bed. Wiped from the day, I headed to my room early, brushed my teeth, and conked the hell out.

BRRRINNGGGG!!! BRRRINNGGGG!!! BRRRINNGGGG!!!

I rubbed my eyes and covered my ears while trying to make out the "1:13 a.m." on the clock in the dark room. I could hear a loud commotion down the hall—the entire senior class was exiting the building because of the fire alarm.

"Is there actually a fire?" I asked Andrew as we walked to the stairwell in our sleepwear.

He shrugged.

We gathered in the parking lot as the alarm continued to blare. There was no sign of fire or smoke anywhere.

I overheard some classmates gossiping.

"I heard Jimmy say Greg Couch pulled the alarm!" said one.

"No, no!" said another. "I'm pretty sure it was Kathy B!"

I rolled my eyes and then rubbed them.

Ella and Rachel approached me, still in their day clothes. Clearly, I was the old man of the group. Benny soon joined us, wearing gym shorts and a t-shirt, and full of energy.

After some aimless chatting, Benny's eyes lit up. "Wait a second. I think it's time… for night beach."

"Ugh," I groaned. "I'm so tired."

Rachel stood in front of me and placed her hands on my shoulders. "Arthur. In fifty years when you're old and wrinkly, are you really gonna regret not getting a few extra hours of sleep here and there, or are you gonna wish you made amazing night beach memories with us? I mean, we only have a week left before we might never see each other again!"

"But you don't understand. If I don't sleep enough, I'm gonna feel like there's ants crawling all over me. It's awful."

"No excuses!" said Benny, spinning around and leading the charge toward the sound of crashing waves.

I followed, reluctantly.

We found a nice clean slab of sand near the shoreline and plopped ourselves down.

I started to complain. "I really hate san—"

"WE KNOW," said Ella. "Just be in the moment, Arthur. Look at that sky and listen to the waves. It's magic."

Ella reached into her jacket pocket and took out a rolled joint and a lighter. She took a huge hit.

"Lemme get some of that," said Benny, taking the next hit. "One more, one more… oh yeah…"

Rachel was next. The way she held it in her hand looked surprisingly classy. After three small puffs, she looked in my direction and held out the joint.

"No, thanks," I said. "In fact, I think the alarm stopped. Maybe we should head back."

Rachel didn't budge and nudged her hand up.

"Try everything twice, Arthur," said Benny.

"Is it… hot to the touch?" I asked.

"No," said Rachel. "Just don't touch the tip."

I exhaled. "Alright… just a little."

I daintily grasped the joint between my thumb and index finger, examining it with great trepidation. I put it to my lips and breathed in.

"Did I do it right? My throat feels hot, and it tastes so bad." I breathed in again. "Hmm."

"I don't think you got it," said Ella. "You gotta breathe really deep, or it's just gonna sit in your throat."

I placed the joint further into my mouth and took the deepest inhalation I could muster. It lasted a full four seconds. A few seconds later, I started coughing profusely.

Rachel tapped me on the back a few times. "Atta boy. You got it."

"Well done, my boy," said Benny.

Ella nodded and smiled as I handed her the joint.

"So… how long does it take to start feeling it?" I asked.

"Not long," said Ella.

We all laid down on our backs. Above us, the night sky was impressively clear. The waves crashing, the majesty of the stars… that moment would stick with me.

I smiled. "Heh heh… heh heh. I think… I'm starting to feel it."

The others chuckled.

I laughed. "I feel like there's fishhooks on both sides of my mouth, pulling upwards. It's like inverse gravity. I can't not smile!"

"Ugh, I love this," said Rachel.

"Same," said Benny.

Rachel sighed. "Ya know, despite everything that's happened... I don't think I'd take any of it back. Will I send my kids to Christian school? And do I want anyone else to go through what I went through? No fucking way. But still... without finding myself here, I wouldn't have met y'all, and there's no one else I would've rather gone through hell with. We survived Righteous Christ Academy... together."

"We should get shirts made," said Ella.

"I love you guys," I said. "Heh heh... heh heh."

"I love you all, too!" said Benny, turning our high sky gazing session into a cuddle party.

"Hey, Artie," said Ella. "Look who's coming."

I looked back at the hotel to see Jennifer walking toward us.

"Shut up!" I whispered.

"Hey, guys!" said Jennifer, wearing blue *Sailor Moon* pajamas. "What's goin' on over here?"

"Definitely not getting super high," I said, loudly.

"Oh, ho hoooo!" said Jennifer. "Can I get a hit?"

"Totally," said Ella, lighting a second joint.

Jennifer inhaled. "Thanks, girl."

"UUUUOOOAAAAHHH," yawned Benny, performatively. "Boy, I sure am tired. I think it's time for bed!"

Rachel stood up. "Yeah, I'm beat! Have fun, you two!"

Ella stood up, too.

Jennifer put her hands on her hips. "Oh, okay, I see how it is. See y'all later!"

Benny, Rachel, and Ella left us alone.

Jennifer craned her neck down toward my horizontal body. "Mind if I join you way down there?"

"Please do," I said.

She laid down next to me. "Wow, look at the sky! It's so clear!"

"Yeah, I know! How many stars would you guess we're looking at right now?"

"Oh, I don't have to guess; I already know. There's about ten thousand stars visible in the night sky, but when you think about the ones whose light doesn't make it to us... it's over a hundred billion."

My jaw dropped. "Wha... a hundred... billion?? That's like... so many stars!"

She laughed. "Yeah, it is."

"Do you think there's aliens out there?" I asked.

"Oh, definitely," said Jennifer. "Probably tons."

"I hope we find them before we die."

"Me too."

I took in the night sky and the high without speaking for a while. I thought about how different I was, compared to less than a year ago.

Getting high on a beach with my crush at night after basically writing off my school and church? Utterly insane. Who am I anymore? What do I even believe?

"Hey," I said. "What do you think happens when we die?"

"Hmm... I don't know, Arthur. It scares me sometimes."

"Yeah… I've never had to worry about it before. Maybe a heaven still exists… but I wonder how we'd get in."

"Well," said Jennifer, "if it's full of people like Pastor Robbie, I'll be happy to not be invited."

"Ha ha… true."

"Hey, sit up for a second."

I grunted as I sat up.

"There's this one idea in Buddhism that gives me some peace about dying. See those waves there? Well, if you think about it… a wave isn't really a thing. It's just part of the ocean that takes a different shape for a while. Then, after it's done its job, it just drifts back into the ocean where it came from. The wave never goes away. It just… becomes part of something bigger."

"Are… we the wave?"

"Yeah, Artie. Hey, did you know that every particle in our body used to be part of a distant star?"

My eyes widened. "What?!"

"It's true. There's no such thing as you and me. We're just… a part of the universe that looks like us for a little while. And after a while, we'll just… go back."

"That's… so deep," I said. "It makes me feel all fuzzy inside. It's like… I can feel the Holy Spirit's presence on this beach right now… if I even believe that's a thing anymore."

Jennifer nodded slowly. "Could be. Or maybe, every time you thought the Holy Spirit was telling you to do something, or encouraging you to feel a certain way, it was really just you, being wise enough to listen to yourself."

"Hmm… I am pretty wisdomous, aren't I?"

Jennifer chuckled. "You're cute when you're high."

"Yeah, well… you're cute when you're… not high… and also when you're high."

She laughed, then smiled. "Thanks. It's getting late though. Walk me back?"

We walked to the hotel, and I escorted her to her room.

She smiled. "Save me a seat at breakfast tomorrow?"

"Will do."

She leaned in and kissed me on the cheek. When combined with the reversed weed gravity, I smiled so big.

"Goodnight, Arthur."

17. FPR

"Yeah, I think we got it!" Ella pressed a button, causing the red light on the video camera to vanish. "Great job, Art. I think we have enough interview footage now."

"Are you sure?" I asked. "I thought you said it still wasn't where you needed it to be."

Ella sat down at a computer in the lab and plugged in the camera. "That was then. This is now. I did some more snooping, and I convinced an alumnus through… lucrative incentive… to dig up an ace in the hole for us, so we won't need to rely on the interviews as much. Trust me… Robbie is going down."

"Hell yeah," I said, quietly, as it still felt weird to curse. "I'll leave you to your editing, then."

With most of my finals done, and the chimera formerly known as *Eden* dead and buried, hanging around school past 3 p.m. was pretty boring. Still, there was something introspective and nostalgic about wandering the grounds of Righteous Christ Academy after most students and faculty had gone home. Sure, I'd experienced plenty of crappy moments there, but that place was my life for a stupid amount of years. I was gonna miss it when I headed off to Georgia for college.

As I walked around the exterior of the campus, its after-hours quietness struck me. Without the bustle of school or church, I smiled at many sights that activated fond memories, for so many of them had been made there.

Over by the playground, Benny and I had noticed each other's t-shirts featuring the PlayStation video game *Crash Bandicoot* and became instant friends. I had said I thought *Spyro the Dragon* was the better game, and he put up a good fight.

On the football field was where, on field day, I almost cracked my head open on an extremely long slip-n-slide.

In the old black box theater, I came out of my introverted shell and found my artistic voice, thanks to Ms. Flannigan. Even when not performing, I shared so many fun times with the acting troupe there.

I walked by the school cafe, empty and dark. There, I won a costume contest for my Linguini from *Ratatouille* outfit—a chef's coat with a plush rat doll strapped to my head. The cafe was also where Travis Caster told my crush of the time I was into her. Not a great memory, but it was part of my journey.

The Daily Bread restaurant—I would miss their whipped potatoes, and the senior year lunches where Benny, Ella, and I would speculate about Rachel's disappearance.

Staring up at the enormous illuminated Righteous Christ sign, my smile faded. My church used to bring me great comfort. It was where I went to learn, to seek community, and to love. After senior year, all I could see was a modern paint job and an enormous waste of tithe money. I could just picture a room full of business executives, asking the pastors how they'd line their pockets in the coming years.

If Jesus saw what his legacy had turned into… what would he do? Oh gosh, I'm turning into Ella!

I perused one of the two bookstores and felt like I was shopping at Walmart. Book after book promised to teach young children how to love. I picked one up about Noah's ark that I remembered Ella commenting on the first day we met her. It was a story of actual genocide, painted as a good thing, with kid-friendly illustrations.

As I placed the book back on the shelf, my eyes welled up. It wasn't because of the story, or the bittersweet feeling of my high school years ending. I was in a state of emotional shock and hadn't processed it yet.

Over the past year, so much of what had anchored me to reality for my entire life had come undone. I'd pushed away the authority figures in my life that I used to look up to more than anyone. I'd adopted friends that lived worldly, sinful lives every day, and I, too, had partaken in some of those lifestyles.

What if my recent revelations were wrong? What if the world had influenced me like Pastor Robbie always warned us about? Am I maybe just a worthless sinner, unworthy of God's grace?

I had so many great times on that campus, but the dominant feeling had since turned from joy to anger. What used to be sources of inspiration for me were to be defended against. Yes, the reasons for my significant doubts were valid. But was my life any better with my new perspective? I honestly didn't know.

I sat on my favorite ledge to let my mind unwind. It was in an obscure corner outside the school building, between the computer labs and the parking lot. The way the green railing cascaded down the stairs next to it provided a great armrest.

"Hey, Arthur," said Ella, walking out of the building with her messenger bag over her shoulder.

"Oh, hey. You finished editing?"

"Almost. Just need to make a few minor tweaks and she should be good to go."

"Ah, okay. Cool."

"Everything okay?" she asked. "You seem… weirdly deadpan, which, for you, is saying a lot."

"I… just feel lost. All these changes… it's all happening so fast, and I don't even know who I am anymore."

Ella sat next to me and put her hand on my shoulder. "Heyyy, hey, hey, hey. You take all the time you need. I'm sorry if I pressured you to change too much this year. There's a lot to unlearn here, and you tackled it faster than anyone could've expected. Just sit with yourself for a while, ya know? And if you end up realizing you need the comfort of church in your life, I'll do my best to be happy for you. I get that the life of the filthy heathen isn't for everyone. It's not the easy road."

"Yeah… I guess."

Ella continued, "I don't know if I have the right answers. We're all just doing our best to do our best. Just know that I'm your friend, no matter what. Just be true to your genuine self; that's all that matters. Okay?"

It was nice to have such a kind friend, but I was too lost in my head to truly appreciate her in that moment.

"Yeah," I said. "Thanks."

"Alright," said Ella. "I'm gonna head out. You gonna be okay?"

"Yeah, I'll be fine."

"I can finish up the rest of the project myself. Don't worry about what you were gonna help me out with on graduation day; I can get someone else to do it."

I nodded, and then Ella got in her car and drove home.

Before returning home, I took a walk off-campus to a nearby Wendy's. I got a spicy chicken sandwich, though I didn't enjoy it as much as I had hoped.

On the way back to RCA and my car, I took the scenic route to enjoy the sunset, which would allow me to check on something I'd been putting off for a while.

I walked to the midpoint on the bridge and leaned over the side, scanning the stream and its bank for signs of movement. Nothing. I checked the other side. Still nothing.

"Oh, there you are." I said under my breath.

A ways down the stream, a family of not three, but four ducks frolicked in the stream. I couldn't be sure the runt was the same duck an alligator had been eyeing on my last visit, but I told myself it was. Very glad to see the lost duck back with their friends, I smiled.

I didn't spot any alligators nearby. I was sure a few lurked somewhere, but at least for the moment, their threat had vanished.

When I got home that night, a familiar sound greeted me. "You've got mail!"

The subject read, "Staying Vigilant Amidst Satan's Attacks." It was from Pastor Robbie, sent to anyone that subscribed to his newsletter.

His usual recent doomsday fare, about delinquents out to destroy RCA's good name, filled the newsletter. His closing comments stood out to me, though.

"For the wages of sin is death, but the gift of God is eternal life." - Romans 6:23

We must remember: mankind is flawed, and worthy of NOTHING but eternal hellfire. It's by God's grace and mercy that we are saved. We owe Him everything.

"Whoever walks with the wise becomes wise, but the companion of fools will suffer harm." - Proverbs 13:20

We must be extremely careful with who we let into our lives. If we surround ourselves with ungodly fools, it is fools we shall become. Be careful to whom you give your love, my friends. Not all deserve it.

As soon as I read Robbie's words, it became clear which influences in my life would lead to a future full of love and compassion.

I took out my phone and texted Ella: *I'm in.*

*   *   *

The day of graduation had arrived, at last. Looking in my bathroom mirror, I positioned the blue cap on my head, trying to find that one angle where the green tassel draped across my face just right.

"You look so great, honey," said my mom, resting her head on my shoulder. "Have your father and I told you how proud of you we are?"

I rolled my eyes. "Too many times, just this morning."

"Well… it's true. We can't wait to see what amazing things you accomplish in the next chapter of your life."

"Thanks, Mom."

"Good thing we have you here for the entire summer, though." She wiped a tear from her eye. "I'm just not ready to say goodbye to you yet."

"Plenty of time. Ya gotta let me go to school, though. See ya this afternoon."

"Okay, sweetie. Wave to us from the stage!"

I put my cap and gown in my backpack and drove to the school campus for the last time.

After parking, I made a beeline for the computer lab where Ella was putting the finishing touches on Pastor Robbie's goodbye present. She typed into Final Cut Pro *fpr_final_2_forreal*, and hit export.

She threw her arms in the air. "Fucking done!"

"Congrats," said Benny. "Just in the nick of time."

"So, what's the battle plan?" I asked, as Ella safely ejected her flash drive.

"Alright, team. Benny, it's your job to sweet-talk Allison so I can sneak into the video booth above the sanctuary right before they play the highlight reel. It should be toward the end of the ceremony. Think you can handle that?"

"Ella, who do you think you're talking to? She won't stand a single chance."

"How about me?" I asked.

"Arthur, it's up to you to make sure they can't shut off the power from the ground level, or this video will only see a few seconds of life."

She handed me a small backpack. "In here are a bunch of wires just like the ones they use backstage. When you're in graduation rehearsal before the actual show, find an excuse to pop behind Wing C, and drop these on top of the power cables. Get them all tangled up and stuff. If there's other junk back there, throw that on too. Anything to delay how long the video plays for."

I looked at the backpack. It wasn't very inconspicuous. "I dunno… don't you think they might see me?"

"Trust me, nobody is gonna be on the lookout for the graduate smuggling in sabotage gear. Everyone's gonna have backpacks."

"Hmm, all right. I got this."

"Yeah, you do!" said Benny, slapping my shoulders.

"So, what about Rachel?" I asked.

"She's got a lot going on with catching up on the classes she missed. I let her off the hook for this one. It's just gonna be us three, the OG RCA troublemakers."

"One last ride, huh Arthur?" said Benny.

"Let's do it. Also, just thinking ahead… what happens if we get caught, or the plan doesn't work?"

"On graduation day?" said Ella. "Stern looks? Eye rolls? Who cares? We're home free."

I smiled. "We're free… I like the sound of that."

Before the ceremony, we met up with Rachel in The Daily Bread for one last group lunch. I got the whipped potatoes, of course. We talked about food, the fond memories we'd made at

RCA, and what face Pastor Robbie would make if… no, WHEN… our plan went off without a hitch.

On the way out, Rachel tapped me on the shoulder. "Hey, Artie?"

I spun around. "What's up?"

"So, on the bus ride back from senior trip, I sat next to Jennifer Carrera, and she told me about what happened with you two at the Hell House."

"Oh," I said. "I'm sorry about that. I know I have a lot to learn about… a lot of topics."

Rachel shook her head. "No, no. I wanted to say thanks. I go to RCA too, Artie." She lowered her voice. "I know what they teach about abortion here. It's hard to challenge what we've been taught, and I think you should be proud of how far you've come."

My cheeks turned red. "I… thanks… I really appreciate that."

"Of course! Plus, you, like… snuck around Pastor Robbie's office for me? What the heck? So sweet! Ya know, I may have told Jennifer about your sleuthing and I think she got a little hot and bothered…"

"HA!" I blurted out. "No way."

"It's totally true! And I'll always put in a good word for my besties." She hugged me. "Now… are you ready?"

"Yeah. We got this."

*   *   *

"Okay, students with last names beginning with M through P, please head backstage. As your name is called, you will walk up to Principal Randall and Pastor Robbie, who will be standing on stage.

Hold the diploma with them, turn to the audience for photos, and walk off stage left. For this practice run, just pretend the pastor and principal are there."

Ella was wrong—hardly any graduates had backpacks with them. As I walked onto the sanctuary stage and through the side door, I held the backpack over my far shoulder. My heart was already pounding.

As the students' names were called, I examined my surroundings. The backstage area was full of various carts and props. Electrical wires ran up and down the winding area. Over my shoulder, I read two signs: *Wing A* and *Wing B*. I leaned to the side to try to see around the corner, but with little luck.

"Arthur Morton…"

Crap.

I walked onto the main stage area and posed for the hypothetical cameras. The backpack whacked the teacher standing in for Pastor Robbie and Principal Randall, but thankfully, he didn't seem to care. I shook his hand and headed off stage left.

As soon as I entered the other side of the backstage area, I saw an open door right in front of me, leading to the sanctuary where the student before me had promptly headed. There was no one else in sight. I spotted *Wing C* and ducked behind its curtain.

Low to the floor on the wall was a thick wire coming out of a locked socket. Above it was a small label that read "Projector Power."

I peeked around the corner and saw Austin Prudent walk off the stage and toward the sanctuary. I didn't have much time before someone would notice I was gone.

I unzipped the backpack and dumped the gaggle of wires right on top of the power cord. I tied some of them in knots around each other, plugged a few into empty sockets nearby, and pushed the real cable down to the bottom. Then I ripped off the "Projector Power" label and stuck it on another socket. I also grabbed a folded curtain from a nearby cart and draped it loosely over the area. I didn't cover anything too much to avoid suspicion.

After the last student in our group exited the backstage area, I pulled out my phone and acted like I was on a call as I walked back out to the sanctuary. I bumped right into a teacher helping with the ceremony and dropped my phone.

"Jeez, watch where you're going!" he said. "Sheesh."

He seemed far too busy to care why I was dilly dallying. I scurried back to my seat by Benny and Ella.

"So?" asked Benny.

"Mission accomplished," I said, shaking the empty backpack.

"Atta boy," said Ella. "Now we just need to time Benny's flirtations just right so I can get into the booth up there." She pointed up at a small window that overlooked the enormous sanctuary.

"Easy peasy," said Benny. "Thankfully, Ella and I have last names that start with letters early in the alphabet, so we've got plenty of time for sabotage after getting our diplomas."

"Ha ha, suck it, M name," said Ella.

"It's two letters after Kent…"

Ella shrugged.

The teachers helping run the event then ordered us into rows based on names.

A few minutes later, the doors opened. As families and students filled the sanctuary, my teeth clenched. I had just taken part in sabotaging my high school's graduation!

What if there were cameras back there? I thought. *What if they don't let us graduate? Guess it's too late to turn back now… Operation FPR is a go.*

The band on stage played as the ceremony's start time drew close. The selection of songs was not Christian, surprisingly. They started with some Beatles, then moved on to the theme song from *Friends,* and ended with "Hallelujah" by Leonard Cohen.

The last one in particular gave me the feels. Sitting in the sanctuary where I had been moved by so many worship performances over the years, and hearing the same band sing secular music, I realized something: those feelings weren't the Holy Spirit moving through me; live music is just really powerful sometimes.

As the song ended, Principal Randall stepped up to the podium. "Another year, another fine group of young disciples, prepared to spread God's love throughout the world. Thank you all for being here today. This year, in particular, has been challenging for a lot of us. Before we hand out the diplomas, please welcome our own Pastor Robbie to the stage, to share some hope as we look to the future."

Principal Randall returned to a seat on the side of the stage as Pastor Robbie strutted to the microphone while adjusting his necktie. The audience's claps drowned out Ella's and Benny's boos. Robbie brushed his flowing hair out of his eyes and leaned on the podium.

"Ya know, every time a year ends, I look back and think about how grateful I am that God blessed me with the opportunity to nurture the kids that cross my path here at Righteous Christ Academy. I get down on my knees every night and thank him for choosing me as his knight, to charge with sword and shield in hand at the devil and scream 'NO!' "

I assumed Ella was rolling her eyes.

"These truly are the end times we're living in. The sin that runs rampant in the world threatens to infect this very school every single day. Thankfully, you parents have nothing to worry about. God's plan is just and righteous, as are the men He appointed to prepare your children for the world. Let us pray."

Robbie raised his hands to the sky and closed his eyes. "Lord God! We thank you for the strength you bestow upon this holy place. We are sinful creatures, and we deserve nothing from you… but you still gift to us your mercy at every turn, and that blows me away every day, Father God. Please continue to give me and the faculty of Righteous Christ the strength to continue to fight the sinfulness of the world, and expunge all who dare stand against us. Let this army of God continue to grow and grow, so that they may slay the wickedness that infests the hearts of so, so many."

He gracefully lowered his arms and said, very slowly, "Amen."

After a few more speeches from faculty that I almost entirely tuned out, a teacher asked the first group of students to hustle through the backstage entrance, which was covered by some curtains on stands.

After the first few students received their diplomas and posed for the cameras, the loudspeaker announced, "Benny Bertrand."

I clapped as Benny skipped across the stage, pumping his arms in the air. As the camera zoomed in on him, something colorful caught my eye. Adorning his robe was the rainbow pin we picked out together. Robbie and Randall didn't seem to notice. As Benny walked offstage, I smiled to myself, and felt no shame whatsoever.

A few students after Benny, Rachel was called up. Robbie took a step back and folded his arms, allowing Principal Randall to hand her the diploma. Randall's smile looked incredibly insincere.

A while later, Ella's group was up. She wore the same rainbow pin as Benny. As she approached the center of the stage, Robbie stepped toward her with her diploma. He held it out for her to grab, but just as she reached out, he dropped it. She bent over to pick it up as he scowled. She held it up and smiled at the cameras. As she walked past Robbie, she stomped right on his foot with her boot. As he grimaced, she looked back, put her fingers up to her mouth, and mouthed the word "sorry."

Next up was my group. As I stood in line backstage, I wondered if anyone had noticed my expert level sabotage around the bend, but it was still out of sight.

"Arthur Morton."

I walked onto the stage and accepted my diploma. Principal Randall and Pastor Robbie were cordial, but didn't smile much. I shook their hands and headed offstage, waving to the corner that my mom told me she and my dad would sit in.

Before walking through the second door to the sanctuary, I poked my head behind Wing *C*. Everything was still in place.

I headed back to my seat and noticed that Ella and Benny were not in theirs.

Not much time now, I thought.

After Peter Zulu accepted his diploma, Principal Randall returned to the podium.

"Let's have a round of applause for the new class of Righteous Christ Academy!"

The crowd clapped and cheered.

"Before the band comes back up to play us out, we have one more surprise for you. The yearbook team has put together a video featuring highlights from the past four years. Enjoy!"

I sat upright in my seat and looked over at the dark video booth window, wondering how things were going for Ella and Benny.

The projector screens displayed a wide shot of the school, while "Landslide" by Fleetwood Mac played. The video alternated between footage of students laughing, worshiping, and studying. A few slideshows of photos were featured too. One of Benny and me playing *Halo* on Xboxes connected to projectors in one of the conference rooms after school made me smile.

Nothing was out of the ordinary so far. I wondered if something had gone wrong. After all, Ella wasn't exactly RCA's most adored student lately. If someone had seen her sneaking around where she wasn't supposed to be, they might find it suspicious.

As the song faded away and the video lingered on our class photo, Randall and Robbie stood up and started walking to the microphone.

When the screen faded to black, a new video started playing. A handheld camera floated across the Righteous Christ campus at a fast-forward speed. The color editing and film grain brought with it an artsy, professional vibe. The pounding strings of Coldplay's "Viva La Vida" filled the room with a sudden boost of energy and emotion.

Randall and Robbie shrugged at each other and sat back down.

Rachel looked back at me, raising her eyebrows. I smiled, having no idea what we were in for. It was our moment, for better or worse.

The camera cut to another handheld shot. The camerawoman held out a microphone to a girl in an RCA polo shirt and asked, "So, what's your favorite thing about being an RCA student?" Ella's voice was more bubbly than I had ever heard it—almost unrecognizable.

"Umm… I would have to say, my teachers."

As the student continued to talk, Ella had spliced the interview with surprisingly beautiful footage of classrooms.

"I feel like they really care about us and have a lot of knowledge to share."

On the screen, Mr. Crumbull gestured passionately at a whiteboard.

Ella's camera then sped over to a boy student and asked the same question.

"My favorite thing here is the library. I can come here any time I want, and read whatever I want. They have so many versions of the Bible here, too."

The camera zoomed in on a Bible passage I recognized as a story about King Solomon, who, to solve a local dispute, threatened to cut a baby in half with a sword, and give each half to the two women claiming to be the mother.

Interesting choice, Ella, I thought.

The camera swished to the side and transitioned to a static shot of Benny, sitting in a chair with an unfocused background.

"My favorite part of RCA used to be hearing all the wisdom of the pastors. They shared such loving words with us."

The video cut to footage from one of Pastor Robbie's sermons. In it, he smacked a fist against the pulpit.

"That's the thing, though!" said Robbie in the video. "God's love isn't fair… we don't deserve Heaven. Yet still, He only asks one thing of you. One thing! Just believe, and He will pull you out of that lake of fire we all belong in."

Pastor Robbie shuffled in his seat on stage.

The video cut back to Benny, who sat in silence for a moment. "I wish I knew… how to choose what I believe."

New footage appeared again, showing teenagers running through the rain, all sporting oddly thick, nut-colored hair.

Wait a second… this is Cocoon! Ella's secret ace! Holy cow!

"Jesus didn't eat for forty days!" screamed a rain-drenched Robbie. "You can make it through one!"

In the sanctuary, I could hear murmuring throughout the audience. Robbie stood up and walked over to an employee wearing a headset and began whisper-yelling at him. The man then disappeared backstage.

Oh crap…are they about to try to cut the power?

In the next shot of the video, Robbie stood over the out-of-shape Lily, who struggled to do a single push up.

"Only twenty more! This is what you deserve for destroying the temple God gave to you!"

I shuddered as I noticed myself in the background, struggling to do just a few push-ups.

We then saw dark footage of Samuel screaming in horror as he realized a counselor had placed a large snake around his shoulders.

I glanced around my vicinity in the sanctuary. Samuel's head faced downward, not moving at all.

Rachel's interview was next. "When I dated Samuel... his dad, Pastor Robbie, made me feel like part of the family. He even covered my medical expenses for me."

The camera followed Rachel into a medical office. She walked up to a receptionist and held up a picture of Robbie.

"You remember when I came in here to get an abortion, right? Was this the man that came in with me?"

"Yeah, that's the guy," said the receptionist. "What's this all about?"

The audience's murmurs erupted into full-on conversations, as more than a few parents took their young children by the hand and speed-walked to the exits.

The church employee returned from backstage and whispered something to Robbie, who had been pacing back and forth next to the stage. Robbie screamed something at the employee and stormed toward the back of the sanctuary; I assumed, to the video room.

Okay... so far, so good.

The video cut back to Robbie's sermon, and zoomed in close on his face. "Without God, you are nothing. Are you hearing what I'm saying? You are running out of time. Declare Him as Lord, repent of your sins, and He will welcome you with open arms."

To my right, two hunched-over bodies snuck back to their seats. It was Benny and Ella.

As the song entered its melancholy final moments, the video cut to a husky young man in a chair, shuffling around to get comfortable. It was me.

"So," said Ella from behind the camera, sounding less performative than before. "What's your favorite thing about going to RCA?"

"I'd have to say… my friends."

Ella chuckled from behind the camera.

"I used to feel like such a failure, but then they, and you, came along and showed me that even though humans aren't perfect, we all deserve to be loved."

On-screen, Ella walked out from behind the camera and hugged me tightly from the side. Rachel and Benny then zipped into the frame, transforming it into a group hug.

In the sanctuary, Ella, Rachel, and Benny all looked over their shoulders. We exchanged enormous grins and laughed uncontrollably as our projected selves continued to embrace.

Just then, the video feed cut out, replaced with a blue screen and text reading *Input 3A*.

Almost all my classmates stared at Benny, Ella, Rachel, and me. Before anybody could say anything, microphone feedback blasted our ears. I placed my hands over my ears until it subsided.

Robbie's voice filled the sanctuary speakers from the video booth. "Please, uh… forgive the technical difficulties. This… isn't what it looks like… Ella Kent is an expert at video stuff, and… sound… making. She's manipulated it to look like… I would never… The Lord says that—"

The audio feed cut out, along with the sanctuary power. It was a total blackout. The audience filled with loud, concerned conversation.

I figured an IT guy must have given up any hope of disassembling my expert-level sabotage, and stepped outside to reset the power, not realizing that Robbie had stopped the video.

Moments later, the lights came on and the blue projector screen lit up. Without skipping a beat, Principal Randall speed-walked to the pulpit and leaned into the microphone.

"Please stay calm. This is all just an unfortunate mishap. If you remain in your seats, I think Pastor Robbie can clear all this up for—"

Randall pressed his palms to his ears as microphone feedback again filled the room. Over the speakers, Robbie's voice came through loud and clear.

"—and then the power went out, and… No, there's no way they'll believe that ridiculous propaganda video. If she thinks for one second that it's gonna convince anybody of anything, that BITCH has another thing—Wait, I'm what? Oh, no…"

After Pastor Robbie muttered what I sincerely hoped were his last-ever words to the students of Righteous Christ Academy, the audio feed cut out one last time.

The audience gasped in near unison after hearing one of their divinely inspired leaders use such an offensive slur toward a student. Principal Randall tried to settle them down, but the absurd volume of the crowd almost entirely drowned out his voice.

Benny, Ella, Rachel, and I laughed voraciously and cried tears of cathartic joy as the audience around us filed out in droves.

*   *   *

As the crowds exited the sanctuary, I lost sight of Ella and Benny. I avoided eye contact with basically everyone as I funneled out.

Noticing many concerned faces looking at me, I bought some time before dealing with impending confrontations by swinging by my car.

Reaching into the trunk, I grabbed my yearbook and a pen, though I wasn't sure how many former classmates would want to sign it after what just went down. I also put my cap and gown inside before closing the trunk.

"Hello, Moto," *brummm… brummm… brummm* rang my cell phone.

"Hey, Mom. No, I don't wanna talk about it right now. That's fine, I'll see you at home. Yes, we can talk about it then. Yes, I'll be fine. Bye."

I couldn't quite get a read on how upset she was, but it was for sure less anger than the porn fiasco.

When I headed back toward the main church campus, the energy felt like a festival that had been canceled for rain as soon as it began. Everyone was yelling at each other or gossiping about something. Nobody was posing for photos or shaking hands. I supposed it was partially my fault, but I'd feel guilty about that later; I had blank yearbook pages that needed filling.

I squirmed through the crowds, vaguely looking for someone that might not hate me. By The Daily Bread, I noticed two familiar faces deep in conversation.

"Hey, Mr. Crumbull. Hey, Ms. Flannigan."

Their conversation stopped dead when they saw me. Clearly, they were talking about me, or at least about the events of the day that involved me.

"Hey, Arthur," said Mr. Crumbull. "Some day, huh?"

"Yeah… hey, can you sign my yearbook?"

Ms. Flannigan chuckled as Mr. Crumbull took the yearbook and pen that I held out. "Ya know, no matter how much you've changed, you're still all business. Straight to the point. No fluff allowed. I like that about you."

"Heh… thanks."

Ms. Flannigan signed as well.

I look at the page. In swirly handwriting, I saw, *Ah, high school. I laughed, I cried, it was better than* Cats! *-Ms. F*

Further down the page was a horrific clown face smiling at me, signed, *Your teacher and friend, Mr. Crumbull.*

"Thanks!" I said. "For everything."

They hugged me.

Ms. Flannigan said, "If you ever decide to get into theater down the road, Arthur, look me up."

"Will do."

She chuckled and shook her head as I walked away. "Funny kid…"

I wandered around a bit more, still avoiding eye contact with anyone I didn't think would want to sign my yearbook.

I spotted a friend. "Hey, Andrew!"

"Oh… hey…" he said, while glancing around.

"Wanna sign my yearbook?"

"Uh… sure."

Andrew, he wrote.

"Eloquent," I said, sarcastically.

"I'm sorry, Arthur. I gotta go find someone. Good luck with everything."

"Yeah… you too."

I guess ya can't please 'em all…

Next up was someone I never would've expected to want to remember after graduation. "Hey, Samuel. Wanna sign my yearbook?"

"Definitely, my dude," he said, taking the book and pen.

"So… how ya feeling after all that?"

"I… am feeling…" He spoke sporadically as he wrote. "I'm great, actually. Yeah. I can't tell you how satisfying it was to hear my dad just flail like that. Makes me feel like I can actually stand up to him, ya know? So, thank you for that."

I blushed. "That's… I mean… I didn't do much. That's good to hear, though."

"Yeah, man. I'm eighteen now. I don't even think he can legally force me to join the military, so… yeah, screw him."

He handed me back the book.

I smiled. "I'm glad you're feeling better."

Samuel nodded and patted me on the shoulder as he walked away. "You're a good dude, Arthur. Good luck with everything."

Looking at the yearbook, I saw the small new addition.

I'm sorry for being a dick. You rock.

-Samuel

PS: FPR!

"Hey, Artie."

I turned around to see a very welcome face. "Hey, Jenn."

We both chuckled for a moment.

"So…" she said. "Definitely didn't have THAT on my senior year bingo card. Especially from you. Not sure I would've had the guts to do that… but I'm proud of you."

"That means a lot. Thank you for everything. Honestly, I don't know if I'd have come this far without your deep talks."

"Oh my god, they actually helped? Ugh, that makes me so happy!"

"Heh, I'm glad. Maybe we can stay in touch? I'll call you whenever I'm confused about the universe or something."

"I would love that," she said.

I smiled. "Sign my yearbook?"

"Umm, duh! Let's see… Dear Arthur. You're… cuter than you think. Have some… more confidence… next time. Jennifer."

I blushed. "Thankssss…"

She ended her message by drawing a heart.

She then gave me a big hug. "Don't be a stranger, kay? Maybe we can hang out this summer before college."

"Definitely. See ya around."

She waved and vanished into the crowd.

"Hey, movie star." Benny strutted up to me, hyped up on adrenaline.

Ella and Rachel were with him.

I raised my arms in the air. "Y'all… holy crap. That was amazing. I can't believe it worked."

"It was all this amazing lady," said Benny, pointing at Ella.

"I mean… he's not wrong," said Ella. "Y'all helped too, though."

"So, do you think he'll get fired over this?" I asked.

"Honestly," said Ella, "I have no idea. You know better than anyone that it takes time to reconfigure what you think you know about the people around you. My goal with the video was just to communicate to the RCA parents that if they want their kids to be surrounded by love… maybe this isn't the best place for them. Arthur, your interview footage really helped sell that, so… we'll see what happens."

I smirked. "Hah… you're welcome. But what about when he called you a… bitch?"

Ella chuckled. "Oh, yeah. That… might help."

We all laughed.

Rachel looked around. "Ya know, I hate to be the party pooper… that's normally Artie's job… ha ha… but I'm kinda over all these eyes on us. Wanna take this party somewhere else?"

I nodded. "Absolutely."

*   *   *

"You're really gonna miss this place, huh?" asked Ella, unbuckling her seatbelt.

I put my car into park. "It's the best queso. Am I wrong?"

"Uhh… to each their own. Oh, look. Rachel and Benny are inside already."

Ella opened her door.

"Hey, wait a sec," I said.

"What's up?"

"I, umm…" I fiddled with my fingers. "I just wanted to… ugh, I'm so bad at sappy stuff."

"Oh no," said Ella.

"I just wanted… to thank you."

Ella scoffed. "Oh, it was no big deal. I wanted to make that video for myself and Rachel just as much as you, so—"

"Not for the video. For… being a great friend to me this year. I don't really think I deserved it."

Ella smirked. "Thanks, Arthur… That's nice. But don't be so hard on yourself—if I told you half the things I did at my old school… hoo boy."

I nodded. "Right, Ella the delinquent… here to corrupt all us nice Christian boys."

She punched my shoulder playfully. "I think I did a pretty good job."

"I wholeheartedly agree."

"You were a pretty good friend, too," said Ella.

I smiled. "Thanks."

We exited the car and headed inside.

Afternoon at Chili's was a different experience than I was used to. There was no line, a different waitstaff, and the menu wasn't quite the same. Luckily, the lunch menu still had queso.

"So," said Rachel. "Do they have Chili's in Georgia?"

"Great question," I said. "I'll have to look that up. Might be a deal breaker."

"I'll bet," said Rachel. "By the way, y'all… are we all sticking around here for the summer?"

"I will be, yeah," said Ella. "My pool's always available.

"Count me in," I said.

Benny grimaced. "Actually… I'm heading out to New York in two weeks."

"Whaaaat?!" we all said in unison.

"Yeah, they have an early summer theater program I hear lets you get a jump start, especially with singing, which… as you know… not my best skill."

"It's true," I said.

"Well damn," said Ella. "Gonna be a pretty boring summer without ya. My video editing program doesn't start until October."

"That's so far!" said Rachel. "I'll be out in late August. Though with summer school catchup, I won't have too much free time."

"September for me," I said. "Oh no… do you think this is our last group Chili's ever?"

Benny shrugged. "It's possible."

Rachel held up a chip dipped in queso. "In that case, I'd like to propose a toast to us. The yearbook team may have snubbed us for any flattering awards, but I have some of my own I'd like to give out."

"Oh my God," said Benny.

"Okay, actually…" Rachel ate her chip. "I'll grab another chip in a minute cause this is gonna take a bit, and I might need my hand to wipe a tear or three."

Ella rolled her eyes and smiled.

Rachel cleared her throat. "Benny, you are a vibrant lighthouse in a sea of cynicism. Your award is 'Most Likely to Improve the Lives of Everyone He Meets.' I hope we can have three-hour phone calls every week for decades to come."

"You know it, girl," said Benny through misty eyes.

Rachel sniffled. "Arthur. You surprised me this year. You showed true strength and maturity. It's not an easy thing to hear out challenges to your deepest beliefs, but here you are, an enlightened young man who values kindness and empathy over blind loyalty and obedience. I'm so proud of you. To you I present… 'Most Courageous.' "

"Aww… thank you, Rachel… I don't know what to say."

"You're welcome, Arthur."

"And last, but certainly not least… Ella, my wife from another life. You have literally saved me. You showed me selflessness when everyone around me treated me like a vehicle for their own salvation. To you, I bestow the honor of 'Biggest Lifesaver.' Thank you for everything."

"My pleasure," said Ella, placing her hand on Rachel's. "You made it easy."

"Awwwww!" said Benny. "My heart can't handle this!"

"Oh hey," I said, not realizing how carelessly I was derailing the moment. "Can't forget to get you all to sign my yearbook." I placed it on the table and opened it to a blank page.

Ella thought for a second about what to write. She then dug into her backpack and pulled out blue and red sharpies. She drew a sleek alligator in blue, with demon horns and a pitchfork in red. Underneath it she wrote, "Long live the Alligator Heretics!" followed by her name.

"Oh, that's perfect," said Rachel, grabbing the pen to add her own name next to Ella's drawing.

Benny and I did the same.

Rachel dipped a tortilla chip in the queso dip. "A toast to us."

"And to our bright, bright futures," said Benny, raising his chip. "We survived so much together, and it's all smooth sailing from here on out."

Ella joined in. "To our debaucherous futures. Long may we swear, read Harry Potter, sleep in on Sundays, and most importantly, love whoever we want, how we want, without shame."

I dipped my chip into the bowl and scooped a meaty chunk of queso. "And to our continued friendship. As we leave our bubble and find where we belong in the world, may we always cherish what we found here. Long live the Alligator Heretics."

We all tapped our chips together. "Long live the Alligator Heretics!"

Epilogue: Second Coming

Even as an adult in my late twenties, I wasn't much of a drinker. I tolerated the taste and enjoyed the effects when necessary, and that night was one of those nights. I had a date, though as was par for the course with online dating, it was hard to say if my match was looking for romance or something more provocative.

My romantic history post-high school included some love adjacency, some hurt, and plenty of frustration. I frequently found myself on a pendulum of desire, swinging back and forth from passionate partner-seeking to utter burnout, which often led to an empty hunger for carnal ecstasy, though it rarely found an outlet.

She had chosen the bar—a small dive in her neck of Los Angeles. The lighting was generated from a few antique electric lanterns hung from the ceiling. The ambiance did its job; I almost immediately forgot about the stresses of adulthood and looked forward to drowning my sadnesses in inebriation and, hopefully, some sensual companionship.

Erica sat at the far end of the bar. She wore a tight skirt, a black leather jacket, and a t-shirt featuring The All-American Rejects, a band from my high school years that we had bonded over on Tinder. Other topics discussed prior to our rendezvous included a mutual appreciation for Neapolitan style pizza, puppies, and Erica's convenient obsessions with full beards like mine, and "hashtag dadbods"—stocky male physiques commonly found in fatherhood, a stage of life far removed from my aspirations.

Avoiding eye contact, I mumbled a faint, "Nice shirt."

"I thought you'd like that," Erica responded. "Your shirt is really nice too! I love polka dots," she added, gently brushing my shoulder.

By no surprise, Erica, a self-proclaimed heavyweight of boozy consumption, finished her glass of wine first. "We gotta catch you up. Excuse me, can we get two shots of Jameson?"

I put a slight effort into hiding just how much the thought of pure whiskey hovering anywhere near my face caused me to retch. "Oh god… okay, I'll do it, but only for you."

"It'll be fun. I promise."

I chose to read into the subtext, but instead of flirting back, my borderline obsession with honesty pushed me to elaborate on the backstory. "Well, I was kind of a late bloomer with alcohol. Booze just wasn't around much in my formative years."

Erica seemed mildly surprised. She scoffed, "What, did you go to boarding school or something?"

"Not… exactly. I went to a private Christian school. There were definitely plenty of students drinking, but they knew better than to invite a tattle tale like me."

"Ooh, juicy. So you were the little altar boy, always following the rules, never naughty?"

I chuckled, and glanced at my empty shot glass, lost in thought for a moment. "We didn't have altar boys, but yeah, more or less." I smirked and locked eyes with Erica. "Sometimes I feel like it delayed my social life for years, and now I'm spending my late twenties trying to make up for all the, uh… naughty moments I've missed."

Erica placed her hand on my thigh, leaned in and whispered, "I think I can help with that."

Thirty minutes later, she welcomed me into her studio apartment. "Ugh, sorry for the mess!"

"It's totally fine, it's… super nice," I assured her, an obvious white lie.

Wrinkled blouses and jeans covered much of the floor.

Erica ignored my low-key insult and added, "It's okay, we can just hang out on the bed. Oh, actually, one sec."

She swung by the kitchen and came back with two glasses of Chardonnay. We sat on the bed with drinks in hand.

"Cheers!" I hid my reaction to how unpleasant each sip tasted.

A few minutes was all it took to leave our slightly awkward conversation in the past. Erica turned on some Spotify vibes, and a few minutes later, we were lost in each other's arms.

After a few minutes of heavy macking, passion escalated predictably. First, tops were lost, then bottoms.

Using my hands, I tried to ensure Erica had a good time first, but wasn't sure if her reaction was genuine.

After a while, Erica said, "Your turn."

As she touched me, I enjoyed myself as best I could, but my mind wandered. I worried Erica would expect me to pleasure her orally, something I had never tried in my very limited sex life, out of fear that my hypersensitivity would cause me to be grossed out by the experience, offending the recipient. Most of all, though, I stressed about why I wasn't hard yet.

"Is something wrong?" asked Erica with concern.

"No, you're like… so hot right now. It just… takes a while sometimes." My anxiety increased; the pressure was on.

A few moments passed, and I couldn't help but dwell on how a *normal* man would be fully aroused by the amazingly attractive woman currently willing to sleep with him.

Erica asked the question I dreaded, having already heard it during a few similar encounters. "Is it… me?"

"I swear it's not you. I want you so badly right now, but it's not working. I don't know why. It's happened before. I think I'm just in my head. Alcohol isn't the only thing I'm a late bloomer with. Sex is still a learning experience for me, and since I know that's not what people in their late twenties wanna hear, I get a lot of anxiety over it."

I braced for impact.

Erica smiled and reassured me, "Hey, I get it. Definitely don't feel bad! We can cuddle; it's nice just being here."

I breathed a sigh of relief. "Thank you. I can't tell you how many women have reacted extremely negatively to this. And every time that happens, it means the pressure for it to work the next time is even higher."

"Well, they suck."

I hadn't made eye contact in a while. "Yeah, I guess. I just wish I understood it more. Sometimes I wonder if maybe it all goes back to the way I was raised. Maybe it fucked me up more than I think. But I guess that's normal; I mean, even public schools were really into abstinence-only sex ed back then. Then again, public schools didn't have purity conferences."

"What's a purity conference?" Erica asked.

"Oh gosh, it was so weird. They separated the guys and girls into two auditoriums and had the male faculty talk to us, and vice versa. The guys' room was a bunch of fear mongering about how masturbation was a crime against the creator of the universe. Ya know, the usual."

"Um, that's not very usual."

"From what I hear, the girls' room was even worse. Telling them that one of their main God-ordained purposes was to provide pleasure to their husbands, and that it's their fault when men lust and stumble."

"Dude… that's some fucked up shit. Maybe you should unpack this with a therapist."

I sat up. "Oh, sorry if that was too much. I know you're not my therapist. And I do have one, by the way."

Erica chuckled. "It's okay." She glanced at the clock on her nightstand. "But also, it is getting late…"

"Ah, sorry. I'll let you get some sleep." I hurriedly stood up and got dressed to avoid any more awkwardness. "So, maybe we can try this again soon?"

Erica smiled awkwardly, and responded, "I… don't think so. But hey, I really do hope you find some peace."

I struck a forced smile and replied with a dry demeanor, "Yeah… me too. See ya."

I spent the drive home mentally beating myself up over my ongoing romantic failures.

When I arrived home, I stopped by my apartment building's mail room. I turned the key extra quietly, to avoid waking any neighbors. I grabbed the pile of envelopes and headed up to my apartment.

Most of the mail was bills I could've sworn were supposed to be paperless. One blue envelope had a stamp with an alligator logo on it. It took me a second, but I didn't have to read the address to know it was from Righteous Christ Academy.

I opened it and gave it a quick skim. It was an invitation to my class's ten-year reunion.

Oof, I thought. *I don't know if I'm gonna fly all the way across the country for this. I don't even know if they'd let me in these days…*

I opened the Instagram app on my iPhone and typed *Benny Bertrand* into the search, though his profile popped up before I finished. His latest post was an album of him and his boyfriend at a swanky NYC restaurant, celebrating the opening of Benny's latest off-Broadway show. They were clinking champagne glasses in the first photo, and kissing in the second.

Ella uploaded maybe three photos to her account each year. The latest was at a premiere for a movie she had worked on. There was no significant other in sight.

At least she and I can bond over our ongoing singleness, I thought.

Ella also lived in Los Angeles, though we had only caught up once or twice in the past few years.

Rachel didn't have any social media presence. Occasionally I'd hear about her giving conference talks about surviving purity culture. I'd watched all of them. Lately she'd also spent a lot of time fighting for trans rights alongside her husband, which Ella would sometimes share clips of on her Instagram story.

One social media account I was very sick of seeing was Rachel's brother's podcast. *Holy Alpha ft. Wesley Bristol* made me want to vomit whenever social media algorithms decided "pro-male" doomcasting was what I needed to see more than anything. Wesley devoted his efforts to fighting against the *#MeToo* movement, cancel culture, and "radical feminists," a buzzword for, well, any woman fighting for equal rights. He also loved to encourage his male audience to take back their God-ordained leadership roles, the lack of which was apparently responsible for all the evil in the world.

People like Wesley made me SO grateful I lucked into making the friends I did while at RCA. Speaking of, Jennifer and I stayed in touch occasionally. She was a NASA engineer in Washington, DC. We would occasionally text about nerdy movies and the like. We shared our mutual disappointment with *The Hobbit* movies and checked in after most season finales of *Game of Thrones*.

I checked my iMessage conversation with Benny. My last text to him was four months ago, congratulating him on a show. He had replied, *Thanks, bud! Let's get together soon!* which I had reacted to with a heart.

Ya know what? I thought. *Screw it.*

I pressed Benny's face, and then the green call button. The dial tone repeated a few times.

"No. Way. Arthur, my boy. How the hell are ya?"

"Hey, dude," I said. "Not too bad, I guess."

"I was actually JUST thinking about you. Did you get the invite to the reunion?"

I glanced at the sheet. "Yeah, I just got it. You're not actually thinking of going, are you?"

"Ya know what, I really wasn't, but then I heard about a performance going on down there during the same week as the reunion, and now I'm like… I think we gotta go. I'm sending you the link to tickets… right… now… okay, sent."

I put Benny on speaker, pressed the new text notification, and then the Eventbrite link.

"No fucking way," I said. "That… sure is something. Lemme think about it, okay?"

"Yeah, bud. Just lemme know. It would be so fun to catch up, even if we don't stick around the actual reunion too long."

"Will do. See ya."

*   *   *

When I stepped off the plane in South Florida, it was like being smacked with a hot towel.

Wow… I did not miss this, I thought.

I swiped around Tinder in my hotel room until the reunion had already started, so I could avoid being one of the first RCA alumni to arrive. I got zero matches.

Doo DOO went my phone. It was a text from Benny.

Hey, I just parked. Where you at?

Shit, I typed. *Running a little late. Be there in a few.*

I threw on a button-down, took the elevator downstairs, and hopped into my rental car.

Driving down the streets I used to know so intimately was bizarre. Everything was smaller than I remembered, and also dirtier. Even my old neighborhood looked slightly different as I drove past it.

The entrance to Righteous Christ hadn't changed, though. Ten years wasn't enough to warrant a logo change, apparently. I parked in the same lot I did every school day, for the nostalgia. As I got out of the car, I thought about the time Ella and I stole Rachel's sweater out of Mr. Crumbull's car, just a few feet to my left. I chuckled.

I walked across the campus toward the gym where the reunion was taking place. Much of the visual landmarks felt familiar, but no longer held any meaning for me. I was struck with a conviction that I didn't belong there.

As I walked into the gym, I kept my head lowered, not wanting anybody to recognize me unless I was fully prepared for the conversation. Not exactly a reasonable expectation at a high school reunion.

"Hey, have you checked in yet?" said a voice.

To the side was a table with a sign-in sheet and blank name tags.

"Oh, no… I haven't."

Thankfully, I didn't recognize the volunteers running the booth. I signed my name on the sheet and wrote *Arthur* on a name tag. I kept it sloppy for discretion.

The gym was less full than I expected. Reunions weren't as popular as the movies made them seem, especially when roughly half the alumni no longer supported the beliefs of the school. The lights were dim, and streamers and balloons adorned the walls. It reminded me of our prom, but on a smaller budget.

Over the speakers, classic Righteous Christ worship music played. My whole body shuddered with discomforting nostalgia.

While making myself a drink, I heard someone calling out to me. "Hey, Arthur! Is that you?" A tall, bearded man in a white shirt and blue tie approached me and shook my hand. "It's me! Andrew!"

"Holy shit! I mean, holy cow. I barely recognized you. You're looking so pro!"

"Thanks, man. And don't even worry about the cursing; I've changed so much since the old days."

"Oh yeah? How have you been? I heard you married Jade Parnacle a while back?"

"Yeah, that did NOT end well. We started dating the summer after graduation. We were still so gung ho for God at the time, so we got married after dating for like a year, basically so we could have sex."

"That sure is a reason," I said.

"Yeah, no… we really didn't know what we wanted, so we rushed into things. We realized pretty quickly that if we hadn't been pressured by the church into getting married, we probably wouldn't have made it that far."

"But… you got to have sex at least, right?"

"Ehh, a little. Ya know, in those purity conferences, they made sex sound so simple, like if you save yourself, your wedding night is gonna be magical and perfect. Nope! Turns out when you spend your life telling yourself that sex is evil, your brain listens! Jade uh… really struggled with… let's say… welcoming me with open arms."

"Okay, no need for details."

I was fairly certain he was referring to vaginismus, a neurological condition where a woman's vagina muscles tighten in response to the fear of being penetrated, among other reasons.

"Yeah, we eventually got there, but it took a lot of patience and therapy. And now it's all over, so… yeah. Purity culture, man. Shit's fucked!"

I took a sip of my drink. "You're tellin' me…"

Andrew continued, "I've been good these days, though. I'm on the dating apps, and I'm going to a progressive Christian church. Get this… the pastor is a lesbian!"

My eyebrows raised. "That's… refreshing."

"Yeah, it's a great place; it's really filling a void for me."

"Sounds like they actually practice the love that they say their god is all about."

"They totally do. So, where did you end up with all that stuff?"

"Well," I said, "I'm certainly not religious. As for whether I believe in a god, I think it's a fair hypothesis, but that's it. I guess you could say I'm agnostic to the general god concept, but an atheist toward the modern interpretation of the Christian God. That dude was definitely created in the minds of men."

Andrew chuckled. "Right on. Well, I'm glad you found your way through all that. I remember you were really struggling with it senior year."

"Thanks, dude," I said. "And yeah, that was a tough year."

"You're welcome. I'm gonna make a few rounds, but hey, it was so great catching up. Good luck out there!"

I raised my glass. "You too!"

As I paced around the event, I had a harder time than expected recognizing faces, especially since roughly half the men sported full beards, myself included. To my elation, I didn't notice any familiar teachers who would judge me. I had heard that most of them left RCA over the past decade.

Finally, I spotted Benny. He looked almost exactly the same, but dressed more extravagantly. He wore a loose button-down covered in floral patterns, untucked over slim slacks, and some very shiny white shoes.

"Hey, dude," I said.

"Arthurrrrr!" He hugged me. "It's been WAY too long."

"It really has," I said, smiling.

"So, how's life in LA? I saw your name in the credits of the Disney movie that came out last year. So fucking cool!"

"Hah, thanks. It's fine. Not super passionate about animation now that it's work, but it pays the bills."

"Right on, right on," said Benny. "So… how have you *really* been? Like, being here now… I find myself thinking about how much this place impacted my life. Does this place still haunt you? Cause it sure haunts me!"

I shrugged. "Hmm. Kinda, yeah."

"Yeah, man… sometimes I wonder if our lives would've been easier if we never… went astray, as they say. Would be nice if I could visit my parents for the holidays without them staging spiritual interventions. Speaking of which, please don't tell them I'm in town."

"Hah, I haven't talked to them since high school. But damn, that's rough. Sorry to hear that."

"I mean… it's my choice to avoid them these days," said Benny. "It's just… too much." He cleared his throat. "Ah… sorry for the rant. How 'bout you, though? You mentioned a while ago you were seeing a therapist, unpacking all this shit?"

"Yeah, it's nice just having someone to talk to sometimes. I don't think I was traumatized as much as some other alumni, especially the girls, but there are plenty of little things that affect my adult life." I leaned in to his ear. "Like… I can't get hard easily when I'm with a real-life human woman. I don't know if it's because of being raised to view sex as this evil thing, or being such a late bloomer, or too much porn, or anxiety, but…"

"Dude, I have been there. Well, except for the woman part."

"Really?"

"Absolutely," said Benny. "Maybe it's the purity culture, maybe it's genetics. Hard to say. But just ask your doctor for some pills for that. They even have chewable ones these days. Even if it's just in your head, that's no reason to avoid treatment."

"Okay, that makes me feel better. Maybe I'll try that."

"You boys talking about erectile dysfunction?"

Ella approached us in leather pants and a denim jacket. She even sported a new nose ring since the last time I saw her.

"Oh my god!" screamed Benny, throwing his body onto hers. "I can't believe we're all here! The Alligator Heretics ride again!"

"Hey, don't forget me!" came a voice from behind.

Rachel approached us, wearing a casually professional pantsuit.

"RACHELLLL!!!" said Benny, flailing his arms around.

We all came together for a group hug.

"This is so trippy," I said. "It's like no time has passed at all."

"Yeah…" said Ella. "Kinda wish it felt like we'd had more distance. Being here… it's not fun, y'all!"

"Yeah," I said. "It sucks that such a formative period of our lives has so much baggage behind it. Kinda feels like my high school years were stolen from me."

"I know, right?" said Rachel. "I'm half expecting Pastor Robbie to walk through those doors and shut this whole thing down."

"Pretty hard to do that from Texas," I said.

Ella shook her head. "It's insane they let him run another Cocoon camp at a Righteous Christ church."

Benny draped his arms around Ella and Rachel. "Well, at least we saved the future kids at THIS Righteous Christ from his shenanigans. You're welcome, Florida!"

"Fair," I said.

"Hey," said Rachel. "Did you guys hear about Pastor Tom?"

Ella shook her head. "Nah, I don't keep up with this place at all anymore. What happened?"

"It was like, just a few days ago. This massive story got published in a local South Florida paper. A bunch of former mistresses came out and said he had affairs with them."

"Holy shit," I said.

"Yeah," continued Rachel. "And with some of them, he, like, seduced them while in counseling sessions and shit."

"That's fucked up," said Ella.

Benny laughed, awkwardly. "Jeez. Sounds like he deserved it."

Rachel shook her head. "But… I really wouldn't be surprised if they do some big video where he says the devil got ahold of him, and that through Bible study and deep reflection with the other pastors… he's been cured by the grace of God!"

"Kill me now," said Ella.

"So," I said. "Now that we're all here… we don't have to stick around RCA, do we?"

"Hell no," said Rachel. "I thought being here could be some sort of cathartic brute force therapy or something… nope! Super bad call." She shook her head vigorously.

"Agreed," said Ella.

"Let's get outta here," said Benny.

*   *   *

Benny, Ella, Rachel, and I entered a downtown theater as we continued to reminisce about old times. The lobby wasn't very large, but whoever decorated it did a great job evoking the regal feeling of a Broadway venue. Against the otherwise bland walls sat bronze statues of lions. Vibrant red curtains hung throughout.

We grabbed some popcorn and drinks from the bar and took our seats in the theater. It wasn't as large as the RCA theater, but without those big God bucks, what can ya do?

"I can't believe this is really happening," said Rachel.

"Yeah," I said. "Trippy."

An usher came around, handing out playbills to the people seated at the end of the row to pass down. When they reached me, I took one and passed them on. The front cover was very professional. The illustration was of a forest at night, under a purple sky. The text was gold and luxurious. I smiled as I read the title: *Melinda Flannigan's EDEN.*

The orchestra lit up and the large red curtain parted. The stage was dark.

"In the beginning," boomed a voice, "there was nothing."

BLAM! went the horns.

The stage lights turned on and illuminated a gorgeous set. At first glance, the trees looked real. How they got the ground to look like it was covered in actual dirt and grass, I had no idea.

"And then I got bored, snapped my fingers, and made some playthings."

BLAM!

A shirtless Adam jumped out from behind a tree and struck a masculine pose. A small, leaf-covered speedo surrounded his crotch.

"Just a man?" said the voice of God. "Surely I can do better."

BLAM!

The man retched and gestured across his chest as Ms. Flannigan, barely dressed and looking hot as hell, jumped out from behind him, striking a feminine pose. Her red hair against the dainty green costume reminded me of Poison Ivy from *Batman*.

God continued, "From one useless rib… perfection."

An unseen chorus sang, "Hwuuuuaahhhh!!!"

From behind the trees, twenty dancers dressed as animals flew onto the stage and swarmed Adam and Eve. The opening number only gained more energy from there.

Eden was barely recognizable. The music was even more catchy than I remembered, though to be fair, I hadn't heard it in ten years. The direction, choreography, stage lighting, effects, and performers all brought us into Ms. Flannigan's world immediately.

After the opening number blared to its conclusion and the lights blacked out, the audience burst into applause. Benny belted one "oww!"

When the applause died down, a single spotlight illuminated Eve at the center of the stage, as violins created a sad ambiance.

"Who am I?" sang Eve.

She continued on to sing the passionate *I want* song that I hadn't heard sung since before Pastor Robbie forced Ms. Flannigan to cut it. The audience barely made a peep throughout its three-minute length. Occasionally, the voice of God would butt in with a joke, and Eve's playful dismissal of him always earned a laugh.

The music crescendoed. "Someday when I find myself, I'll take up arms and get off this shelf. Someday. Someday. The man in the sky, and the man in my bed… they'll flex their arms, and wonder why I fled."

The story followed most of the same beats, from what I could recall. Adam and God constantly gaslit Eve, trying to convince her that her aspirations were confusion implanted in her mind by the snake, who just so happened to be the one character in the show that spoke the truth plainly.

The snake's song, which I almost remembered word for word, sent chills down my spine, thanks to the actor's stage presence. "The power of knowledge is the power to love. Question him, question me, question every proposition, into infinity."

At the end of the show, Adam and Eve were cast out by God for not obeying his one rule: to avoid eating from the tree that provided knowledge, the ultimate weapon. They covered themselves in full clothing, suddenly ashamed of their naked bodies, because reasons. In the version I remembered, Adam blamed Eve for not listening to his leadership, and they walked out together, ending the show. But in this version, the curtain didn't fall.

"No," said Eve, turning to Adam. "I'm not doing this anymore!"

BRUMP! Trumpets sprang to life.

Eve clenched her fists and walked toward Adam. "You say you're smart, you say you're wise. But if I ask for patience, you refuse to compromise. You say that my body will distract and make you stumble, but all I really hear is mumble, grumble, mumble, grumble."

The orchestra climbed, and electric guitars raised the energy by a million. The stage lights dimmed as a spotlight followed Eve to the front of the stage.

She spoke without song. "The garden was beautiful. The animals were all so peaceful. The food was nourishing, and I had a super hot guy at my side. But the rules were a prison, designed to keep me quiet and the men satisfied. In the end, that one forbidden fruit was the most delicious fucking apple I've ever eaten."

Eve ripped her baggy clothes off, revealing the leafy green cloth from earlier scenes. As the orchestra blasted one final note, she spun around and slapped her ass with her hands. The spotlight went black.

We stood up and clapped unreasonably loud. Even I joined Benny in his energetic cheering.

Was *Eden* going to be Broadway's next big hit? Doubtful. Too cheesy? Yeah. Was it a little on the nose? Probably. But for the Alligator Heretics, that revival was the niche closure we never knew we needed.

After the curtain closed, it opened again to a fully lit stage. The entire cast made their way into the light to take their bows to great applause.

After the bows were done, Ms. Flannigan approached the microphone. "Thank you SO much, everyone. I can't tell you how long this has been in the works. Actually, yes I can. It's been TEN LONG YEARS!"

The audience clapped.

"Thank you," she continued. "Believe it or not, this idea started back when I worked at a Christian high school. Yes, that's right. I was a devout Christian woman, turning my head as the men around me yelled at girls for wearing skirts two inches too short."

Ella chuckled.

"For a while, I thought *Eden* was a lost cause, crushed by the patriarchy that surrounded me. But then, the amazing students I thought I was there to educate showed me I was in need of growth, too… and here we are."

I exchanged glances with Ella, Rachel, and Benny. We smiled.

"Remember, everyone," said Ms. Flannigan. "Follow love wherever it leads you. Thank you."

The curtain closed once more, and we joined the audience in one last round of applause. We walked out, beaming ear to ear.

We said hello to Ms. Flannigan behind the theater, who was ecstatic to see us. We didn't get much face time as she had to greet many individuals whose lives she had touched just as much as ours.

"I am beyond grateful that you made the time to come by," she said, hugging us tightly. "I love you all and sincerely hope you've been able to find peace in your lives."

I smiled, but it faded as I reflected on the lack of fulfillment in my adult life.

The Alligator Heretics and I walked around the theater to the sidewalk out front. We faced each other in a circle, smiling.

"So," I said. "Anybody up for Chili's?"

"Actually," said Ella, "my partner is waiting back at the hotel. I should probably get back."

Benny grabbed her shoulder. "Partner?! Oh my god, you better text me some photos."

"Absolutely not."

"Unfortunately, I really can't," said Rachel. "My flight is leaving extremely early tomorrow, so I'm gonna get some rest."

I put my hands on my hips. "Now Rachel, in forty years, are you really gonna be worried about the extra sleep you didn't get?"

"I'm almost thirty, Arthur. You can't turn those words back at me anymore!"

"Okay, okay," I said. "It was amazing seeing you all. Let's make sure the next reunion is sooner than ten years."

Ella hugged me. "Absolutely. We're basically neighbors, so we have no excuse. Stay awesome, friend." She kissed me on the cheek.

"See you very soon," said Rachel, coming in for a hug. "Promise."

"You two are my drug," said Benny, as Rachel and Ella squeezed him from either side. "Don't ever change."

Ella and Rachel waved goodbye and headed back to their respective lives.

I turned to Benny. "So, Chili's?"

"Ya know what, Art… we could go. But I dunno… maybe it's time to let the past be the past. I don't know about you, but I kinda feel like I got what I came for."

"I guess. I just kinda feel like… I don't know what I'm going back home to. You've all found love, and have these full lives. I don't know what I'm doing wrong."

Benny placed his hand on my shoulder. "Arthur. You are one of my favorite people in the whole goddamn world. You are so fucking authentic, and I love that about you. Maybe because of that, it's harder for you to put on a face for the world, masking the struggle. But I promise you… we are all still struggling to overcome obstacles put in our lives by RCA."

I smiled. "Thanks, dude. I appreciate that."

"Yeah, man. We gave too much of our lives to that place to let it continue crippling our confidence. You're amazing, and you have such a bright future left to discover."

I blushed. "Thanks, Benny. But also, I hardly ever get to see you. We really gonna cut this short for a symbolic cutting of ties to the past?"

"Hell no, Art. Let's make some new memories. Cheesecake Factory?"

"That depends. Do they have queso?"

Benny chuckled. "Arthur, there is more to the culinary world than Americanized queso dip! Tonight begins your new obsession: spinach artichoke dip."

I grimaced. "Vegetables?! We'll see about that."

*   *   *

Twenty minutes into the meal, I raised my hand and ordered a second spinach artichoke dip.

"Do I know you, or what?" said Benny.

I smirked. "Yeah, yeah."

Benny and I reminisced for the better part of an hour, and it felt like we had graduated yesterday. We talked about how far video games had evolved in the past decade, our reactions to the *Lost* finale, his plans to propose to his boyfriend, and our love-hate relationships with social media.

The nostalgic catch-up sesh was made even more fun because, for the first time in our lives, we got drunk together. Few activities are as liberating as inebriation with someone you survived a sheltered childhood with.

As the wine flowed, the smiles grew bigger, and the laughs louder. After Benny told the embarrassing story about how he lost his virginity, I let loose an enormous guttural laugh.

The family at the table beside ours shot us judgmental looks whenever we talked loudly about general debauchery or made a ruckus.

I overheard an elderly man mutter, "Kids these days just need to go to church more."

We burst out laughing.

The Real Alligator Heretics

If you made it this far, you have my sincerest gratitude. *Alligator Heretics* is my metaphorical soul on paper, and I am so honored to have shared it with you.

Although fictional, the story drew influence from my personal journey from fundamentalist Christian to, well… whether I refer to myself as an atheist, agnostic, secular humanist, or some other label, depends entirely on who I'm talking to. Each definition comes with its own baggage. Let's simply say I'm not religious anymore.

My journey wasn't as concise as Arthur's, though many of the major beats were similar. I was raised in Christianity from as young as I can remember. During the final months of high school, I pondered a thought that everyone eventually thinks: *Is what I was raised to believe actually true?*

Unlike Arthur, it took a few more years for my opinions on religion and spirituality to solidify, and they're still evolving. Actually, that's one of the biggest reasons I fell away from Christianity—the realization that anyone who claims to know all the answers, without room for adjustment, is almost certainly wrong.

Throughout my time attending a secular art college, I met many unique individuals, both religious and not. Some were loving, and others were hateful. There was no clear correlation between those who fell into religious circles and those who didn't. I quickly realized, while away from my South Florida bubble, that the world is much larger, more diverse, and more beautiful than I presumed.

Thanks to friends that surrounded me during high school, college, and beyond, I very slowly realized that my religious ideologies, which frequently led to actions, negatively impacted real people. It became clear that loving each other is not a complicated concept, and, if anything, was hindered by the rules my Christian associates claimed to have been instructed by God to follow.

As many heretics do, I became frustrated when I realized what I was taught was hurtful, and likely untrue. I went through an "angry atheist" phase and thought the best use of my time was to share my newfound knowledge with as many people as possible. I don't scowl at those who still do that, but it is no longer for me.

I find myself ranting on social media about world issues a few times a year, but I always regret it. There are many injustices in the world that are worthy of fighting, but personally, I try to focus more on what we have in common than what divides us. When occasionally succeeding at this mindful goal, peace finds me.

Realizing you no longer believe in philosophies that represented a stable backbone your entire life can be overwhelming, and I can't blindly recommend it to everyone. I was lucky enough to avoid receiving much backlash from family and friends, but that's not always the case. Religion exists because early humankind excelled when we joined forces under the banners of mutual beliefs. In a time before science, religion was the best we could do. It makes sense that it's so deeply ingrained in our culture, but that means when doubting its truth, the personal toll can be great.

Many friends have been shunned by their spouses, families, friends, and even their employers. Those who structure their lives around their religion, such as church workers or private school teachers, may find an insurmountable mountain to climb in front of them, if they begin to doubt.

For me, leaving my faith was the right path, but it never really felt like a choice. The places I found myself in, and the people that surrounded me, pushed me toward this fate, and the rest unfolded organically, based on the simple fact that I care if what I believe is true.

We're all products of influential variables, most of which we have no control over. I think that means everyone is worthy of empathy, regardless of where on their journey they find themselves, and which journey that even is.

I could write a bunch more long-winded paragraphs filled with anecdotes and ruminations, but that's not in character with my autistic self. Instead, I'll leave you with five short suggestions for a peaceful life.

1. When your friends tell you you're hurting them, listen.

2. Those who tear you down don't deserve your friendship.

3. Question everything.

4. It's okay when someone disagrees with you.

5. There is no wrong way to love.

Good luck out there.

- Josh

If you enjoyed this book, please consider leaving an honest review!

Alligator Heretics was self-published by Joshua Sobel, and as such, the marketing budget is zero. It would be a huge help if you could leave a rating and/or short review on Amazon, Good Reads, and anywhere else that books are sold or reviewed. Social media posts are also a major help. Thanks so much!

Want to stay informed on Joshua Sobel's future books? You can find social media links at the website below.

artiehousebooks.com

About the Author

Joshua Sobel works as an animation tech artist in Los Angeles. Despite thriving in a creative industry, the bug to tell stories bites frequently. Alligator Heretics is his first novel and draws inspiration from his high school experiences.